Bound
by Ivy

SK.Quinn

SK.Quinn
UK

Copyright © by SK.Quinn

First Edition 2013

Designed by: Devoted Books Ltd.
Manufactured in the UK.

For my readers - you are amazing

'Sophia Rose,' Marc says. 'Will you marry me?'

Oh my god. Oh my GOD. I stare into Marc's beautiful blue eyes, and they've never looked more intense.

I put a shaky hand to my mouth.

My gaze drops to the huge pear-shaped diamond glittering in Marc's fingers. In this room, surrounded by ivy and roses, I couldn't imagine a more perfect setting for Marc to propose. But it's still a shock.

This scene couldn't be more out of a fairy tale if it tried. I'm standing here in my blue Belle dress with its big sticky out skirt, and Marc kneels before me, a handsome prince in a tailored black suit and crisp white shirt.

'Marc,' I whisper through my fingers, a smile growing on my face. I'm so utterly surprised that I can barely make my lips work.

Marc's eyes hold mine, and I feel like I'm falling into them.

I glance at the ring again. My god, it's beautiful. He's beautiful. This is real. This is really happening.

CLICK.

The sound of the dressing room door makes me jump.

'Hello?' I call out.

Marc looks at the door with a questioning frown. 'Did you invite someone down here?'

I shake my head.

Light spills onto the dressing room floor, and a pale, pointy female face appears.

I don't quite register who it is at first, because the face is so out of place in my dressing room. But then the icy blonde hair, sharp nose and cold eyes all come together.

It's Cecile.

'You bitch.' The words are hard and low, and hit me right in the stomach.

Marc stands and clamps an arm around my shoulder. He snaps the ring box closed and slides it into his pocket. 'This is Sophia's private dressing room.'

Cecile is wearing a fitted red-wool dress with long, white gloves, and her shiny hair is piled up on her head with diamante pins. Her eyes are red and angry, and her body is all tensed up.

'Giles is being charged with kidnapping,' she hisses at me. 'Because of you. Because of the lies you told.'

'I didn't tell any lies about Getty,' I say. 'He's a dangerous man. And he's where he needs to be.'

'You *knew* what he was to me,' says Cecile. 'And you couldn't stand that, could you? You couldn't stand that I was involved with someone famous too. So you had to ruin things.'

I let out a startled laugh. I don't mean to, but … Cecile is talking crazy.

'You didn't want to be involved with him,' I say. 'You said he was a monster.'

'He's the father of my child,' says Cecile. 'But there'll be no wedding now. No marriage. I'll be a single parent …'

She turns to Marc, her whole face changing, her eyes lost and desperate. 'Marc, oh, Marc. Why can't you see what Sophia really is? She's nothing more than a liar. She has no class. No money. I would have been so much better for you.'

Her thin fingers go to Marc's shirt, making little white fists as they grip the fabric. '*Please*. I have no one now. There's still time. Choose me.'

My body stiffens.

'Cecile, you should leave,' I say, in a low voice. I reach forwards and pick her fingers from Marc's shirt.

She falls back, her eyes wild now, darting back and forth over my face.

Suddenly, I notice what a mess she is. Her makeup, usually so carefully applied, is wonky in places, and her face is so heavily powdered that she looks like a dusty ghost.

Her dress isn't sitting right either. It's twisted at the waist, so the hips are all puckered.

She turns to me. 'You ruined my LIFE!' she shouts, her eyes bulging. 'You don't deserve Marc. You don't deserve anyone. And you'd better believe you'll pay for what you've done.'

She turns and charges out of the room, slamming the dressing room door behind her. I hear the fast click of high heels running down the corridor outside.

I go to run after her, but Marc's arm tightens like a vice around my shoulders.

'Leave her.'

'I don't want to leave things this way,' I say, struggling under his arm. 'I need to straighten things out.'

Marc holds me firm.

'Marc, *let me go.*'

He doesn't. Instead he grasps me firmly by both shoulders and turns me to him. 'You're not going anywhere until you calm down.'

'I … thought I was calm.'

'If you were calm you'd realise that it's dangerous to go after someone in that state. She doesn't know what she's saying or doing. She might hurt you.'

I put a hand to my chest and feel my heart is racing.

Marc moves his face closer to mine.

'Now isn't the time.' He gives me a firm kiss on the lips. 'Okay?'

I let out a long breath. 'I will be.'

'Now tell me what's going on,' says Marc. 'What business does Cecile have defending Giles Getty?'

My eyes drift over Marc's shoulder to the roses and ivy strewn around the room. 'She's pregnant,' I say, 'and he's the father of her child.'

Marc's eyebrow shoots up. 'Good god. Tell me you're joking.'

'No. I'm not.'

'Why didn't you tell me earlier?'

'She told me in confidence. There didn't seem to be any reason to mention it.'

'God.' Marc's eyes cloud over. 'That bastard. He doesn't care who he hurts.'

'She was so scared when we talked about it,' I say. 'Her family will disown her if they find out she's pregnant. Unless she marries the father.'

'Unlikely, since Getty's on his way to prison.'

'Yes,' I say. 'Hopefully for a long time.'

Marc takes my fingers and grips them tightly against his chest. 'I won't let him get anywhere near you, ever again. I have the best legal team in the country working on keeping him behind bars.'

I feel my fingers warming against his body.

'I will always protect you, Sophia. Always.'

I give a little shudder. When his voice goes all deep and intense like that, it does things to my body, even when my mind is all churned up and running around in circles.

'Cecile really was acting crazy,' I murmur. 'I guess she must have snapped.'

'We all have a breaking point.' Marc's brows pull together and the smile leaves his face.

'Marc?'

'If anything ever happened to you, it would destroy me.' He drops his hand to his trouser pocket and pulls out the ring box, turning it in his fingers. 'I don't want that little scene ruining your memory of getting engaged. I'll ask you another time. When the moment is right.'

'You're not going to ask me again now?'

'No. The timing should be perfect. Patience Miss Rose.' He drops the box back into his pocket. 'There'll be another moment.' That spiky, quirky Marc Blackwell grin appears on his face. 'Would you have said yes?'

'I just might have done.'

Marc's grin turns into a little smile that shows his dimples, and he scratches his temple. 'I'm pleased to hear it.'

I hear music floating down the corridor outside, and realise the party must be starting. I think of my Dad, Jen and everyone else up there, waiting for us.

'Does anyone know you were planning on proposing today?'

'Just your father. I asked his permission.'

'Was he surprised?'

'Very, very surprised. And a little shocked.'

'But he said yes?'

'He said as long as you were happy, he was happy.'

'It's important to me that he approves.'

'Oh?' Marc raises an eyebrow.

'Mum was a real believer in family approval. She wouldn't marry Dad without permission from her family. And when she was dying, she told Dad that he and I should always pull together. I know she wouldn't want me marrying anyone without Dad's blessing.'

The music outside gets louder.

'I should change,' I say.

I have my most comfortable jeans and Converse waiting in the wardrobe, and can't wait to put them on. 'Weren't you worried that Dad might have refused you?'

Marc squeezes my hand. 'Terrified.'

After I change, Marc and I head to Leo's dressing room.

My dressing room is in the old part of the theatre, but Leo's is in the new, modern part, which is all carpeted and clean.

Marc frowns. 'Your dressing room should be here. In the newer part. The air quality is better.'

'I guess I'm not a big star like Leo.'

'You're every bit as important to the show. I'll make sure your dressing room is changed.'

'No really. It's fine. I like my dressing room. Actually, I prefer it to Leo's. It's more me.'

Marc raises an eyebrow. 'You've been to Leo's dressing room before?'

I sense by his tone that he's not happy with that idea.

'Yes,' I say, as we head into the modernised part of the theatre. 'A few times. It's all bright lights, red carpet and framed show bills. It's nice. Very Leo.'

Marc's jaw grows tense. 'I trust he was the perfect gentleman.'

I hesitate. Marc's idea of the perfect gentleman might be a little different to Leo's.

'You've got nothing to be jealous of,' I say, by way of an answer.

Marc's eyes darken. 'I'm glad to hear it.'

'You and Leo worked together years ago,' I say. 'You should know what a nice guy he is.'

'All I remember of Leo Falkirk,' says Marc, 'is that he was unreliable and often turned up late. I wouldn't trust him with anything important. And that includes you.'

'Leo was a teenager when you knew him,' I say. 'He's

never been late for anything since I've known him. He's a good guy. I promise.'

'In my opinion, that has yet to be proved. Especially after that little publicity stunt he pulled with you outside the theatre. When he led you into a crowd of baying photographers.'

'That was an accident. He didn't know I'd trip.'

'A responsible man would never have let you get anywhere near that crowd.'

We walk on in silence for a moment.

'I loved the ring,' I say.

Marc's jaw loosens a little. 'It was my grandmother's, then my mothers. Of course, as soon as my father found out it was a real diamond, he sold it. It took me years to track it down again. In the end, I found it in a pawn shop in Whitechapel.'

I squeeze his hand. 'You're an amazing person, Marc Blackwell. After everything you've been through ... the childhood you had ... to be the man you are ...'

'The most amazing thing about me is you.'

We reach Leo's dressing room and hear the murmur of voices and the dim sounds of Johnny Cash.

Marc drops my hand and pushes the door open hard. A little too hard. I can't help thinking he's imagining it's Leo's face.

The dressing room is large, but there are so many people crammed inside that it looks pretty tiny right now. Three tuxedoed waiters squeeze through the crowd handing out glasses of champagne and topping up glasses.

'Hey.' I grab Marc's hand back. 'Be nice, okay? You and Leo aren't enemies.'

'Aren't we?'

'No. He's in awe of you. He thinks you're amazing.'

'It's what he thinks of *you* that worries me.'

We walk into the room, and I see Jen and my Dad squashed together with Tanya and Tom.

Tom is chatting away in his loud voice, and Tanya, Dad and Jen are listening and laughing.

Jen looks amazing in a cream bodice dress with gold embroidery. Tanya and Tom are in evening wear too – Tanya wearing a subtle black dress with a pretty solitaire diamond necklace, and Tom, flamboyant as ever in top hat, tails and red dickey bow.

My dad looks a little uncomfortable. He's wearing his very smartest jeans – the black ones with no stains on them – and a white shirt that I remember him buying for my grandparents' wedding anniversary fifteen years ago. He's clutching his champagne glass by the bowl, like it's a pint of beer, and he's staring at the door.

Leo and Davina are standing by a huge stereo system that I guess must have been brought in for the party. Leo is roaring with laughter, and swigging from a bottle of champagne.

'Soph!' Jen sees me first and pushes through the crowd. Her shoes are so high that every step threatens to tip her over, but she just about manages to stay on her feet.

She reaches me and throws her arms around my shoulders. 'Oh my god, you were amazing. Just amazing! Come on! Everyone's dying to tell you how well you did.' She drags me across the room by my arm.

Marc follows, keeping a firm grip on my hand.

When we reach Dad, Tom and Tanya, Marc's grip is tighter than ever.

'Sophia!' Tom's booming voice nearly knocks me over. 'What a performance. Absolutely terrific. You were sensational. All those rehearsals really did pay off, didn't they? You and Leo were on level pegging up there. I'd never have known he'd been in the business any longer than you.'

'You were very good, love,' says Dad. He looks a little tired, and keeps glancing at the door, like he's waiting for someone.

'You were great, Soph,' says Tanya, giving my shoulder a squeeze. 'I loved it. And I usually hate musicals.'

'*Tanya*,' Tom chastises.

'What? It's true. I do hate musicals.'

'But that's hardly what Sophia wants to hear right now.'

'It's fine, it's fine.' I smile. 'I take it as a compliment, believe me.'

'So what happens over Christmas?' Tanya asks. 'Do you have to perform on Christmas day, or what?'

'Not on Christmas day,' I say. 'But I will on Boxing Day and New Year's Eve and then all through January.'

Tom's eyes widen. 'How do you feel about *that*?'

'I'm trying not to think about it. I love Christmas. But it's just one year. And at least I get to spend Christmas day with my family.'

'You'll be back at the cottage for Christmas then?' Jen asks.

'Of course. I always spend Christmas there.'

'Well, you never know. Fame might have changed you.'

'I'm not *famous*. I'm notorious. And I wish I wasn't.'

'You may not be famous yet,' says Tom, 'but I'm guessing when January is over you'll be well on your way.'

'What are you two doing for Christmas?' I ask Tom and Tanya, eager to change the subject.

They look at each other, and Tanya gives a sheepish grin. 'My parents are spending Christmas in Spain this year, so I thought I'd hang out with Tom's family. They've got an estate out in Surrey, so there's plenty of room for me.'

'Our first Christmas together,' says Tom.

'God, I'm terrified,' Tanya says. 'Aren't you?'

'Not in the slightest.'

'But what if your family don't like me? What if they can't understand the way I talk?'

'They'll love you. And I can translate. I understand northern now.'

Tanya rolls her eyes. 'It's not a foreign language!'

'Not foreign, my love. Exotic.'

Tanya laughs.

'I'm going to miss you two over Christmas,' I say.

Jen puts a hand on my shoulder. 'Don't worry, you won't be lonely. I'll come round yours for a drink on Christmas day, just like always.'

'Will Mr Blackwell be joining you for turkey?' Tom asks.

4

'I … I don't know,' I say, glancing at Marc and feeling embarrassed.

I haven't asked Marc about Christmas yet and I really have no idea what his plans are. I know I want to go back to the cottage, but I don't know if Marc will want to come with me.

'You must be so proud of Sophia, Mr Blackwell,' says Tanya with a grin. 'After all, she's your pupil.'

'I'm extremely proud,' says Marc. 'But I always knew how talented she was.' He moves his thumb around my palm.

I catch my breath, feeling his thumb all the way through my body. My cheeks redden and I throw him an 'easy tiger' glance.

He rewards me with a 'I'll do what I like' twitch of his eyebrow.

'So how's the PR going?' Jen asks Marc.

'Not perfectly. But hopefully I'll have things straightened out soon.' The pressure of Marc's thumb increases against my palm.

'We should tell Dad that we didn't get engaged yet,' I whisper, my voice growing weak as Marc's thumb pushes harder. I try to slide my hand away before things get too hot, but Marc holds it firm.

'Fine with me,' says Marc, sounding totally business-like.

The pressure of his thumb is making my knees go weak.

'Before things get out of hand,' I say, my voice beginning to break.

'I wouldn't want anything to get out of hand,' says

Marc, his eyebrows spiking up in that stomach-melting Marc Blackwell way.

I swallow, feeling a glorious dull pain throb across my palm. I want to close my eyes and moan, but instead I press my lips tight together.

Marc slides his hand from mine, his fingers running up my hand. He grasps my wrist tightly.

My skin tingles and shivers, and suddenly I want him so badly that I can hardly stand straight.

God damn it.

Marc accepts a glass of champagne, all cool, calm and collected.

I wish I had his self-control.

'Mr Rose,' says Marc, taking a neat little sip of champagne and catching my dad's eye. 'May Sophia and I have a word with you?'

'A word?' Dad drags his gaze from the door.

'Marc and I just wanted to talk to you for a moment,' I say.

'Oh. Talk. Yes.' Dad's eyes flick to the doorway again. 'What about?'

'Shall we take a seat?' Marc suggests, nodding towards the couch at the back of the room.

Dad holds out his glass to be refilled by a passing waiter. 'Yes. Okay.'

Marc leads us through the crowd and gestures to a sofa made of carved, golden wood and upholstered in red silk.

Dad dusts his jeans before he sits down, and perches on the edge of the couch as though he's afraid he'll crush it.

I sit down too, but Marc stays standing.

'Are you okay?' I ask Dad. 'You seem a little ... not quite yourself.'

'Oh, just ... Genoveva was supposed to be here.'

'Who's looking after Sammy?'

'A babysitter.'

'Is Genoveva okay?'

Dad downs his champagne. 'As far as I know.'

I throw Marc a quizzical look.

'If this is a bad time—'

'Not at all,' says Dad, glancing at the door again. 'What did you want to talk to me about?'

'I ... we just wanted to tell you that we're not engaged yet.'

'Engaged?' Dad blinks at his empty champagne glass. '*Oh*. Right, yes. No, I didn't expect ... I mean, you're far too young, and you've only known each other five minutes.'

'We sort of got interrupted.'

Dad's eyes widen. 'Sophia, you weren't ... I mean, were you going to say yes?'

'I would have done.'

'But ... Sophia, you're such a sensible girl.'

'Dad, what are you saying?'

Dad's eyes flick back towards the door. 'In all honesty, I think you should wait a year or so before thinking about something as long-term as marriage.'

'But you gave Marc your permission.'

'Of course I did. It's your decision love, not mine.'

'But Dad, don't you understand? It's not just your permission I want. It's your blessing.'

'That's a bit harder to give. Things have happened very quickly. And you're so young. I just don't want you getting hurt.'

'I would never hurt Sophia,' says Marc. He has his hands in his pockets and his forehead is locked into a frown.

'Dad, you look so tired,' I say. 'Is everything okay?'

'Oh, just—' He glances at Marc. 'Family stuff.'

'I should leave you to talk with your father,' says Marc, his hands still buried in his pockets. 'I'm going for a walk'

'Marc—'

'I'll be back soon.' Marc gives me a light kiss on the cheek.

I watch him stride out of the door, the long lines of his body moving through his clothing, and feel the usual disbelief that this Hollywood star, with his beautiful, handsome face and taut body, is my boyfriend.

I turn to Dad. 'So what's the story?'

5

Dad focuses on his champagne glass, both hands clutching the crystal bowl. 'Genoveva and I had an argument. That's all. No big deal. Look, I know I gave Marc permission, but … I never dreamed you'd say yes.'

'Dad, you really don't sound like yourself right now—'

'He seems very controlling of you, love. Very protective. The way he looks at you … it's all very intense.' Dad stares at the door. 'I wouldn't want you making a mistake. And getting hurt.'

I follow his stare. 'Dad. Where *is* Genoveva? Why isn't she here?'

'This is your party. Let's talk about you.'

'We were,' I say, taking a sip of champagne. 'But that didn't turn out to be much fun.'

'Sophia, if you really want to marry Marc, I can't stop you.'

'I would never marry anyone without your blessing. You know that. After what Mum said to us …'

'I'm going to get on home and let you enjoy yourself. We'll talk about this another time.'

'Dad, are you okay?'

'Just tired, love. Will you be coming home for Christmas?'

'Of course. The play runs on Christmas Eve, but I'll come to the cottage straight afterwards and we'll all spend Christmas day together, just like always.'

'Will he be coming? Marc?'

'I don't know. I haven't asked him yet.'

Dad hesitates. 'He's so much older than you.'

'I love him, Dad. I want to be with him. That's not going to change. If Marc comes to the cottage for Christmas, will you be okay with that?'

'I'll be okay with it.' He stands up. 'See you on Christmas Eve. Enjoy your big night. Don't worry about me.' He kisses me on the head. 'Well done love.'

I watch Dad head towards the door, but before he can leave, Jen corners him. She's probably trying to work out what we were all talking about. She's so nosy. The perfect PR girl.

I feel the couch jiggle beside me.

'Hey pretty girl, why the serious face?'

I turn to see Leo. He's still holding a champagne bottle, and takes a long swig from it.

'What's up? Where's Mr Marc Blackwell? Out hunting vampires?'

'He's gone for a walk.'

'A walk? In the moonlight? Without taking the love of his life? I've never seen a man so crazy about a woman. He doesn't take his eyes off you.'

'He's protective.'

'More than just protective. I thought he was going to rip my head off when he walked in here earlier. What did I do?'

'He didn't like that I'd been to your dressing room before,' I admit. 'He doesn't know whether to trust you yet. But he will.'

'Does that mean my dressing room is off limits now?'

'Of course not. I don't do everything Marc tells me. He's not my keeper. There's no reason for me not to hang out with you. Marc has nothing to be jealous about.'

'Oh no?' Leo's words are playful, but he slides a little closer.

I laugh and slap his shoulder. 'No! We're just friends.

You know that.'

'I guess I can't compete with Marc Blackwell.' Leo lifts my chin and affects a deep, serious voice. 'Oh Sophia, Sophia. Where for art thou, Sophia?'

I feel eyes on me, and turn to see Marc in the dressing room doorway.

Leo follows my gaze and drops his fingers. 'Uh oh.'

Marc stalks towards us at such speed that waiters and guests step aside.

'Sophia.' Marc glares at Leo. 'Is he bothering you?'

'No. Of course not. We were just talking.'

'He doesn't need to touch you to talk to you.' Marc's voice is hard and angry.

'Leo was just messing around.'

'He can mess around with someone else. Someone who isn't spoken for.'

'Hey.' Leo stands up. 'We were just talking. No hard feelings, huh? She only has eyes for you right now.'

'*Right now*?' Marc's voice is positively boiling.

'Marc.' I put a hand to his chest.

Over Marc's shoulder I see Dad watching. He has a look on his face that tells me he's not impressed by what he's seeing.

I lead Marc away from Leo. 'We were just talking.'

'Are you okay?'

'Of course I am. Well ... except for everything with Dad. I'll talk to him over Christmas. Hopefully he'll be his old self again by then.'

Marc wraps an arm around me. 'I'll talk to him too. And I'll keep talking to him until he understands just how much I love you.'

'Oh Marc,' I sigh. 'Why can't life ever be easy? All I want is to be with you. Why can't Dad see that we're meant to be together?'

'He will. You look tired. I should take you home.'

'But I've hardly spoken to anyone yet.'

'Sophia, you'll wear yourself out. It's been a long day.'

'I need to at least thank everyone for coming.' A yawn catches me by surprise, and my hand shoots to my mouth.

'Come on,' says Marc. 'Say your goodbyes. I'm taking you home.'

After I've said goodbye to everyone, Marc and I head to the limo.

Keith is waiting in the car, reading a crime paperback and eating a bag of liquorice allsorts. He gives a joking salute when he sees us and leaps out to open the back door.

'M'lady.' He bows to me. 'You were terrific. Wonderful. I nearly cried at the end. Don't tell anyone'

'You saw the show?'

'Wouldn't miss it. Marc made sure I had a good seat.'

'I thought the tickets were all sold out.'

'Mr Blackwell bought plenty of reserves,' says Keith with a wink.

'Maybe Marc was the reason they all sold out,' I say, with a tired smile. 'He bought all the tickets.'

'Hardly,' says Marc, helping me into the car.

Once we're inside the limo, I fall against Marc's shoulder, realising how truly tired I am. Marc sits upright, slipping his arm around me and pulling me into him. I feel his chest moving against my cheek and feel warm and safe.

'Marc?' I say. 'I wanted to ask you something earlier. About Christmas. What are your plans?'

'That all depends on you,' Marc says. 'And what you want.'

'I want to be with you,' I say. 'But I always go back to the cottage at Christmas to see Dad and Sammy. And Jen – she comes over on Christmas day too. I was wondering ... would you like to spend Christmas day with me? At my Dad's cottage?'

'Would I be welcome?' Marc's voice rumbles against

my cheek.

'Dad said he'd be okay with it,' I say, chewing a thumb nail. 'So? Will you come?'

'If you feel I won't be creating an uncomfortable situation. I don't want to be disrespectful to your father.'

'I ... he said it would be okay.'

'Just okay?'

'He really wasn't himself tonight.'

London lights flicker through the tinted car windows, and I find myself closing my eyes.

'I wish I could visit Dad tomorrow,' I say. 'Make sure he's okay. But I promised Leo we'd rehearse.'

Marc stiffens. 'You never mentioned that.'

'Didn't I? I meant to. I forgot. Leo asked me during the interval. He wants to use the audience reaction to guide us.'

'Nice to know he's acting like a professional for once.' There's an edge to Marc's voice, but I'm too tired to worry about it. Instead, I relax into his shoulder, feeling my eyes closing again as the car jogs through London. Soon sleep overtakes me.

When I open my eyes again, I'm in Marc's townhouse. He's carrying me up the stairs, and I feel my hair swaying beneath me. My eyes sleepily glide over the building pictures lining Marc's staircase.

I need to do something with this place, I think sleepily. *Give it some heart and soul. Grow some plants. Make it warmer.*

Now we're on the landing.

Marc pushes open his bedroom door with his shoulder and carries me to the bed. He pushes the duvet aside with his elbow and lays me on the silk sheet. I look up at his handsome face, seeing concern pull at his blue eyes.

'What's wrong?' I ask.

'You're tired,' he says, in a low voice. 'But god ... if you knew what I wanted to do to you right now ...'

I feel the familiar warmth building. I'm still tender from our time in the dressing room earlier, but I want him so badly.

'I'm not that tired,' I say, stifling a yawn.

Marc circles the bed, taking off his suit jacket and throwing it over a chair. 'Yes,' he says. 'You're tired. Far too tired for what I have in mind.'

'What do you have in mind?' I murmur.

'It can wait.'

The warmth turns to burning. 'I can stay awake.' I try not to yawn again.

'No. Sleep now. The quicker you do, the quicker I can fuck you the way I want.' Marc goes to the foot of the bed, undoes my shoelaces and slides off my shoes. It's not like the time he undressed me at the hotel, when his movements were deliberately seductive. He's quick and functional, flinging my footwear to the floor.

Then he undoes my jeans and pulls them from my legs, pausing for just a moment to look at my bare skin, before tearing his eyes away and throwing the duvet over me.

'Put your arms up.'

I do, and he lifts my sweater over my head.

I don't think he means to turn me on, but the roughness of his hands make me ache for him.

I lie back on the bed.

'Marc. I'm awake. I promise.'

He goes to the bedroom window, loosening his tie and kicking off his shoes. Then he stares out at the dark London sky.

'Aren't you coming to bed?' I ask.

Marc turns. 'I was going to wait until you'd fallen asleep,' he says. 'So I won't be tempted.'

'You can be tempted,' I say.

He smiles. 'If you knew what I had planned, you wouldn't be saying that. Trust me. You're too tired.'

'I'm not.'

He comes to sit on the bed, reaching out a hand to stroke my cheek. 'My job is to take care of you. And right now I'm taking care of your physical health instead of your physical pleasure.'

'Kiss me,' I say.

'Sophia—'

'Please.'

Marc's hand hesitates on my cheek. His eyes burn. Then slowly, he leans forwards and presses his lips against mine – a long, slow goodnight kiss.

I love the feeling of his lips. Before I can think about it, my mouth opens and I'm kissing him fully, passionately, reaching around his shoulders to pull him closer.

'*God*,' Marc moans into my mouth, kissing me back,

pushing me hard into the bed. 'Sophia, you might regret this.'

'I won't.'

Marc unbuttons his shirt and flings it off, kissing me harder, sliding his fingers into my hair and clenching his hand into a fist, pulling my hair tight. He moves so his knee comes between my legs and his body weight presses against me.

My scalp stings where he grips my hair, and he tugs his fist down until I moan.

'Oh, Marc.'

'I'm not going to do what I planned right now,' Marc murmurs against my mouth. 'You're too tired. But I have to see you come.'

He kisses me harder, clenching his fist tighter. A bruisey pain moves around my scalp and neck, and my head is totally immobilised. I'm held by him, completely in his power, his body weight holding me to the bed.

Marc pushes his knee harder between my legs while he pins my shoulders to the bed with one hand and grips my hair with the other. I'm getting so wet that I know my panties are almost soaked through.

'Oh god Marc, please,' I beg. 'Please fuck me.'

Marc's hand moves between my legs and I gasp and moan as he pushes my panties aside and forces three fingers deep inside me in one swift, hard movement.

'*Oh*,' I moan.

He turns his fingers back and forth. Then he slips in a forth finger, and I lose all sense of anything except pleasure building up. I'm sore and full all at the same time, and it feels so good.

'Tell me if this is too much,' Marc whispers. I feel his thumb push inside me too, and sink into the bed with pleasure and pain.

'It's ... I think I can take it,' I gasp. 'For ... now.'

Marc pushes further, further inside, his eyes locked on mine.

I swallow and shake my head, knowing if he twists his hand like he did before, I won't be able to take it. But he doesn't move. He stays still, watching me, his eyes fierce.

'One day I'll have you begging for my whole hand to be inside you,' he says. 'But not today.'

He pulls his hand out in such a rush that I'm left throbbing and desperate for him.

'Fuck me Marc, please,' I beg.

Marc undoes his trousers, letting go of my hair to struggle out of them. He takes off his boxers too, and I see him, huge and hard, before he climbs back on top of me.

His long arm reaches out to grab a condom from the bedside table drawer, and he rips open the foil and stretches latex over himself.

I open my legs for him, and he groans as he comes into contact with my damp skin. 'Very accommodating Miss Rose. Very, very accommodating.'

He teases me for a moment, rubbing his hardness around.

'Please fuck me,' I say again. 'Please. *Please.*'

Marc thrusts into me. He pushes deep, going all the way inside, further than his fingers could ever manage, reaching dark, sultry places that make my whole body tingle.

'Oh,' I moan, as he fills me up. He's pushing against me, all of me, his groin hard against mine, rubbing me inside and out, and I'm pinned to the bed, trapped by him. I know as soon as he moves I'm going to come. But just like before, he holds me still for a moment, teasing.

'I wish I had your self control,' I whisper.

Marc's eyes are fierce, and he replies through gritted teeth, 'I don't have much of it left. Believe me.'

He slides his hand into my hair again and pulls it tight like before.

'Oh god,' I cry, as he gives my hair a tug.

He starts to move, and with every stroke he pulls my hair harder, until my head begins to move with him and a delicious, dominant pain spreads down my neck.

The pain stops me from coming straight away, but oh god ... the pleasure. Every push inside me, every tightening of his hand around my hair, is making me delirious and I'm lost in him, just like always.

Marc's eyes don't leave mine as he pumps back and forth, forcing my head to move with him, causing electric shocks all over my body.

When he slips his other hand around and grasps my buttocks, forcing his fingers right into the flesh hard enough to bruise, I can't hold on anymore. I want to scream out with how good it feels.

'Oh, *oh*,' I gasp, looking into his eyes and seeing he's close to coming too.

'Sophia,' he moans, his eyes melting and softening, his fingers grasping my buttocks so firmly that he's almost lifting me off the bed.

He gives one mighty thrust, hitting everything in just the right way.

And I come.

In one huge giant wave, my body pushing and pulling all around him. Pleasure flows over me from my scalp all the way down to my feet, and my whole body melts into the bed. Everything feels electric – my scalp, my neck and between my legs.

As I feel wave after wave of pleasure, I hear Marc's breathing go sharp and hear something between a shout and a moan as he comes.

He pushes his body against mine, forcing himself harder between my legs, against my chest.

I feel his breathing soften as his body releases into me. His nose is nearly touching mine now, his eyes lightly closed, eyelids flickering. His lips fall forwards, giving me the softest, sweetest kiss. I feel warmth all over my body.

Marc wraps his arms around me and pulls me onto my shoulder so we're lying side by side. He moves a hand up to gently cradle my head where he was gripping my hair before, his fingers stroking back and forth.

'Not too much?'

'No,' I murmur. 'It felt good.'

'I knew it would.'

There are no more words. I'm too tired to talk. To think. All I can do is feel the warmth of Marc's arms and body. I press myself close to him and fall into a deep sleep.

I wake up the next morning to feel sun shining on eyelids, and know instinctively that Marc is no longer lying next to me. My eyes flicker open and I roll over to see an empty, cold space.

It's a beautiful, crisp winter day, and the sky is white through the criss-crossed townhouse window. The sun is pale overhead.

I pull myself up in the bed, feeling the silky duvet fall down over my bare legs. I'm still wearing my panties and a black vest with coloured stars all over it. As memories of last night come back to me, I feel warmth travel up my abdomen.

What does Marc have planned for me today?

I shiver at the possibilities.

There's a brown trunk in the corner of the room, and I see underwear and a change of clothes laid out on it. My underwear and my clothes. I smile.

Marc had my clothes couriered over from Ivy College after the whole Giles Getty incident, and he arranged a room in the townhouse to store them all. There's a bed in that room too, but of course I've never slept in it.

I'm always in Marc's bedroom.

Some mornings, I wake up and find Marc lying beside me. He's always awake and watching me intently, like I'm made of china and about to fall and break. Other mornings, Marc wakes up before me and lays out my clothes. Then I meet him downstairs in the kitchen for breakfast.

When I wake to an empty bed, I find it a little strange. I think, in Marc's case, leaving me sleeping is a habit left over from the days when he couldn't let go. When he absolutely had to stay in charge at all times. But he can let go now. At least, most of the time.

I'm about to climb out of bed when the door creaks, and I'm treated to the sight of a bare-chested Marc Blackwell in grey sweatpants.

He's carrying a silver breakfast tray and his floppy brown hair looks a little damp. As he comes closer, I smell shampoo and cologne.

'Awake at seven on the dot.' Marc smiles his quirky, deadly smile – the one that has female cinema audiences weak at the knees. His teeth are so perfect, and his lips, the way they curve in that devilish way, are so ... I don't know the words, but let's just say that smile does things to me. 'Your routine is very predictable Miss Rose.'

'Marc, I haven't showered yet.' I'm feeling sleep dirty and wish I could brush my teeth before he comes any nearer. When we wake up in bed together, I don't care that I haven't washed. But if he's already showered, I want to take a shower too.

'I like you when you haven't showered.' Marc places the tray on the end of the bed. 'I love the way you smell.' His low voice hits me in all the right places. 'I want you to eat well this morning. You'll be needing your stamina.'

'Oh?' I raise a teasing eyebrow. 'What for?'

'What would be the fun if I told you? Eat.'

On the tray, I see a bowl of porridge topped with crispy bacon, maple syrup and pumpkin seeds. There's also a plate of Eggs Benedict decorated with a sprig of parsley, under a glass cloche. And a bowl of fresh strawberries and yoghurt. Wow. There's a lot to eat.

Next to the porridge and eggs stand two cut crystal glasses – one full of pink grapefruit juice, the other holding a stem of ivy.

I smile at the ivy. 'Did you pick that from your

garden?' I ask.

'*Your* garden,' says Marc, sitting beside me on the bed and arranging my hair around my shoulders. 'There's no question who it belongs to now.'

I feel myself grinning. 'I love it out there. There's so much more I'd like to do.'

'Write a list of any plants you need. Equipment. I'll have Rodney take care of it. Now eat.'

'It looks amazing,' I say. 'But ... there's so much. I don't know if I'll be able to manage everything.'

'Last night was a long night, and you need to replenish yourself. I have plans for you this morning. Plans that require stamina.' Marc raises an eyebrow.

My stomach flips over, remembering the 'plans' he spoke about last night. When it's finished flipping, I slide the tray of food towards me.

I pick up a silver spoon with square edges and dip it into the porridge.

'Mmm,' I say, taking a mouthful and realising how hungry I am. 'Delicious.' The porridge is laced with cream and warm maple syrup. More like a dessert than a breakfast, but it feels like exactly what I need this morning. Marc's right – I used up a lot of energy yesterday, one way or another.

'Try the bacon with it,' says Marc, holding up a crispy strip.

'I've never had bacon with porridge before,' I admit. 'Does it go?'

'Better than you'd imagine.' Marc holds the bacon to my lips and I take a little bite. He's right, of course. It goes perfectly with the rich porridge and maple syrup. I lean closer, taking another bite that snaps near his fingers.

'Careful Miss Rose,' says Marc with a smile.

'You're allowed to hurt me, but I can't hurt you?' I

throw back, playfully.

'I don't hurt you. I test your limits to heighten your enjoyment.' Marc's eyes darken and fix on mine. 'I'd put you over my knee and spank you at the slightest opportunity. Do you know why?'

'Why?' I squeak, swallowing bacon.

'Because it would make you come over and over again.'

'How do you know that?'

'I can see it in your eyes right now. And by the way your neck and chest have flushed, and your voice has gone up a key. But I've got more planned for you today than just a spanking. Believe me. I've had a length of silk rope ordered especially.'

Oh. God. My desire is written all over my face, I know it is. Part of me hates the fact Marc can turn me on so easily by talking about spanking and tying me up.

I have no idea if I'd be turned on by all this dark, subversive sex if I hadn't met Marc, or whether I like it *because* of Marc. I guess it doesn't matter. I love him and loving him has awakened things in me.

Now that Marc has let go with me, I love him so much that sometimes I can hardly breathe.

When we're making love, I feel like we become one person. I trust him completely. Totally. I want to be part of him, always. The fact he takes pleasure from dominating me, and the fact I love him dominating me, well – it just shows how much we're made for each other.

There's a bleeping sound, and I see a flash of white through the grey cotton of Marc's sweat pant pocket.

Marc frowns and slides out the phone, glaring at the screen.

I feel myself frown too, because he looks so serious all of a sudden. A world away from that beautiful, sexy grin he gave me when he came into the room.

'Marc?'

He doesn't answer. Instead, his eyes flick back and forth over the screen.

'Is everything okay?' I ask.

Marc stands. 'Finish your breakfast. I have to deal with this. I'll be back soon.' He stalks out of the bedroom.

I stare at the door as it bangs shut, wondering what on earth is going on.

I sit watching the door for a while, puzzling over what Marc's message could be. But after a few minutes, delicious breakfast smells start teasing my nostrils and hunger prods and pokes at me.

God, I'm famished. I really am.

I begin spooning up porridge and crunching on strips of streaky bacon, feeling warm maple syrup and creamy oats roll around my mouth.

When the porridge is done, I lift the glass cloche from the Eggs Benedict and dig in with a silver knife and fork.

Wow. The poached eggs and Hollandaise sauce taste so good, and underneath salty, warm ham tops two soft English muffins. I don't think, when I start eating, that I'll be able to finish the plate, but I do with ease, mopping up the Hollandaise with a square of bakery fresh muffin.

I finish up the strawberries and yoghurt too, washing them down with the freshest, cleanest glass of pink grapefruit juice I've ever tasted.

As usual, Marc knows what I want and need better than I do.

When I'm finished, I slide the tray away and lie back on the firm mattress. My body feels relaxed and happy and full of food, but pretty soon my mind begins running an obstacle course again. What was Marc's sudden exit all about?

I just can't imagine that Marc could ever slip back into his old, dark ways. We're so close now. My heart tells me not to worry – at least not on the 'Marc growing cold' front.

My head, on the other hand, begins its usual run through of all the reasons why it's crazy that Marc and I are together. After all, he could have pretty much any woman he wanted.

I remember the pictures of Marc with gorgeous models and Hollywood actresses on his arm. Of course, that was way before we got together. But god, I wish I'd never seen those pictures. Compared to those women, I'm nothing.

Shut up Sophia. You'll drive yourself crazy.

I snap my eyes closed and try to chase all my horrible, ugly insecure feelings away. But sometimes it's tough. Coming from where I came from, it's hard to believe that I can truly stay where I am now – in the home of a billionaire, who also just happens to be drop dead gorgeous. Oh, and I shouldn't forget that I'm also playing a leading role in a major West End musical beside Leo Falkirk.

God, life is crazy sometimes.

I hear the bang of hard feet on the staircase and sit up straighter.

The bedroom door springs open.

Marc strides towards me, pushing his hair back from his forehead.

'Marc?' I swing my legs from the bed.

'Sophia, there have been some developments. I think now would be a good time for you to visit your father for a few days.'

'I'm going to stay with him tomorrow. After the Christmas Eve performance. Leo and I were planning on going over a few songs today. At the theatre. Remember?'

Marc's face darkens. He stalks back and forth, then turns to me. 'Fine. But when you finish your performance tonight, you're to go straight to your father's house. Keith will drive you there. I'll have your things sent over today.'

'Marc, what's going on?'

'Nothing for you to be concerned about. But it's best you stay at your father's place right now. What time did you arrange to meet Leo?'

'I didn't. You know Leo, he's a "let's wait and see" kind of guy. We said we'd play it by ear.'

'Phone him now and see if he wants to meet in the next hour. If he agrees, I'll have you taken to the theatre. You're to stay there until after your performance.' Marc begins pacing again.

'*Marc*. This is crazy. You *want* me to go and spend time with Leo? Last night, you were acting sort of jealous.'

'Jealous?' Marc's eyebrow twitches. 'Of Leo Falkirk? Do I have something to be jealous about?' His voice is low and foreboding.

'No. Of course not.'

'I'm protective of you where other men are concerned,' Marc growls. 'Especially irresponsible men. I didn't like Leo putting his hands on you last night. And I don't like the thought of him entertaining you in his dressing room, away from everyone else. Anything could happen.'

I laugh. 'But it wouldn't.'

'*You* might not want something to happen, but he might.'

'Meaning?'

'Meaning all I know of Leo Falkirk is that he's a boy in a man's body. I don't trust him to behave responsibly.'

'Well I do,' I say, standing. 'He's a good guy.'

Marc comes closer to the bed, towering over me. 'If he ever touches you against your wishes, I'll kill him.'

I feel Marc's hand come into my hair, but I turn away

so his fingers slide free. 'He wouldn't. I told you. I know him.'

A frown cuts into Marc's forehead. 'How well do you know him?' His words have a dangerous edge to them.

'Well enough to know he'd never hurt me.'

Silence. It takes me a moment to realise how Marc could have taken those words, and by the time I see the pain in his eyes it's too late. I've lost him, at least for the moment.

'Marc—'

'Call Leo and see if he'll meet you. I need you to leave the townhouse as soon as possible. There are things I have to take care of.'

I feel sick. 'I didn't mean ... about hurting me ... you've touched parts of me that no one has.'

Marc turns away from me. 'I'll leave you to get dressed. And to make your call. Your phone is on the dressing table.' He heads to the door. 'Call me when you get to the theatre, so I know you're safe.'

'Marc,' I say, knowing my voice sounds fragile and tearful. 'Please. What's happening?'

Marc turns back to me, and I see his beautiful profile. God he's so handsome. So charismatic. I hear that horrible voice again – the voice of my paranoia. *He's getting tired of you. That's what this is all about.*

'It was nothing you did,' says Marc, not looking at me. 'Just ... trust me, this is for the best right now. It's my way of keeping you safe.' He heads to the door.

'Wait,' I call to Marc's retreating back, tears coming now.

'We'll talk later.' Marc leaves and the bedroom door slams closed behind him.

11

I shower and dress, my mind swirling with unpleasant thoughts. Something weird is going on – bad weird. And I hate not knowing what.

Once I'm dressed, I call Leo and ask if he can meet right away.

Leo gives a firm 'yes', and tells me he'll bring doughnuts and coffee to the theatre.

I head downstairs and find Keith waiting in the hallway. He's in his chauffeur's uniform, complete with grey cap, and he touches the peak when he sees me.

My hair is still damp from the shower and hanging around my shoulders. Until my hair dries, I look like a wild woman. But if I use a hairdryer it sends my hair into a wild frizz.

'Good morning Miss Sophia,' Keith calls out.

I smile. 'Come on, Keith. You know it's just Sophia where I'm concerned.'

'I know. Just teasing. I believe I have the pleasure of taking you to the theatre today?'

It's strange seeing Keith in Marc's house. I've only ever seen him in the car or the garage before, but I guess he must come inside pretty often. Marc isn't the sort of man to let his staff wait in cold garages.

A very loyal employer. Isn't that what Keith said about Marc? And he's loyal to Denise too, taking care of her over the years. And I've seen myself how loyal he is. To his students. To the college.

Is he proposing to me out of loyalty? says a nasty voice. *Maybe he's worried he's ruined my reputation and now he has to do the right thing.*

God, what's wrong with me today?

'Marc wants me to go there, so I guess I'm going,' I say, attempting a smile.

'You don't strike me as the sort of girl who'd do everything Marc told you to. In fact, I'm pretty sure that's one of the reasons Marc is so head over heels about you. You have a mind of your own.'

'Most of the time,' I laugh. 'But it's easy to lose my head when Marc's around.'

We head down to the garage, my brain still working at one hundred miles an hour.

*****

When we drive out of the townhouse, I notice black-clothed security men around the gate.

'Do you know why those security guards at there?' I ask Keith, as we swing out into the road.

'Beats me,' says Keith, turning onto the busy main road. 'They weren't here when I arrived. I'm sure it's nothing to worry about. Marc is a "better safe than sorry" kind of guy.'

'Uh ... Keith,' I say. 'Aren't we going the wrong way?'

'Marc's orders,' says Keith. 'We'll be varying our route to the theatre from now on.'

'Oh.' I chew my thumbnail. 'Keith, what's going on? Marc wanted me to leave the townhouse as soon as possible. And then there arc these extra guards on the gate, and you've been told to take a different route. I thought the townhouse was safe ...'

'If I've learned anything over the years, it's that Marc always has good reasons for his actions.'

'If you're sure ...'

'Oh, I'm sure.' Keith's eyes mist over. 'You know, years ago, when I first started working for Marc, he asked me to take what I thought was a stupid route to one of his premieres. He was learning a speech in the back of the limo, and I thought to myself, *he doesn't*

*know London like I do. I'll just drive the quickest way,
and he'll thank me for getting him there faster.*

'So I took my own route, and guess what happened?
Paps blocked the road, and we spent an hour stuck in
traffic with cameras banging on the windows. Marc
knew the paps would be there, of course. He'd planned
a back route for us, but I thought I knew best.'

'Was he angry?' I ask.

'No. He just said it was a lesson to trust him in future.
And I always have.'

12

When we reach the theatre, Keith drives the car right up to the stage door so there are only inches between us and the security guards. Then he gets out and checks the security guards' IDs. Only then does he let me out of the car.

I still get a shiver of fear when I see that stage door, but little by little I'm learning to let the past go.

'Thanks Keith,' I say, climbing out of the car.

'Marc asked me to pick you up after your show to-night,' Keith says. 'And drive you straight to your dad's house.'

I chew at my thumbnail again. 'Will Marc be with you? When you come to pick me up?'

'He didn't mention it. But don't worry. I'm sure he won't let you out of his sight for long. I've never seen him so wrapped up in anybody, and I've known him a long time.'

*****

Inside the theatre, I head up to the auditorium and find Leo lounging on the stage, a steaming cup of coffee in one hand and a glazed doughnut in the other. A box of pink, brown and yellow doughnuts sits beside him.

'My leading lady!' Leo gestures to the space beside him. 'I got you espresso. It sounded like you could use waking up earlier.'

'Thanks.' I sit down on the stage and pick up a tiny takeaway espresso cup, wrapping my fingers around the hot cardboard.

'Doughnut? I bought a heart-shaped one, just for you.' Leo pushes the box towards me with his flip-flopped foot. His feet are golden brown, and a little roughed up around the edges – surfer's feet.

I think about what Marc said earlier, about Leo being irresponsible. I can imagine that, when Leo was a teen actor, he could have been a little too carefree. And he still is, in a way. But that doesn't mean he's not a good person.

I shake my head. 'Thanks, but I had a pretty big breakfast.'

'The breakfast of love, huh?' Leo says, taking a bite of his doughnut.

I don't reply.

'Uh oh. You and Marc on the rocks again?'

'I don't think so,' I say. 'But *something* is going on.'

'Would it have anything to do with all the extra security guards around the place?' Leo asks. 'They frisked me this morning before I could enter the theatre. And I've got to give some dumb password at the door and show my driver's licence.'

I laugh.

'What's going on?' Leo asks.

'I wish I knew.' I take a tart sip of espresso and wince. It's too strong for me, but the caffeine is welcome. I should love strong coffee, coming from an Italian background, but I don't.

My mother used to adore espresso. I remember her buying this huge silver espresso maker for our tiny cottage kitchen. 'I miss *real* Italian coffee,' she'd said. She maybe used the machine once. Then it gathered dust on top of the kitchen cupboards, just like her sandwich toaster, ice-cream maker and a zillion other gadgets.

'You look very beautiful this morning, Sophia,' says Leo.

I blush. 'Leo—'

'Oh come on. You must know you're beautiful, in that natural, Disney-eyed, butter-wouldn't-melt sort of way.

A million guys must have told you so.'

'Not really.' I take another sip of my espresso and wince again.

'A little strong for Miss whiter than white?' Leo grins.

'Whoever said I was whiter than white?'

'I did,' says Leo, 'but then again, you've hooked up with Marc Blackwell, so I guess you can't be all that sweet and innocent. Hey, if you two are on the rocks again—'

'We're *not* on the rocks. I should call him. I promised I'd let him know that I arrived safely.' I take out my mobile, but before I can make the call, Leo reaches forwards and snatches the phone.

'Leo!' I shout. 'Give that back.'

'Oh no. I'm not having you checking it every five minutes to see if Prince Charming has called. I'll hang on to this until we've finished rehearsals.'

'Leo, I promised him—'

'I mean it, Sophia. I'm not going to practise with someone who's getting distracted all the time.'

'God!' I shake my head, exasperated. I've never had a little brother, but I'm beginning to understand what having one must be like. 'Leo, give me my phone. I promised Marc I'd call. He'll worry.'

'He should. If you're with me.'

'Give me the phone Leo.' I try to snatch it from him, but he holds it up high. That does it. I climb up on the stage and wrestle his knees until he falls onto the floor.

We end up in a pile together, me on top of Leo trying to claw the phone out of his hand.

'Okay, okay,' Leo laughs, holding up his long arm so the phone is out of my reach again. 'I'll do you a deal. You can have your phone back so you can call your over-protective boyfriend. But after that, I take the phone for the rest of rehearsals, okay? I don't want you checking your phone all the time. It's distracting.'

'Okay, deal,' I say, trying to catch my breath.

Leo hands me the phone. 'Here. I'll help you up.' He wraps his arm around me and sits up, throwing me into his lap in the process.

For a moment our faces are inches apart, and I feel the hard muscles of his arms and his toned chest.

'Why Miss Rose, you're blushing,' says Leo.

I extract myself from his lap, embarrassed that there actually is a blush creeping up my neck and over my cheeks. Then I turn my back on Leo and call Marc, still out of breath from our wrestle.

'Sophia.' Marc answers straight away.

'I'm here,' I tell him. 'I made it to the theatre.' I glance over my shoulder. 'I'm with Leo.'

'I know,' Marc says quietly, his tone foreboding.

'You do?'

'I'm having you monitored at all times. For your safety.'

'Oh.' I swallow, thinking about that little scene with Leo and praying Marc didn't somehow see it through CCTV cameras or something. 'Then ... why did you ask me to call?'

'I like to play safe where you're concerned,' Marc says. 'Make double sure.'

'Are you going to tell me what's going on yet?' I ask.

'Sophia, it could be nothing at all. I don't want to worry you. But while I'm looking into things, it's better that you're not at the townhouse. That's all I can say right now.'

Silence. I want to tell him I love him and miss him. That I can't wait for him to touch me again. That I can't bear us being apart. But I'm so frightened by his sudden anger and coldness. So instead, all that comes out is, 'When will I see you again?'

'Soon, I promise.'

There's a click, and the line goes dead.

'Now you can give me the phone,' says Leo, bounding to his feet. 'We had a deal, remember?'

I sigh. 'Fine.' Reluctantly I hand it to him.

Leo clamps his fingers around the phone. 'I'm going to store this somewhere you can't get hold of it. And then you can focus on me and me alone.'

13

Leo and I spend the day rehearsing, drinking coffee and hot chocolate, ordering in fresh ham sandwiches and sponge cake from a Soho deli and just talking about all sorts of things that don't matter.

At dinner time, we head out to China Town and eat crispy duck pancakes, egg-fried rice and beef in black bean sauce.

Two security guards follow us and wait outside the restaurant while we eat. But still, we have fun.

Leo tells me about his journey from nobody to famous movie star – how he did all sorts of jobs on the way up, from selling surfboards to making smoothies. He tells me about his artist mother and his father who was town mayor for a while.

I tell him a little about my family and how my mother died when I was young.

When Leo asks me again about the security, I'm half tempted to tell him about Giles Getty and the kidnapping, but something in me just can't get the words out. I'm not ready to talk about that. Not yet.

Jen knows something happened, but doesn't know the details. After the kidnapping, I phoned her to say something bad happened at the theatre, and that I might be too spooked to go through with my opening night performance. But she doesn't know much more than that, and she understands me well enough to wait until I'm ready to tell her more.

What Jen does know for sure is that Marc insisted I stay at his townhouse and that he take care of me. I told Jen about all the therapists Marc lined up, and that was enough for her. As long as she knew I was being looked after, she didn't need to know any more.

*****

Leo and I don't work too hard at rehearsing because we know we have another big performance tonight.

When show time finally comes around, we're well practised, but full of energy and in good form. The crowd react well to us and we fix most of the things we felt didn't work on opening night.

Just like always, time flies when I'm performing and before I know it, Leo and I are doing our final bows and walking off stage.

I'm hoping Marc will be waiting for me in the wings, but he isn't. Instead, Keith is there – which takes me by surprise.

'Keith, what are you doing here?' I ask, picking up the skirts of my costume and walking towards him.

'I've come to pick you up.'

'Isn't Marc here?' I ask tentatively.

'No. Sorry. I know I'm no substitute.'

'You'll do just fine,' I say. 'Thanks for coming to get me.'

Leo appears beside me. 'Where's Prince Charming?'

'I was hoping to see him. But ... I guess he has his reasons for not being here.'

'If you were my girlfriend, *I'd* be waiting for you after every show.'

I give him a sideways glance, raising an eyebrow. 'I doubt that,' I say. 'You strike me as the sort of guy who'd be there the first few nights with the biggest bunch of flowers ever, and then get bored and be off chatting up one of the dancers.'

Leo laughs. 'Oh, so cruel!'

'Can I have my phone back now?'

Leo rolls his eyes. 'Sure. It's in my dressing room. I'll go get it for you.'

14

There are no missed calls or text messages on my phone, and I can't help feeling like something more is happening than just some safety thing. Why wouldn't Marc have called, even just to check that I was okay?

I keep the phone in my lap all the way to my dad's house, but there isn't so much as a bleep or a flash. As we near my village, the reception bar creeps lower and lower until it hovers between one bar and no service. Our village council campaigned to keep a mobile phone mast out of our area, so there's still only reception when the wind blows a certain way.

'Keith,' I ask, as we pull up outside the cottage. 'Has Marc told you anything more about what's going on?'

'Not exactly,' says Keith. 'All I know is that he's been tightening security today. I've been swamped with messages about new procedures and passwords.'

I'm about to climb out of the car when Keith holds up a hand to stop me. 'Wait. I'm to escort you right to the door. New instructions.'

'Okay.' I'm beginning to feel really anxious now. Both about all the security and Marc not calling. When Marc and I are apart my body craves him, and the thought of being away from him tonight ... it almost hurts. I need to call him.

Keith comes around to open the car door and just as he does, I see a flash of black outside the front garden.

'What was that?' I gasp.

'Security,' says Keith, helping me out. 'They'll be surrounding the perimeter of your dad's cottage and stationed on the roads leading down here too. One good thing about these little country places – the roads are very easy to monitor. Not like London.'

I step out of the car, my legs a little shaky.

Keith shuts the car door behind me. 'I'm sure there's nothing to be concerned about. But better safe than sorry.'

I nod, and walk up the gravel path towards the house. Everything's dark, and I realise that Dad has no idea I'm coming down here tonight. In all the weirdness of today, and my phone being locked away by Leo, I totally forgot to call him.

I knock softly on the wooden door and wait for an answer.

Silence.

'Everything okay?' Keith asks.

'It looks like no one's home,' I say, confused.

'Maybe they're all asleep.'

'Not Dad. He works shifts as a taxi driver. He's a night owl. He stays awake until three or four in the morning, usually. I guess he could be at work, but he doesn't usually work weekdays this late.'

I knock again, wincing at the loud noise in the darkness.

Inside the cottage, I hear a clunk and then Sammy starts crying.

'Whoops,' I whisper

The door creaks open and I see Dad, looking sleepy and bleary eyed.

'Dad?' I say. 'Were you asleep?'

'Oh. Hello love. I didn't realise it was Christmas Eve already.'

Now I know something's wrong.

'It's not Christmas Eve,' I say, glancing at Keith. 'I'm a day early. Didn't my bags arrive earlier?'

Dad scratches his head. 'Oh, something did. I just thought it was your Christmas presents.'

He blinks, and I notice that his eyes aren't quite focusing.

'Have you been drinking?' I ask.

Dad blinks again. 'Only a few beers.'

I turn to Keith. 'Thanks so much for the lift. I'm fine now, honestly.'

Keith glances at my dad. 'Will you be okay here?'

'Absolutely fine,' I say. 'Don't worry about me. Get back to your family.'

'If you're sure ...'

'Positive. Go on. Get on home.'

Keith hesitates, then gives a little nod. 'Well. If you're sure. There's plenty of security around here. Call if you want anything. Okay? I can be back here within half an hour.'

'Okay.'

Keith heads back to the car.

I turn back to Dad. 'Come on. Let's go in and you can tell me what's going on.'

15

The cottage is dark inside, and silver moonlight turns the sofas into creepy, lumpy shadows. I smell stale beer and old socks, and feel something I haven't felt in the cottage for a very long time – not since the few years after Mum died.

Sadness.

Sammy's still wailing, but Dad doesn't seem to notice.

My stomach ties itself in one knot after another as I walk through the cottage and trip over beer bottles and clumps of clothing.

'Dad,' I say. 'What's going on?'

Sammy's wailing lessens a little and turns into a dull little whimper. Then he becomes quiet, and I guess he must have fallen back to sleep.

I turn and see my dad's pale, creased up face in the moonlight. His hair is standing up all over the place. His eyes are bloodshot and now I see him trying to walk, I know he's a little drunk. And he's holding himself in that way, that same sad defeated way, that he did when Mum died.

A sliver of sickness runs through my stomach as I remember that awful time. Dad, drinking too much, not taking care of himself, depressed all the time. The house a complete state. Me struggling to cope with it and hold the family together, whilst nursing a big, empty hole where Mum had been.

I still miss her, even now. There aren't many days when I don't think of her, one way or another.

'Everything's okay, love,' Dad insists, his words soft and tired. 'You just woke me up, that's all.' There's a clink as he trips over a beer bottle, and he stumbles around until he finds his feet.

'No it isn't.' I turn on the light and wish I hadn't. I'm not sure I've ever seen the cottage looking so bad. Piles of dirty clothes everywhere. A counter covered in dirty plates and cups. There are even a few flies climbing over rubbish bags by the bin, which makes me absolutely shudder. It's winter. Who gets flies in winter?

An empty whisky bottle lies on the dining table, and drained beer bottles are lined up along the floor by Dad's easy chair.

'Oh Dad.' I turn to him and realise how truly awful he looks. Those bleary eyes are bright red under the light. His skin is pale and tired, and he's wearing the same shirt and trousers from the party.

'You were wearing those clothes in bed?' I ask.

'Yes.' Dad scratches his head. He follows my gaze down to his dirty shirt. 'I was too tired to get out of my clothes tonight. It's ... been a long day.'

'And too tired yesterday and the day before by the looks of it. Where's Genoveva?'

'She's taking a break.'

'Dad.' I cross my arms. 'Are you going to tell me what's going on or am I going to have to force it out of you?'

Dad sighs and slumps down on the sofa. 'Genoveva left,' he says, picking up an empty beer bottle from the floor and trying to drink from it. It takes him a good few seconds before he realises the bottle is empty, at which point he tosses it back down to the floor.

It rolls towards my feet and I pick it up. 'Has Sammy been crawling around all this stuff?'

'No.' Dad rubs his eyes. 'A girl from town has been taking him for half the day while I'm at work. She's not bad. Cheap rates. He seems pretty happy with her. And this place isn't so bad.'

'Not so bad?' I try to stuff the empty beer bottle in the overfull bin, before giving up and placing it on the sticky kitchen counter. 'Dad, it's awful. You can't have Sammy in a place like this. Does Genoveva know what a mess it is?'

'I … she won't take my calls. I keep expecting her to walk through the door. But it's been over a week …'

'Oh, Dad.' I go behind the sofa and put my arms around him shoulders. 'Why didn't you tell me? I would have come and stayed here. Helped out.'

'You couldn't have done, love. You're so busy with your play and everything.'

I hug him tighter. 'I'm so sorry. I should have called you. I was …' I think back to that weird and difficult week after the whole Giles Getty thing. '… pretty busy. But I still should have thought of you. I'm so sorry. I knew something was up last night, but I didn't realise it was this bad. You should have said something. You know how important you and Sammy are to me. I'd drop everything to come help out.'

Dad gives a tired smile. 'That's exactly why I didn't tell you.'

'What happened?' I ask. 'With Genoveva? Did you have a big fight or something?'

'Of sorts.' Dad sighs. He grabs another empty beer bottle and starts picking at the label.

'Dad?'

'She's … been seeing someone else.'

'Oh no.'

'A doctor. He lives in the village. He's married.'

'Oh no.'

Dad nods. 'I feel terrible for his wife. They have three kids together. Three times the heartache.'

'So where's Genoveva now?'

'I don't know. I've heard that she's with him. In one

of his holiday homes. I'm just hoping she'll see sense and come back to us. Sammy needs her. I need her too.'

'Poor Sammy. He must not know what end is up right now.'

'Him and me both.'

'Things will get better,' I say, picking up beer bottles. I line them up around the bin, just like I used to after Mum died. 'Time heals.'

'She'll be back,' says Dad. 'I'm sure of it. She just needs time to realise what a terrible mistake she's made.' He puts his head in his hands.

I put a hand on his shoulder. 'I hope so Dad.' But secretly, I can't see it. Genoveva and Dad often rowed, but she's never left him before. And if she's seeing someone else …

'Sammy's missing her like crazy,' says Dad. 'That's why I know she can't have left for good. She'd never leave him for good.'

I don't know what to say about that. Truth be told, I've always thought of Genoveva as a bit on the cold side. I try to see the best in everybody, but with Genoveva it was a struggle at times. And right now, seeing my dad upset like this, it's a *real* struggle.

Two sides to every story, I remind myself. But knowing Genoveva the way I do, perhaps there really is only one side to this one.

'Oh Dad.' I put my arms around him again. 'Let me make you some hot milk and I'll start getting this place cleaned up.'

'No.' Dad shakes his head and clambers to his feet. 'You must be knackered. You've come all the way from London. We'll both get stuck in tomorrow. You should go to bed. Get some rest. We both should.'

His skin looks so pale and thin – almost see through.

'That sounds like a good idea,' I say, knowing full

well that I'm going to insist Dad stays out of my way tomorrow. He's far more of a hindrance than a help when it comes to clearing up, and by the look of him he needs a good lie in. 'You go get some sleep.'

16

After Dad has staggered off upstairs, I creep up myself and sneak a look in Sammy's room. He's sleeping soundly in his cot, his little arms thrown up above his head.

Sammy's room used to be my old bedroom and I love that Sammy sleeps in here.

It's a perfect kid's room because there's a sloping ceiling that makes it hard for an adult to stand up.

Of course, Genoveva has redecorated so it doesn't look anything like my bedroom anymore. The little fairies I painted around the fireplace have been scrubbed off, and the lavender plants I grew along the windowsill have been thrown out. All the old furniture Dad and I found at flea markets has been replaced with white flat pack stuff.

I watch Sammy sleeping for a few minutes, but just as I'm backing out the door, a floorboard creaks and Sammy mutters and rubs his nose.

'Mama,' he says, wide awake suddenly.

I go to him. 'It's alright Sammy,' I whisper, suddenly furious with Genoveva. 'Don't worry. I'll look after you while Mummy's away.' I rub his back until his eyes close and sing the lullaby my mum used to sing to me – *Somewhere over the Rainbow*.

Soon Sammy is asleep, and I creep downstairs.

*****

When I reach the living room, I call Marc.

He picks up on the first ring.

'Sophia.'

'Marc. I … is everything okay? You didn't call—'

'I've been calling and calling,' Marc barks. 'Why

have you had your phone off?'

'I didn't turn my phone off.'

'I called at least twenty times. Every time it said the number was unavailable. I was going out of my mind with worry. I even came to the theatre, but my security team told me you were out. With Leo.'

'We went out to dinner,' I say. 'It was only for an hour or so.'

'If it wasn't for the fact my security people were there ... Sophia, I don't like not being able to reach you.'

Suddenly it hits me. 'Wait. My phone was in Leo's dressing room, at the back of the theatre. There's no phone reception back there. So I guess no calls could get through.'

'Leo's dressing room?' Marc growls.

'He confiscated my phone,' I explain. 'So I could con-centrate better. Otherwise I'd just have been checking it all day for your calls.

'He took your phone?' Marc sounds furious.

'I mean ... it wasn't exactly like that. I agreed to it. He was right. It would have been a distraction.'

I can hear Marc breathing. Hard.

'Marc?'

'Don't give Leo your phone again.'

I rub my eyes, tired suddenly. 'Marc, you're making something out of nothing.'

'Get some sleep. I'll see you soon.'

'When?' I ask. 'It's Christmas Eve tomorrow.'

'And you have all day free. Until your show at eight.'

'How do you know that?'

'Because I know your schedule.'

'How?'

'Sophia, it's my job to look after you. Don't you think I'd find out your rehearsal and show schedule?'

'Yes, but how?'

'One of my team is very good at extracting information from computers.'

I sigh. 'You could have just asked me. I'd tell you whatever you wanted to know.'

Marc laughs. 'Like the fact you were going out to dinner with Leo Falkirk?'

'That was a last minute thing. I would have told you. It was no secret.' I slump on the sofa, really tired all of a sudden. 'Look, I'm too tired for you to be jealous right now, okay? We're having a bit of a family crisis.'

'What's going on?' Marc's voice is urgent.

'Genoveva left. Dad needs a bit of looking after.'

'Do you need me to send anyone? Staff? Rodney?'

'No, it's fine. Dad isn't the sort of person who likes strangers around when he's down. He needs his family right now.'

'You're a very good daughter.'

'I'm just looking after my dad, that's all. Just like anyone else would do. What did you have planned for tomorrow?'

A pause. 'I was planning on taking you shopping. But if your father needs you—'

'Shopping?'

'For Christmas presents.'

'I've bought all my Christmas presents,' I say. 'Months ago. I like to get my shopping out of the way early.' I don't add, *it works out cheaper that way.*

Marc laughs. 'Very organised. But I didn't mean *your* shopping. *I* wanted to buy Christmas presents for you and your family.'

'Oh Marc.' I feel myself soften. 'That's … lovely. Truly. But please don't feel you have to go to any trouble. My family are just happy to be together at Christmas. And as for me, being with you on Christmas day is the best present ever.'

'I'd never dream of turning up at your family home without Christmas gifts.'

I smile down the phone. 'I understand. I guess I'd feel the same, if I were you.' I hesitate. 'But ... how can you buy a present for me if I'm with you?'

'Very easily,' says Marc. 'You can choose exactly what you like.'

'But then it won't be a surprise.'

Marc laughs. 'I forgot. You like surprises.'

'Yes I do.'

'You like to challenge me, don't you Miss Rose?'

'You're one to talk.'

'Fine. A surprise it is.'

My chest flutters. 'Marc. Don't get me anything too expensive, will you? I mean, I couldn't afford to get you anything too big, so just get me something small.'

'I don't want you to get me a present,' says Marc.

'Why not?'

'I'm not a great receiver.'

'But I want to give you a present. It will make me happy.'

A pause. 'I would never stop you doing anything that made you happy.'

17

The next morning, I'm woken up earlier than usual by Sammy crying. It's a desperate, long wailing that prickles at my heart and has me leaping to my feet.

I trip over toys and towels in the hallway, and burst into Sammy's room, finding that he's pulled himself up in the cot and is howling over the bars.

'Sammy, Sammy,' I say, my face softening. 'What's all this noise about then?' I take him out of the cot, and his chubby little hands grip at my hair. He snuggles himself into my shoulder and calms down.

'Sammy?' Dad comes crashing into the room in his boxer shorts and t-shirt.

'It's okay Dad. You go back to bed. I'll get Sammy his milk.'

Dad rubs his eyes. 'Are you sure love?'

'I'm sure. It looks like you could use the extra sleep. Go on. It's fine.'

'You're really sure?'

'Positive.'

'Well. Wake me if you need anything.'

'I will,' I say, knowing I won't.

I walk Sammy to the window. It's still pretty dark out, but the sky is greying as dawn approaches. 'Look out there Sammy,' I say. 'The sun will come up soon. It's Christmas Eve already, isn't that exciting? Santa's going to come tomorrow and bring you lots of toys.'

I see a flash of someone moving outside the cottage and leap back from the window.

'What the–' I grip Sammy tighter, my heart beating like a drum. When I look closer, I see that the black figure is one of Marc's security team. 'Whoa. Okay,

okay. Just security.' *But they're pretty active for first thing in the morning. I hope everything's okay.*

I walk Sammy to the guest bedroom, grab my phone from the bedside table and call Marc.

'Sophia.' Marc's voice sounds crisp and wide awake, as if he's been sitting by the phone, waiting for my call. 'You're up early. Is everything okay?'

'Sammy woke me. It's fine, but I just had the fright of my life seeing one of your security guards prowling around the cottage. Are you going to tell me what's going on?'

'I told you. It's nothing—'

'Marc.' My voice is stern. 'Just … tell me, please. I'll worry more if you don't. Is it something to do with Getty?'

'In a roundabout way.'

My heart beats faster. 'Did they let him out?'

'No. He's still in custody.'

'He is?' I'm confused now. 'Then what's going on? And how can it have anything to do with him?'

'It's to do with … people he knows. Look. I want this to be a good Christmas for you. I don't want you dwelling on something that's probably not important. Just trust that I'm handling everything and keeping you safe. After Christmas, if security is still an issue, I'll tell you everything. Okay?'

'After Christmas?'

'After Christmas. But until then, I want you to forget that there's security around.'

'That's going to be pretty tough.'

'I know.' A pause. 'How's your father?'

'I don't know yet. I sent him back to bed so I could take care of Sammy and do the housework.'

At the mention of his name, Sammy wriggles a little in my arms, and I rebalance everything so I don't drop the phone.

'Let me send you some assistance,' says Marc.

I sigh. 'It's fine. Really. Like I said, Dad's not in a great place for having strangers around. He needs his family here. It might be best if I stay a while.'

'Can I at least send Rodney over to help you with the housework?'

'It won't take me long. Just a few hours.'

'I don't want you tiring yourself out. You have your show this evening. Unless you'd like me to contact Davina. Tell her you're taking a break for personal reasons.'

'I can't do that. People have bought tickets. I can't let them down.'

Marc gives a little laugh. 'If it were my show, that's what I'd say too. But when I hear you say it, it's different. The show can wait. Your well-being is more important.'

'But I'm fine,' I insist. 'I can manage. And I can't wait to perform again tonight. Leo and I are working really well together.'

'I'm delighted to hear it,' says Marc, and I hear that edge to his voice again.

'Marc, there's no need to be jealous.'

'Not jealous. Protective.'

'Whatever you want to call it, you don't need to be concerned about Leo.'

'I think you and I are going to have to disagree on that one.'

'I wish you could forgive him for that paparazzi thing. He really didn't mean any harm.'

'I'm trying, Sophia. Believe me. The way I feel about you – it's all pretty new to me. Sometimes, I have a hard time dealing with how strong these emotions are.'

'New to you?'

'Love is a first for me. You know that.'

I glance at Sammy, who has dozed a little over my shoulder. 'Same here,' I reply.

There's a moment's silence.

'I love you Sophia,' says Marc. 'Always.'

'Always?'

'Always,' comes Marc's soft reply. 'And your needs will always come first. If you need to be with your father, I'll go shopping alone.'

Oh, the thought of not seeing him today … but if Dad needs me, then that's just the way things will have to be.

'Being away from you is so hard,' I say.

'I know,' says Marc. 'And it doesn't get any easier.'

Sammy begins to fidget, and I start rocking him back and forth until he's still.

'I guess, even if I don't see you today, at least we'll have Christmas day,' I say. 'I know it's probably not your usual Christmas, hanging out in some small cottage in a middle-of-nowhere village.'

'As long as I'm with you, there's nowhere I'd rather be.'

18

When I leave my bedroom, I hear Dad snoring and am happy that he's fallen back to sleep. Better that than he comes downstairs and gets in my way while I'm trying to clean.

'Come on Sammy,' I say, creaking down the staircase. 'Let's get you some milk.'

Down in the kitchen, I find the formula milk tub is dry and crusty and full of lumps. I see a bottle in the sink that I guess Dad must rewash every morning.

Putting Sammy in his high chair, I give the bottle a really good scrub and then sterilise it in a pan of boiling water. I flick the kettle on.

'It's a wonder you haven't been ill,' I mutter, running the bottle under the cold tap to cool it down, and then mashing up formula milk into warm water from the kettle. 'But ... Dad's just not cut out for this sort of thing.'

How could Genoveva leave Dad alone with Sammy like this? She must realise he doesn't know up from down when it comes to childcare.

I scoop Sammy from the chair, noticing his bottom is now stuck with crumbs, and lay him in my arms to drink his milk. Then I go looking for a diaper, because he's soaked through.

In Sammy's room, there are only empty diaper wrappers, but I find a creased up, grey diaper stuffed under his pram and change him.

After I've brushed my teeth with no toothpaste and washed my face with no soap, I decide the first thing Sammy and I need to do is head to the shops.

Sammy has no clean clothes, so I dress him in a baby

ski suit with ketchup stains on it, sit him in his pram and head out to the convenience store to buy supplies.

*****

Half an hour later, I'm back home with a plastic bag of essentials: baked beans, sliced bread, tea and eggs for Dad's breakfast, milk, formula, diapers, baby food and wet wipes for Sammy. I also buy bin bags, toilet roll, washing-up liquid, soap and toothpaste.

I wipe Sammy's chair down, then settle him in there with a rattle and some baby porridge.

When I've fed him, I make myself a hot cup of tea and set to work.

The more washing and cleaning I do, the more jobs I seem to find. Washing the plates, for example, makes me realise how dirty the draining rack is, so I have to stop to scrub it all over. And when I take the bins out, I realise Dad can't have put the wheelie bin on the curb since Genoveva left, so I have to haul the green bin, along with sacks of rubbish, down the front path and onto the pavement.

I wash two loads of Sammy's clothes before I can even start on Dad's laundry, and by ten o'clock I'm sweaty, dirty and my hair is standing up all over the place. But the house is looking much better, and I feel good.

The living room is clean enough for Sammy to crawl around, and he's having great fun trying to pull himself up on the sofa, and chewing the toys that I've washed and dried for him.

I hear Dad creaking around upstairs and set to work on breakfast for both of us – baked beans on toast with a fried egg on top.

When Dad comes downstairs, his eyes light up at the clean house and the breakfast on the table.

'It's good to have you home love,' he says, his words full of emotion. 'I haven't been coping. Well, I suppose that's pretty obvious.' He takes a seat at the dining table.

'It's okay Dad. You haven't had an easy time.'

'You're the best daughter a dad could hope for. You know that, don't you?'

'Oh, I wouldn't go that far. I should have visited sooner.'

Dad sits at the table. 'This looks great, love. First decent breakfast I've had all week.'

'What have you been eating?' I ask, somewhat dreading the answer.

'Cheap bacon sandwiches from the burger van on the industrial estate.'

'What's Sammy been having?'

'Milk and a bit of my bacon roll.'

'I'll go shopping again later. Get some proper food in.'

'Would you write down a few meals that I can do for Sammy?' Dad asks. 'Simple things. You know. That even someone like me can do.'

I smile. My dad can make the simplest cooking complicated. He tried to make sausage and mash once. I still shudder at the places I found mashed potato.

'Of course I will Dad, but you needn't worry for the time being. I'm going to stay here a few days.'

'You are?'

'Of course. I'm not going to leave you and Sammy alone.'

'You'll still do your shows, won't you love?'

'Yes. I can't let the audiences down. But I'll make sure I leave you and Sammy with a good meal and instructions for his bedtime. Do you have someone who can babysit when you're out working?'

'I'm not working right now. I need to get my head together.'

'I wish you'd called me before. What did you think?

That I'd turn up on Christmas day and not notice what a state the house was in?'

'I thought I'd have it cleared up by then.'

'Ever the optimist.' I smile, and I'm happy to see Dad give me a tired smile in return.

'Something like that.'

19

After I've cleared away the breakfast things, I hang out the washing and spend the rest of the morning stocking up on supplies and playing with Sammy.

I make a simple lunch of soup and sandwiches – finger sandwiches with marmite for Sammy, and cheese and pickle for Dad and I, washed down with mugs of milk from the local farm.

While the three of us eat, I watch my dad and realise how glad I am to be here taking care of him.

This last week must have been really stressful for him. He doesn't have a clue when it comes to housework and cooking.

He loves Sammy to bits, but he's all fingers and thumbs when he changes diapers, and he can never quite remember how much milk Sam should have, and all the other practical things about looking after a baby.

It's really not his fault. It would be like asking me to drive Dad's taxi. I'd have no idea how to work the metre, or the best route from the high street to the train station.

'I wish I had time to get you a Christmas tree,' I say, looking at the empty corner of the lounge where we'd usually put a real fir. 'We went to the village earlier, but the grocers had sold out.'

Dad chews a mouthful of cheese and pickle sandwich. 'Sorry love. I meant to get one, but somehow Christmas Eve came far quicker than I thought it would. So when's your fella coming to stay?'

'Marc? I'm hoping he'll come tonight. After the show. It's going to be weird having him as a guest here. But good weird, I hope.'

There's an awkward silence.

'Are you angry at me?' Dad asks. 'About not giving the two of you my blessing yet?'

'Not angry,' I say. 'Just … I guess a little confused. I love him so much, and he loves me. I don't know how you can't see it.'

Dad sighs. 'Genoveva and I moved in together quickly. And now I realise that maybe I didn't know her at all. For her to leave Sammy like that … she's not the woman I thought she was.

'I couldn't stand for you to be in the pain I'm in right now. You and Marc … it all seems very … I don't know. Sudden. He's so much older, and you've hardly known each other five minutes. I don't want you making a mistake.'

'When you know you know. Isn't that what you always said with Mum? That you were young, but you both knew you wanted to be together forever?'

'And is that what you want? With this Marc fellow? A forever kind of thing?'

'More than anything.' I look down at my sandwich. 'He's the most amazing person. So amazing. Sometimes I wonder what he's doing with someone like me.'

Dad laughs. 'Haven't you seen the way he looks at you? He's crazy about you.'

'But maybe one day he'll realise that I'm not anyone special.'

Dad drops his sandwich and reaches across the table to take my hands. 'You're very, very special, Sophia Rose. You're one of the most special people going.'

'Thanks Dad, but I think you might be biased.'

'I can see that the man cares about you. But maybe you should take things a bit slower, that's all. Go easy. There's no rush. To talk about marriage already … it seems a little crazy.'

'It doesn't feel crazy to me. It feels right. But I need your blessing as well as your permission. I couldn't marry him without both.'

'I didn't say I wouldn't give my blessing, exactly. But … there are certain things I'd need to be assured of before I said yes.'

'Such as?'

'Marc and I can talk about that on Christmas Day. What does he drink? Brandy? Port?'

'Whisky, I guess. And champagne. But he's not a big drinker.'

'I'm pleased to hear it.' Dad tags a swig of milk. 'So. What are your plans for today? It's Christmas Eve – don't you and Jen usually get up to something?'

I twiddle my hair. 'Marc was going to take me shopping, but there's still more washing to put on so … I was just going to stay here, keep you company.'

Dad sighs. 'At the risk of completely going against what I just said, I don't want you stuck here cleaning the house on Christmas Eve. You go out with your fella and enjoy yourself. Did you say he was going to take you shopping?'

'Yes.'

'Don't you hate shopping?'

'This is a different sort of shopping,' I say. 'I'm helping him choose presents.'

Dad pushes away his empty plate. 'You enjoy yourself, love. Don't stay here with me, moping.'

I lean over to wipe Sam's face. 'You're sure? You won't be too lonely? And you'll be okay with Sammy?'

'I'm going to have you all day tomorrow. That's more than enough.'

'Sure?'

'Absolutely positive.'

'Okay. I'll leave some snacks out for Sammy. And I'll

leave supper out for the two of you, and clean bottles for Sammy's bedtime.'

'You go out and have fun, love.'

'I'd better call Marc.'

20

Marc says he'll pick me up at three o'clock in the limo.

At half two, I pace around the garden, checking my watch every minute and watching time tick by.

When the limo finally pulls up outside the cottage, my chest begins to flutter like there's a nest of birds inside it.

I run out of the house, flinging my coat around my shoulders.

Before I can get to the car, the back door opens and Marc steps out.

He's wearing a fitted black suit, black shirt and black tie, and his hair is thick and loose over his forehead.

Reaching me in two short strides, he lifts me clean off the ground and buries his head into my neck.

'God, you smell good.' He inhales deeply.

'I missed you,' I whisper, holding him equally tight.

Marc scoops me into his arms and carries me to the limo. When we're inside, he places me on the seat and kneels in front of me, his chest pressed close to mine, arms around my neck.

'I've been driving myself crazy thinking about you,' Marc says.

'Oh? And what you have been thinking?'

'I've been thinking about you tied up, gagged, begging me to fuck you.'

I swallow. 'And they say romance is dead.'

Marc gives me a deadly smile. 'What isn't romantic about making you come over and over again?'

The limo pulls out onto the road, and I sway in Marc's arms.

'You do realise what a dangerous situation you've just walked in to?' says Marc.

'I thought your job was to keep me safe,' I reply.

'From everyone but me.'

'Luckily I don't want to be safe with you,' I murmur. 'Exactly how unsafe had you planned on being?'

'I hadn't made any plans at all,' says Marc. 'Except to fuck you in the back of this limo.'

'Here?' I whisper.

'You had no complaints before.'

'I did, if you remember.'

'Ah yes.' Marc slides my hair behind my shoulder and starts running his lips along my neck.

I shiver.

'Our first argument,' Marc murmurs against my skin. 'I remember it fondly.'

'What else do you remember?' I whisper, melting as his lips do their work.

'Fucking you that night, even though I swore I wouldn't. Being amazed by how irresistible you were. How you broke down my self control.'

'You were pretty tough to break,' I say, feeling shivers run down my neck as Marc works around it, grazing the skin with his lips. He pushes his lips firmly against my throat and sucks gently.

I give a little unexpected '*oh*' as the pressure does its work.

Marc sucks harder, running his tongue back and forth. Then he slides my coat from my shoulders until it's bunched up behind my back.

Underneath I'm wearing a long red sweater and my usual skinny jeans – dark black today. I'm not wearing Converse, though. It's too cold. Instead, I've chosen scrunched up grey ankle boots in suede leather.

Marc works both hands under my buttocks and pulls

me too him, kneeling higher so the hardness at his groin presses between my legs.

He pulls off his tie in one elegant movement and holds it up in front of me. 'Hold out your wrists.'

21

'Marc, really? Here?'

'Now,' Marc barks.

Oh god. It's such a turn on when he takes charge of me.

Obligingly, I hold my wrists out, and Marc takes them in his hands, rubbing his thumbs over the delicate white skin. He presses his thumbs tight against my pulse points until I let out a little moan.

His eyes hold me, watching me with such intensity that my insides are turning softer and softer.

Still looking straight into my eyes, Marc presses the insides of my wrists together and holds them tight with one strong hand. Then he strokes the tie back and forth over the backs of my hands, teasing me.

'Are you going to tie me up?' I whisper, feeling hot to the point of exploding.

'Do you want me to?' Marc asks, with a quirky tilt of his lips.

'Yes.'

'Then tell me.'

'I want you to tie me up.'

Marc groans, and his eyes cloud over, going all soft and carnal. His lips drop open. 'God, I love hearing you say that…'

He looks down at my wrists and wraps the tie tight around them, pulling the two ends hard so my wrists snap against each other. Then he ties a complicated knot with a long, loose end.

'Another quick release knot?' I say, my voice hoarser than ever.

'Of course'

'You must have been a great boy scout.'

'Funnily enough, I never joined.'

'So where did you learn to tie knots?' I ask.

'Someone taught me.'

'Who?'

'A woman.'

'Oh.'

Marc runs his fingers up and under the sleeves of my red sweater, slowly and gently. 'It's okay. It's not what you think. I worked backstage when I was a teenager. Between acting jobs. I'd help set up the stage and move equipment. There are a lot of knots backstage. The stage manager gave me a first class course in knot tying.'

He moves his hands back down to my wrists. 'It was very useful training.'

'I guess it would be,' I murmur, feeling his fingers through the cool silk of his tie.

'God,' Marc moans, gazing at my bound wrists. 'You look so good tied up like that.'

I feel him throb between my legs.

He fixes those deadly blue eyes on me, then in one swift movement he lifts my arms high above my head.

'Oh!'

He's bound my wrists in just the right way, so when they're above my head they feel like they belong there.

There must be a suit hook in this part of the car, because when Marc lifts my wrists they catch on something, and when he lets them go, I'm held in place.

I pull my wrists left and right to test the theory and I find I'm held fast.

Marc's eyes darken. 'Is it wrong that I like seeing you struggle like that?'

'Only if I wasn't into it.' And I am. Oh god, I am. Being restrained like this, with Marc watching me like a tiger about to pounce, totally helpless and at his mercy

... I can already feel how wet I am, and Marc has barely touched me.

Marc is breathing hard, watching me. His eyes are hungry, and I know mine are too.

When the car turns a corner and I'm thrown around a little, his breathing gets even harder, and he lets out a moan and dives forwards, tugging off my boots, unfastening my jeans and flinging them off. He rips my panties off too, and lifts my jumper and my bra so he can play with my breasts, squeezing them together and pushing his lips against my nipples.

I can feel him so hard between my legs that his trousers must be straining to bursting point.

'Oh Marc,' I moan, as I feel his warm mouth and strong fingers on my breasts.

He responds by pulling back, taking a condom from his pocket and freeing himself from his trousers. I watch, completely turned on to see him working on the condom, the rubber straining all over.

I'm breathing so hard that I think I might faint, and I just don't think I can bear another moment without him inside me.

'Please Marc,' I whimper.

The car turns another corner and I'm thrown forward into him, my body loose and limp against my restraints.

Marc pushes his body against mine. He puts his lips to my ear and breathes, 'I was going to tease you. To make you wait. But I can't. You're completely irresistible to me, Sophia Rose. Irresistible.'

He plunges all the way inside me in one stroke, and I gasp and let out a moan of pleasure.

Then he begins to pump back and forth, effortlessly, smoothly, his breathing quickening with every movement.

I'm in a world of pleasure, bound and held captive

while he does what he wants. Which also happens to be just what I want.

Oh god, oh god.

He's moving stronger and deeper now, pressing his groin harder against me, rubbing so tingles of pleasure shoot all over my abdomen.

After a few hard strokes that leave me breathless with pleasure, he stops and pulls back, panting and pushing thick brown hair from his forehead.

'Marc, please—'

But before I can protest, Marc lowers his head between my legs. His tongue begins circling just above where he entered me in quick, electric strokes that drive me absolutely wild. But it's too raw. Too sensitive. And I'm almost in pain.

'It's too much,' I beg. 'Please. Stop. I can't take it.'

Marc lifts his head. 'I know *exactly* how much you can take.'

'Marc, *please*.' Restrained as I am, there's absolutely nothing I can do but endure the sharp shocks of pleasure that are shooting up and down my body. I wriggle and fight, but Marc simply holds me steady with one hand and continues his torture.

'Oh, *oh*. Please Marc. Please stop.'

Little by little, the sharpness begins turning sweet, until soft waves of pleasure lap around my thighs.

'I'm going to come,' I moan. 'Oh god Marc. Oh god.' I can feel my neck and cheeks are flushed, and my eyelids are half closed and flickering

Marc pulls back. 'Not yet.'

He kneels up again so his groin is level with mine, and I see him huge and hard, inches from me.

God, I want him inside me. I'm absolutely aching for him. But he doesn't slide in. Instead, he puts his hands under my buttocks and pulls me towards him so I'm slouching in the seat.

My chin is almost touching my chest, and my arms are stretched up, up.

Marc opens my legs wide apart. Then he opens up my buttocks, and I realise what he has in mind.

22

'Marc,' I gasp. 'You can't be serious. In the car?'

'You're ready for this,' says Marc. 'And from where I'm sitting, you're not in much of a position to argue.'

'If I did argue, would you listen?'

Marc frowns. 'You know I would. Tell me to stop and I'll stop.'

I bite my lip, and feel my buttocks throb at the thought of him inside me.

'Don't stop.'

Marc moves in closer, widening my buttocks with his hands and sliding himself between them. 'I'll pull out if it gets too much.'

'*Ooohh*,' I moan as he begins to work his way inside, little by little.

'Feels good?'

'Y—yes.'

Marc's eyes begin to close as he inches in further.

'Oh god. Oh Sophia, I can't—' He hesitates, breathing hard. 'Wait,' he says, more to himself than me. Then after a moment, he says, 'Okay. Okay.' He begins inching further inside so slowly and carefully that, although it's a little tight and sore, it mainly feels good.

Marc moves his thumb between my legs, where his tongue was a few moments ago, and begins pressing and circling until I'm absolutely out of my mind with pleasure.

'Oh. *Oh*. Marc. Oh. *Oh*.'

When he begins to slide in and out of me, I can't take any more.

'Oh Marc. I'm coming. I'm coming.'

I come in places I never knew I could come, and the

pleasure that washes over my body is like nothing I've ever known in my life.

I feel like I've been dipped in syrup, and the intimacy of what we're sharing … it makes me feel closer to Marc than ever.

Marc groans and gives one last little push inside me, moaning into my ear, shouting my name and wrapping my hair around his hands.

'Sophia. Oh Sophia,' he shouts, as my body throbs all around him and warmth spreads from my neck all the way down to my toes.

'I love you,' I manage to say, my voice soft and deep.

'*God*. I love you too,' says Marc.

We stay like that for a moment, clinging to each other. Then I feel him loosen inside me and slide free.

Marc reaches up and, in one swift movement, frees my hands, taking hold of my wrists and rubbing them to get the circulation going.

He kisses the red skin and strokes my wrists. Then he scoops a hand down and removes the condom. He places it in a paper cup and slots it into a little bin fitted below one of the seats. Then he takes me in his arms and holds me close.

'I never thought I could be any closer to you. But just then, I lost myself a little bit more.'

'I know,' I whisper into his neck, loving his warmth and his strong arms. 'I felt closer to you than ever just then.'

After a moment, Marc helps me back into my panties and jeans, and does up his trousers. Then he threads the tie effortlessly around his neck in the most casual way, as if it had been hanging innocently in his wardrobe this whole time.

I laugh. 'You're really going to wear that tie now?'

'Of course I am. It's just become my favourite tie.'

Marc sits beside me and pulls me close. 'Are you okay? I didn't take things too far?'

'No, it was just like always,' I say, a smile creeping onto my face. 'Almost too far, but in the end, just far enough.'

'With you, going just far enough is getting harder and harder,' says Marc. 'I worry that one day, I won't be able to stop myself.'

'*I'm* not worried,' I say. 'I trust you.'

Marc's eyes fix on mine. 'How did I deserve someone so perfect?'

The car drives on into central London, and we stay wrapped up in each other's arms, watching London rush past.

23

The limo eventually comes to a stop at a beautiful stone square with a fountain at the centre, right in the heart of West London. The square is lined with tall trees, their feathery branches hung with elegant red jack-o-lanterns and white fairy lights.

'Where are we?' I ask Marc, as he helps me out of the car and into my coat.

'Sloane Square.'

'That's Chelsea, isn't it?'

'Absolutely correct.'

I remember seeing a documentary about Sloane Square once. It talked about women called 'Sloane Rangers' – girls who live in posh Chelsea flats and hang around Sloane Square buying designer clothes and looking for rich husbands.

I look around the square. Perfectly groomed women in Vogue-magazine clothes walk purposefully along, swinging their gorgeous, shiny hair and designer hand-bags. Instinctively, my hand goes to my unruly waves and I twiddle and tug.

'It's okay,' says Marc, slipping an arm around my shoulder. 'Don't be nervous.'

'Do I look nervous?'

'A little.'

'I guess I just feel a bit out of place.'

'You're not out of place. You're very much in place.'

'I don't know about that. It's … the people around here are very stylish. Beautiful. Classy. And here I am in my jeans …'

'Believe me. You have more class and beauty than any of these women.'

We walk past a huge Christmas tree, hung with ceramic gingerbread men and twinkling lights. It's beautiful, but it's had its roots cut off and the sawn tree stump sits in icy water.

'I always get sad when I see real trees without their roots,' I tell Marc. 'In our family, we buy the whole tree and replant it in the garden or the woods when Christmas is over. Well. Except Dad didn't have time to get a tree this year. It's a shame. I would have liked you to see the cottage all Christmassed up. It looks cosy.'

'As long as *you're* in the cottage, I couldn't care less about the decorations.'

Marc steers me off the main square, down a narrower side road buzzing with black cabs.

'Where are we going?' I ask.

'A friend of mine owns a shop here. A toy shop. I thought you could help me choose something for Sammy.'

We come to a stop by a glossy window full of beautiful, handcrafted wooden toys. The window is set into a tall, red-brick building, and a gold coloured veranda hangs from the wall with the words 'Peter's Toys' printed onto it.

I stare at the window display. There's something truly magical about the toys here.

They're all made of solid wood, and I can tell they've been crafted by someone who loves what they do.

There are dolls houses, push trolleys, building blocks, a wooden tricycle … even a logging truck, complete with hand-painted logs on the back. I know Sam will *love* pushing that around.

'This shop is just perfect for Sammy,' I say. 'I can't wait to go inside.'

'You like it?' Marc asks, as I gaze through the window.

'Peter makes most of the toys himself. It's a real labour of love.'

'And I love it,' I say.

'Good. Let's go inside.'

24

The bell jangles overhead as we enter the shop, and inside there's the most gorgeous smell of apple wood and sawdust. The floor is strewn with red wood peelings, and toys are arranged on carved wooden tiers and sliced tree-trunk shelves, complete with bark. It's like walking inside a hollowed out tree.

A tall, thin man with white hair and round glasses comes striding towards us, pushing up the sleeves of his striped shirt. 'Marc. How the devil are you?'

'Peter,' Marc replies, shaking the man's hand. 'Great to see you.'

Marc keeps one arm around my shoulder, which causes Peter to look at me with interest.

'Well I never. Marc Blackwell out in daylight hours with a young lady. *You* must be someone very special.'

'This is Sophia Rose,' says Marc, tightening his arm around my shoulder. 'And yes – she is very special to me. Very special indeed.'

'I'm glad to hear it,' says Peter. 'It's about time you found a good woman.'

'There's no better woman than Sophia.'

'Good, good. Well, let me get you both a sherry. Celebrate the season.' Peter goes to the back of the shop and returns with a bottle of Lustau sherry and three crystal tumblers.

Placing the tumblers by the cash register, he pours generous measures in each and hands glasses to Marc and I.

'Good stuff isn't it?' he declares, taking a swig of his own. 'I've been looking for an excuse to open that bottle since November.'

'Delighted to give you the opportunity,' says Marc, taking a sharp sip.

'Thank you.' I take a sip of mine and it's delicious. Dry and crisp and incredibly warming on a winter's day. It rolls down my throat so smoothly that I'd hardly know it was alcoholic, but the heat that follows tells me otherwise.

'Well. How can I help you today?' Peter asks, taking another swig of sherry. 'Something for the nephew again? Or are we furnishing a nursery?' He gives me a sideways glance and a wink.

I sneak a look at Marc, and am relieved to see he's smiling.

'Not just yet,' he says. 'We're after a toy for a one year old.'

'I think I already know what he'd like,' I say, casting my eye around the shop. The intricacy of some of the toys is just stunning. It kind of makes me wish I was a little girl again, so I could play with the doll's house and the beautiful hand-carved furniture suite inside.

'That logging truck in the window,' I say. 'It's just perfect. He'll love pushing it along, then taking the wood off the back and chewing on it.'

'He can chew away,' says Peter proudly, hooking his thumbs into his trouser pockets and rocking back and forth. 'All natural dyes. Non toxic.'

'You make such beautiful things,' I say, looking around the shop again. 'It must have taken you a lifetime to carve all these toys.'

'Years,' says Peter, putting his sherry glass on a shelf and walking to the window. He plucks the logging truck from the window display, holding it with two hands. 'This is one of my favourites. I'll be pleased to send it to a good home.'

He carries it carefully to the wrapping area, and

lovingly folds sheet after sheet of brown tissue paper around it. Then he pulls free a sheet of gold wrapping paper decorated with holly leaves, and expertly gift wraps the truck, sticking a real sprig of holly to the paper.

'It's young holly,' he explains, passing Marc the parcel. 'So the little one won't prick himself on the leaves.'

Marc takes the parcel in one hand and places his sherry by the cash register. Then he takes out his wallet.

'No, no, put your money away,' says Peter. 'I wouldn't dream of it.'

'Peter, giving to your charity is entirely different from buying things from your shop.'

'Not when you donate thousands of pounds it isn't.' Peter turns to me. 'Marc has been *very* generous to Woodlands. Very generous indeed.'

'Woodlands?' I ask Marc, raising a curious eyebrow.

'Peter's charity,' says Marc, in a voice that tells me he wants to end this conversation as soon as possible.

'It supports the tree farmers who supply my wood,' says Peter. 'Makes sure they get a fair rate of pay, good housing, that sort of thing.'

'Sounds like a good cause,' I say.

'It *is* a good cause,' says Marc. 'Which is why Peter and I always have this argument when I come in here.'

'Marc wins every time,' says Peter, with a little wink. 'But what he doesn't know is that whatever he pays me I put straight into the charity bucket.'

'In that case, I'm going to have to pay you double,' says Marc, with a smile.

Peter slaps his forehead. 'Fine, fine. You win as usual.' He takes the handful of notes that Marc passes him, then hands him back his sherry. 'How's Denise?'

'Good. Enjoying life at the college.'

'But?'

'But nothing.' Marc takes another sip of sherry. 'A woman of her years and experience is allowed to choose the lifestyle that suits her.'

'And you think it suits her? Living alone?'

'That's what she tells me.'

'And you believe her?'

'It doesn't matter what I think. Denise's choices are hers and hers alone to make.'

'Well *I* think Denise is a wonderful woman and it's criminal that she never remarried.'

'She's never expressed any interest in finding someone new.'

'Not to you, but you're like the son she never had,' says Peter, wiggling his white eyebrows. 'Parents don't tend to talk to their children about their dating affairs. Would you like me to play matchmaker? I know a friend of Valerie's who lost his wife a few years ago. A lovely fellow. Plays the violin. Likes the theatre. What do you say, shall we match them up?'

'I'd say we'd be interfering in Denise's life,' says Marc.

'Shame,' says Peter, draining his sherry glass. 'I do like a bit of interfering from time to time.' He gives Marc a wicked grin.

'Denise will find someone when she's ready,' says Marc. 'Until then, she seems perfectly happy. Or at least if not happy, then content.' Marc finishes up his sherry, and I drink the last of mine too.

'Nothing wrong with content,' says Peter.

Marc places his empty glass by the cash register and shakes Peter's hand. 'It's been great to see you again. We should catch up soon.'

'Always a pleasure,' says Peter, shaking Marc's hand heartily.

'Have a wonderful Christmas.'

Peter looks bewildered. 'Have a wonderful Christmas? What have you done to him Sophia? He usually pretends Christmas doesn't exist. Does everything he can to avoid talking about it.'

'I didn't know *that*.' I throw Marc a playful smile.

'There are still plenty of things you don't know about me Miss Rose.'

25

When we leave the shop, Marc holds Sammy's gift-wrapped toy in one hand, and pulls the door closed with the other. I shiver as the cold winter wind hits me, and Marc puts an arm around my shoulder and pulls me close.

'Don't you feel the cold?' I whisper, warming myself against his chest.

'At times.'

'Why don't you ever wear a coat?'

'Because I like the sting of cold weather.'

'Why?' I rub my fingers together to keep away the chill.

'I had it stolen from me. The cold. When I was a child. I was taken to LA in the baking sun, and missed year after year of ice and snow in England. So now I want to feel the cold. Every bit of it. As much as I can.'

'It must have been awful for you,' I say, as Marc steers me along the road and back onto the main square. 'To leave your old life behind like that. When you were so young.'

Marc shrugs. 'When you're young, you accept what's happening because it feels normal. But I was messed up for a long time. A long, long time. I wasn't like you, taking care of everyone.'

'Oh I don't know.' I smile at Marc. 'You took care of your sister. And Denise. Maybe you're not such a big bad wolf after all.'

'No, that's exactly what I am. A big bad wolf. And if you're not careful, Sophia Rose, you'll get bitten.'

'I'm not afraid of you,' I say, meeting his eyes, a half smile on my lips.

'Perhaps you should be.'

'Oh? And why is that?'

'Because I'm still a controlling monster at heart. Despite the fact that I'm learning to let go. My way of coping when times are hard is still to take charge and be in control. When it comes to your safety, I find it hard to ease off.'

We walk across the square.

'Marc? I wish you'd tell me what's going on. With all the extra security and me not being allowed in your townhouse right now.'

'Right now there's nothing to tell. And there may never be anything to tell.'

'And Getty's still in custody?'

'Yes. And he will be for the foreseeable future.'

We're not on the square anymore, but heading down a busy road. Marc swerves me down a side street, where I see a bustling open-air market. The smell of fresh bread, coffee and Christmas puddings fills the air.

'Are we on the right track, Mr Blackwell?' I say with a smile. 'This is a food market.'

'Exactly right. They say the way to a man's heart is through his stomach. Well. I thought I could warm your father to me by filling his house with food. And of course, I know you love cooking. So you might like to pick out some ingredients for Christmas dinner.'

I snuggle against his suit jacket. 'You're a very clever man, Mr Blackwell. Had you ever thought of becoming a teacher?'

'The thought crossed my mind.' Marc steers me through pretty wooden stands with colourful striped awnings, and we stop in front of a butcher's stall laden with giant corn-fed turkeys, aged joints of beef and bright pink hams.

'Had you picked out your meat yet?'

'There's a turkey I took out of dad's freezer earlier,' I say. 'I bought it on special a few months ago. I was going to use that. But ... this meat looks amazing.'

Marc points at a sign above the stand. 'I hadn't forgotten the foie gras incident. Cruelty free. These animals have been well looked after.'

I smile, noticing the free-range sign. 'You remembered.'

'How could I forget? I wouldn't want to buy you a roasting joint that ends up in the trash.'

I laugh.

'Choose whatever you like,' Marc says.

I blink at the choice of beautiful birds and roasting joints. 'Wow. I've never seen meat that looks so good. Those birds ... they're just huge. I don't think I'd be able to get them in the oven. But ...' I point at a giant turkey that's only medium-sized by the standards of this stall. 'That one looks like it would fit. I bet it will taste delicious, too.'

Marc gets the butcher's attention and nods at my choice. 'Bag this one for us, please. Thank you.'

He hands some notes to the butcher and takes the turkey under his arm, wrapped in white paper and string.

'What does your father like to eat?' Marc asks.

'Anything that's bad for him. And sweet things – he likes his desserts.'

'So we'll buy him a Christmas pudding. They're very good here.'

'Great idea.'

26

We buy Dad a huge Christmas pudding laced with brandy, stout and golden syrup. It's wrapped in muslin and almost as big as Sammy.

Marc also orders a box of organic vegetables to be delivered to the cottage today, and a whole host of biscuits, cheese, champagne and chocolates.

'Peter was saying you don't like Christmas,' I challenge, a teasing look in my eye. 'What's the turnaround?'

'The turnaround is you. Anything you love, I'm going to make my business to love too.'

'Oh really?'

'Really. So what else do you love, Miss Rose?'

'Isn't it obvious?' I say, staring up into his blue eyes. They're clear and light with the cold today.

Marc holds my eyes for a moment and strokes hair from my face.

I spy something over his shoulder.

'Mistletoe.' I pull him towards a stand of beautiful silvery green plants.

'You like mistlctoe?' says Marc, with a smile. 'I might have guessed.'

'I think it's one of the most beautiful plants ever,' I say. 'And very romantic.'

'I take it you've been kissed under the mistletoe before?' says Marc, raising an eyebrow.

'Once or twice.' I blush.

Marc bends down to press his lips against mine. For a moment the cold marketplace vanishes and all I can see and feel is him. When he pulls away, I'm disorientated and it takes a moment for the shapes of market stalls to reappear.

'But not like that,' I breathe.

'I should hope so.'

I twiddle my hair. 'You're going to make it your business to love anything I love?'

'Correct.'

'And what about like? Will you like everything I like?'

'Perhaps. What did you have in mind?'

'Leo Falkirk.'

The smile leaves Marc's face. 'I suppose miracles can happen.'

'I wish the two of you could get along.'

Marc gives a little laugh. 'He's got a lot of growing up to do before that will happen.'

*****

After we drop the shopping off in the limo, Marc takes me to Fortnum and Mason – the giant and very expensive department store on Piccadilly.

The whole place is decorated with clear glass baubles hanging from lilac ribbons. The store smells amazing – like apples and lemons, and some exotic spicy perfume.

'I thought this might be a good place to buy Jen a present,' says Marc. 'And Genoveva. If that's still appropriate.'

'You're going to buy Jen a present?' I say. 'That's so thoughtful. She'd probably love anything from this store – even a key ring. And Genoveva would too. But ... well you know about the family situation right now.

'I don't want to be petty or anything by not getting Sammy's mum a present, but I don't want to upset Dad either. How about we get her something, but don't label it? That way, if she turns up to see Sammy, we'll have something for her. But Dad won't notice the present and get all gloomy.'

'If you think that's the right thing to do.'

We're not in the store for more than a minute before a

man in a tailored black suit heads towards us.

'Mr Blackwell. Apologies. We weren't told you'd be visiting us today. I'm so sorry there was no one to greet you. May I assist you with your shopping?'

'No apology needed,' says Marc. 'This was an un-planned visit. But yes, some assistance would be good.'

The man nods, and moves discreetly behind us.

I notice some of the shoppers are staring at Marc as we walk through the store. They nudge each other and whisper, '*Is it? It looks like him, but ... and the girl with him, in the newspapers ...*'

I keep my head down and stick close to Marc.

'People are staring at us,' I say.

'You'll get used to it,' says Marc.

'Will I?'

'Yes. And don't worry. There are security all around.'

'There are?' I look around the store, but see no one from Marc's team.

'In plain clothes. They've been following us all day.'

'Oh.' I think about the kiss we shared in the market, and me snuggling against Marc's body as we walked around the cold winter streets. 'That's sort of embarrassing.'

'Embarrassing?'

'You know. That they were watching us. Being together.'

'Sophia, if you want to have a successful career as an actress, your private life will be on show to a certain extent. To more than just security guards.'

'I guess I'd better get used to it.'

'You will,' Marc assures me. 'Sooner than you think.' He waves a hand around the store. 'What do you think Jen would like?'

I walk towards a gorgeous 1930s style tea set, painted mint green and decorated with gold leaf fleur-de-lys. 'She'd love this.' I hold up one of the cups to the light, and see the shadow of my fingers through the fine china. 'It's bone china.'

Marc comes to stand beside me. 'You're an expert in china, Miss Rose?'

I smile at him. 'Not exactly. But my grandmother had a bone china tea set, and she taught me how to tell bone china from the regular kind.'

'Hidden talents.'

'You're one to talk.'

Marc signals for the assistant, and he takes away the tea set to be wrapped.

'That was the easy part,' I say. 'Now Genoveva.'

I spy a stand wrapped with beautiful chiffon scarves and walk over to it. 'She really likes scarves. She wears them all the time.' I pluck out one covered in white doves. 'Doves mean peace, don't they? That's what we all need as far as Genoveva is concerned.'

Marc signals the assistant again, and the scarf is removed, wrapped and bagged.

'Is there anyone else I need to buy for?' Marc asks me. 'Any long lost cousins or sisters?'

'No. We're a small family now my grandparents have passed away. It'll just be me, you, Dad and Sammy on Christmas day. And Jen in the afternoon.' I think about that. 'It's going to be weird without Genoveva. Well, weird for Dad anyway. Especially if you and I are all lovey dovey.'

'Is that how you'd describe us?'

'How would *you* describe us?' I ask.

Marc turns so he's facing me, and when his blue eyes fix on mine I feel like we're the only two people in the whole world.

'I would describe us as totally, obsessively in love,' he says, his voice lowering to that tone that makes my stomach tighten.

I gaze up at him, lost in his eyes and his words. Marc makes me feel things I've never felt before. There are times when I feel like I've become a part of him and he a part of me.

His hands reach out and find mine, and we stand right in the middle of the department store, looking into each other's eyes. He was right. I am getting used to being on show.

'Come on.' Marc leads me towards a counter, where the assistant is waiting with our purchases. 'I have plans for you this afternoon.'

As we leave the store, I think about Dad, all on his own this year, and how lonely he'll be with just a couple for company. This is the first year I've ever brought a boyfriend home. Typical that it had to be the year that Dad ends up on his own.

'Marc,' I say, as we walk down Piccadilly. 'You know what Peter was saying earlier? About Denise living alone right now. Do you think she'd like to come over for Christmas? It might make Dad feel a little less like a third wheel if there's someone nearer his age there. And it's great to have lots of people over at Christmas.'

Marc frowns. 'She usually arranges to go away over Christmas. But I could ask.'

'Would you?' I hesitate. 'And what about your sister? What will she be doing at Christmas? Would she like to come over? I'd love to see her.'

'She'll still be in hospital,' says Marc.

'Oh.' I look ahead at the wide, icy pavement. 'I'm glad she's getting better, but I'm really sorry I won't see her. Christmas in our house seems to get smaller every year. I would have loved to have some of your family over.'

'She's making vast improvements. And pretty soon she'll be allowed visitors.'

'Great.' I look around. 'So. Where are you taking me?'
'Just wait and see.'

27

We spend the rest of the afternoon ice skating at Marble Arch, drinking champagne cocktails at Park Lane and eating spaghetti at a quiet Italian restaurant hidden away in the narrow streets of Covent Garden.

When Marc drops me off at the theatre, I don't want to leave him, even to perform. But I know I have to. And I also know that tomorrow I'll get to spend all of Christmas day with him.

Wow. That's going to feel *very* surreal. But very nice.

The performance is fun, but it feels long, and when it's finally over I'm hoping to see Marc waiting in the wings. But he's not there, and I'm confused.

Didn't he say he was going to come to the cottage with me on Christmas Eve? Did I get that wrong?

I head to my dressing room and check my phone, but there are no messages. I'm so disappointed not to see Marc that I barely hear the knock on the dressing room door.

'Is there a leading lady in there?' calls Leo.

'Coming,' I say distractedly, pulling on my jeans and sweater. I yank the door open.

Leo's elbow is resting against the door frame, one of his knees a little bent.

'Great show tonight,' he says. 'No Marc?'

'I thought he was coming,' I say. 'But ... I don't know where he is.'

'I came to offer season's greetings,' says Leo, holding up a sprig of mistletoe. 'I'm flying out to LA in an hour's time. I'll be back, but I couldn't go without saying happy Christmas.' He leans forwards and kisses me on the check.

His lips remain on my skin just a little longer than they need to.

'Happy Christmas Leo,' I say. 'Love to your family.'

'Yours too. Hey. Sophia?'

'Yes Leo?'

'Have fun.'

*****

A security guard walks me to the stage door, and I find the limo waiting outside. I feel another heave of disappointment when I notice Marc isn't by the car.

'Hey Keith,' I say, climbing into the passenger seat. 'How are you?'

'Good,' says Keith. 'Looking forward to Christmas tomorrow. Um. Sophia, you might want to hop in the back tonight.'

'Why? I like talking to you when we drive.'

'Just ... jump out and have a look in the back of the car.'

'O-kay,' I say, climbing out of the vehicle. 'What's going on?'

Keith doesn't answer.

*****

I go to the back door, my heart beating fast. I like surprises, but where Marc Blackwell is concerned, I have no clue just what sort of surprise I might be getting.

When I open the limo door, I close my eyes, readying myself. When I open my eyes, I find myself letting out a long breath and an even longer, 'Oooo.'

The back of the car is stuffed with mistletoe. It hangs from every corner – the most beautiful icy green in colour, its round white berries glowing under the moonlight. And under all that mistletoe is the most beautiful thing of all.

Marc.

I dive into the car and throw myself into his arms. 'I

thought you weren't coming,' I say. 'When you weren't waiting in the wings.'

'I wanted to be there,' says Marc. 'But I had a few last minute surprises to arrange. For tomorrow. Keith and I have only just arrived.'

'More surprises …'

'You'll like them. I promise.'

28

We spend the drive to Dad's cottage wrapped up in each other's arms. But when we arrive at my old village, Marc becomes more upright and alert, gripping me tight and watching the streets.

When we reach Dad's cottage, Marc won't let me leave the limo until he checks the surrounding area. Finally he lets me out, but insists I walk close to him all the way to the front door.

'Do I have something to be nervous about?' I whisper, giving the door a soft knock.

'You have nothing to be nervous about. I'm the one who needs to be nervous. And alert.'

When Dad opens the door, he doesn't quite manage to disguise his discomfort at seeing Marc. But he's welcoming enough, calling us inside and asking Marc if he'd like a drink.

The house is still pretty tidy, and I'm guessing Sammy must be fast asleep upstairs because I can't hear him.

'Is Sammy okay?' I ask.

'Fine,' says Dad. He's wearing his dressing gown and pulls the cord tighter. 'Ate everything you left for him and went to bed nice and early.'

I go to the fireplace. 'No carrot for Rudolph?' I say, looking at the empty grate.

'I didn't do all that stuff this year,' says Dad tiredly. 'Sammy's a little young and I'm a little old.'

'That's a shame,' I say.

'I'll leave you two to settle in. See you in the morning.' Dad clumps upstairs.

'You're going to bed already?'

'I'm liking my early nights right now.'

'Okay. Sleep well.' At least he's not sleeping in his clothes tonight.

'So.' I turn to Marc, a little dizzy to see him in my family cottage again. It seems so unreal. And to have him staying over – this big Hollywood star in our little place. It's very different from his townhouse. No en suites. No staff. 'Here we are. At my house.'

'I like seeing this part of you,' says Marc softly. 'We should go upstairs. You need to sleep.'

'Okay.' I take his hand. 'What about you? Won't you be sleeping?'

'I want to stay awake for a while. Keep guard. With the two of us here ... I want to be extra safe.'

'Marc, you're making me nervous.'

'Don't be.' Marc kisses my forehead. 'It's just me being ultra cautious.'

The two of us climb the stairs, and I show Marc the guest bedroom. It's supposed to be a double room, but it's a really small double, so the bed is barely big enough for two. There's a dresser in the corner and an easy chair.

I notice that Dad has piled up my bags by the dresser, and I see an unfamiliar black bag, which I'm guessing must belong to Marc.

'I can keep watch in that chair,' says Marc. 'If I lie next to you ... let's just say I may get distracted.'

I sit on the bed. 'You're really going to spend the night upright in that chair, rather than in the bed next to me?'

'Yes. I need to be alert.'

'God Marc, now you really are making me nervous.' I glance at the window and the black night sky. 'Sammy's in the next room. Is it safe us being here?'

'Yes,' says Marc. 'I just don't believe in taking any chances. Get into bed Sophia. Get some rest. I want you to enjoy tomorrow.'

'Okay,' I say, pulling off my shoes. But inside I feel uneasy. I know Marc would never do anything to put Sammy in danger. But why won't he tell me what this is all about?

After Christmas. That's what he said. Just enjoy Christmas. And trust that Marc has your best interests at heart.

29

When I wake up the next morning, I see Marc sitting bolt upright in the chair opposite.

He smiles as my eyes open.

'Happy Christmas Sophia.'

I feel that stillness that always flows around on Christmas morning. The whole world feels quiet, and there's magic in the air.

'Happy Christmas Marc.' I rub my eyes and sit up. 'Did you sleep?'

'A little. You did. Soundly. I love watching you sleep.'

I slide myself out of bed and go to sit on his lap. He wraps his arms around me. Marc being here is the best Christmas present ever.

'Where you in that chair all night?'

'Yes.'

I kiss him fully on the lips. 'I'm so glad you're here,' I whisper. 'It's kind of weird, though. Waking up to see you in my old home.'

'Good weird?'

'Good weird.' I stretch my arms, stand up and pull him up out of the chair. 'Come on. Let's get cleaned up and then I can make breakfast.'

'You don't want to open your present?' says Marc, going to the black bag in the corner.

'Oh no Mr Blackwell.' I shake a finger at him. 'In our family, we don't open our presents until after the Christmas dinner. That makes the day last just a little bit longer.'

Marc smiles. 'It's good to know that you can exercise that sort of patience.'

'There's a lot you don't know about me Mr Blackwell,'

I say, mimicking his words to me yesterday.

'And a lot I can't wait to find out. Well. If I have to wait until after Christmas dinner to give you your present, it's lucky I have a few surprises lined up before then. Let's go downstairs. There's a surprise waiting for you there.'

*****

With Sammy and Dad still sleep, I creep downstairs, pulling Marc behind me.

'Slow down Sophia,' says Marc. 'You're going to fall down the stairs.'

'I'm too excited to slow down,' I whisper back.

'The surprise is in the lounge,' says Marc, squeezing my fingers.

I pull Marc into the lounge area, and then stop dead, staring.

'Oh, *Marc.*'

In the corner of the lounge is the most amazing Christmas tree, with gorgeous thick feathery fir branches. It looks like it's been plucked straight out of the forests of Norway.

The branches hang with hand-painted wooden holly leaves and delicate baubles painted with 1950s Christmas scenes.

'How did you do this?' I breathe, taking a step forwards and feeling the thick green branches of the tree between my fingers.

'While you were at the theatre. Hence my late arrival. The security team helped me decorate it.'

I give a little laugh at the idea of Marc and his team creeping around in the dead of night, hanging Christmas decorations.

'I can't believe you did all this,' I say, still staring.

'You like it?' Marc asks.

'I love it. And Sammy's going to love it too.'

As if on cue, there's a little choked cry from upstairs.

I smile at Marc. 'I'll go get Sammy up. And Dad. Then I'll make us all breakfast.'

30

For Christmas breakfast, I make pancakes with winter cherries and flaming brandy sauce. I serve them with whipped cream and fresh coffee.

Dad is as surprised as I am by the tree, and I can tell he's secretly happy. He loves Christmas almost as much as I do.

My dad is wary of Marc over breakfast, but the two of them manage a stilted conversation about the roads around the village, and their mutual love of cars. Dad isn't being all that talkative, but Marc does his best.

When breakfast is finished, Dad stands up.

'I've got a big apology to make to the two of you.'

'You have?' I sit up straighter, thinking that maybe Dad is seeing sense about Marc and I getting married.

Dad clears his throat. 'Yes. You might be wondering why I didn't bring any Christmas presents downstairs. Well, look I'm embarrassed to admit it, but I didn't manage to go Christmas shopping this year. I've spent so much time moping that I've forgotten there are other people in the world apart from me. But that changes. As of now.

'I'm going to stop thinking of myself and my heart-ache, and start thinking about everyone else again. And I just hope the two of you can forgive me for being so thoughtless.'

'It's okay Dad,' I say. 'We know you've had a lot on this last week. It's been a tough time. I wasn't expecting a present. And I'm sure Marc wasn't either.'

'No. Not at all,' says Marc.

'You're both very understanding,' says Dad, taking a seat.

There's an awkward silence.

'Dad,' I say, after a moment. 'Had you thought any more about Marc and I getting married? Are you ... still feeling the same way?'

Dad glances at Marc, then looks down at the table.

'I still need a little more time to think,' he says. 'But I'm happy Marc is here. It'll be a good chance for me to get to know him. And you never know, by the end of Christmas I just might be able to give you both my support.'

'That would be amazing,' I say, feeling hope warm my chest. 'Let me get everything cleared up.'

We let Sammy open one present after breakfast. That's another rule in our family – the children can open one gift first thing, and then they have to wait for the rest like all the adults do.

I'm not sure Sammy really gets that the day is special or anything, but he chooses Marc's toy to open first, and he smiles and smiles when we help him tear off the paper and he sees the logging truck.

'Nice gift,' says Dad, getting down on his knees to help Sammy release all the logs, which go rolling around the living room rug. 'Thank you.'

'My pleasure,' says Marc.

After breakfast, we go for our traditional Christmas walk around the country lanes, with Marc pushing Sammy fast over the bumpy mud, and Sammy whooping with delight. Then we head home and I start on the Christmas dinner. I put the turkey in before we went for our walk so, in between chopping vegetables, I baste it and add more seasoning.

Dad plays with Sammy in the living room and, to my surprise, Marc comes and joins me in the kitchen.

'I have a starter planned,' he says, opening the fridge.

There's a white parcel inside that I don't recognise.

'Where did that come from?' I ask, as Marc takes it out and cuts the string.

'I had it sent over yesterday. Rodney bought these at London Bridge market.'

The white paper falls open to reveal eight fat red lobsters.

'Wow.' I look at the seafood. 'They look amazing.'

Marc brushes hair out of his eyes and goes to the knife rack. He effortlessly sharpens a knife on the steel, and I watch him, surprised.

'You look *very* at home in the kitchen, Mr Blackwell. I thought you couldn't cook.'

Marc throws me that delicious spiky smile. 'I don't recall saying I couldn't cook.'

'But doesn't Rodney do all your cooking for you?'

'Yes. Mostly. I'm sensible enough to stand back and let a master do his work. The same goes for when you're in the kitchen.'

'So you *can* cook?'

'I wouldn't go that far. But I can prepare certain things. Lobster being one of them. And I can sharpen a knife.'

'Where did you learn how to do that?'

'I toyed with the idea of opening a restaurant in LA for a while, and I thought if I was going to do that, I should learn everything there is to know about the restaurant business.'

'A perfectionist in everything you do,' I say, with a smile.

'I always give one hundred per cent,' says Marc, his eyes fixing on mine and sending shivers down my arms.

'Am I one of your projects, Mr Blackwell?' I ask. 'Something you give one hundred percent to?'

'I wouldn't call you a project.'

'Oh? What would you call me?'

'My soul mate. The only woman in the world who could break down my barriers.'

'I don't think I've broken down *all* your barriers,' I say. 'At least, not yet. But I'm working on it. Especially when it comes to trust.'

'Trust?'

'Leo Falkirk.'

'I trust *you*,' says Marc. 'It's him I don't trust.'

'I'm hoping that will change. So. Tell me more about how you learnt to cook.'

Marc gives a half smile. 'I can't cook. But I learnt everything I could about professional kitchens. The equipment. The quality of the food. How the best chefs prepare seafood and meat.'

'You learned to prepare lobster just by watching a chef do it?'

'Not just one chef. Lots of chefs.'

'Impressive.' I watch him twist the lobster tail from its body. 'You're a fast learner, Mr Blackwell. I could never learn anything just by watching.'

'Oh I don't know about that. You pick things up pretty quickly.'

'Why thank you.'

I watch Marc twisting and manipulating the red lobster in his strong fingers, revealing white meat under the shell.

'Aren't the best lobsters still alive when you buy them?' I say. 'And uncooked?'

'I bought these pre-cooked,' Marc tells me. 'I didn't think you'd appreciate me cooking a live animal in front of you.'

'You're right. I wouldn't have liked it.'

I watch in fascination as Marc slices each side of the lobster tail, then peels apart the shell and artfully cuts the flesh to remove the green and black parts.

'You're very good at that,' I say.

Marc laughs. 'Wait until you've eaten it before you judge.'

As Marc cracks and peels, and I prepare vegetables, there's a knock at the front door.

Marc lifts his head. 'Surprise number two.'

I grin at him, dusting my hands on a tea towel. 'Who is it?'

'Go to the door and see.'

31

My grin broadens as I walk to the front door and pull it open.

'Oh my god.' I throw a hand to my mouth and beam at the two guests standing on the doorstep. 'I can't believe it. Oh wow!'

Standing right outside our little cottage are Denise and Annabel.

'Happy Christmas Sophia,' says Annabel, smiling shyly. 'I hope you don't mind us coming.'

'*Mind*? I thought you couldn't make it. Marc said ... something about the hospital, you being kept there. I'm so happy to see you. And Denise ... Marc told me he'd ask you to come, but he never said you'd be here for certain. I'm so happy. Come in, come in.'

I grab both their arms and drag them into the living area. 'This is my dad. And Sammy.'

Dad looks up and smiles warmly to see two new people in the house. He's the same as me – he likes the house full on Christmas day.

Denise and Annabel say hello and shake hands, and Sammy crawls around so he can get a better look at the new guests.

'And of course, Marc you know,' I say, smiling as Marc comes in from the kitchen area and gives them both a kiss on the cheek.

'Take a seat,' I tell Denise and Annabel. 'Make yourselves comfortable.' I just can't stop grinning now. 'It's so good to have you here.'

Denise is wearing a sparkly black Christmas dress that has a V at the neckline and really flatters her fuller figure. She smells of exotic perfume and has fixed her make-up so it sparkles too.

Annabel still looks a little thin, and is dressed simply in a blue turtleneck sweater and jeans. But she looks so much better than she did. Much healthier, and her eyes are happier and more alive.

It feels great to have the house full of people. It hasn't been like this for a while. Not since my grandparents and my mother passed away.

'It's so good to have you here,' I say again. 'Let me get you both a drink.'

*****

'You look happy,' says Marc, as I return to the kitchen area and hunt around the fridge.

'Very, very happy.' I pause to wrap my arms around him and bury my head against his chest. 'This feels like the Christmases we had when I was young. The house all warm and full of people. Mum would have liked to see the house so alive again. And she would have loved to meet you.'

Marc's arms come around me. 'You don't usually talk about your mother.'

'Don't I? I thought I talked about her all the time. I'm always thinking about her. Especially at Christmas.'

'No.' I feel Marc's head shake against my hair. 'You don't mention her often. But I understand. You learn to keep your thoughts to yourself when you've lost a parent. Most people don't understand how it feels to have that part of yourself missing.'

'That's a good way to describe it,' I say. 'Is that how you feel too?'

'Yes.'

I grip him tighter.

'But I have you now,' says Marc. 'So there's nothing missing anymore.'

32

Usually we drink beer on Christmas day, and maybe a cheap bottle of port. So it's weird to rummage around the kitchen and find expensive sherry and bottles of champagne. But since we're celebrating the arrival of honoured guests, I decide to pop open a bottle of Dom Perignon.

We don't have any champagne glasses, so I serve the champagne in red wine goblets that used to belong to my grandparents.

'Drinks,' I call, heading into the lounge.

I notice my dad has taken a seat on the sofa next to Denise.

'Wonderful.' Denise takes her glass, and pats my arm. 'Just the thing.'

Annabel looks at the glass warily. 'Sophia. I'm so sorry. But I can't drink. It's part of my rehab programme.'

I look at the champagne. 'Oh god. That was stupid of me. Annabel, you've got nothing to be sorry about. I don't know what I was thinking.'

'Annabel, we've got some nice fresh orange juice if you'd prefer?' says Dad. 'Or tea?'

'Tea sounds great.'

'I'll get it for you.' Dad seems to have really cheered up now guests have arrived. He's acting much more like his old self. Maybe, just maybe, by the end of the day he'll see sense and give Marc and I his blessing after all.

Dad clambers up from the sofa, and I take his seat.

'I'm so glad Marc invited you both,' I tell Denise and Annabel. 'It's just the best Christmas present, having you arrive on the doorstep.'

Denise smiles. 'My pleasure. Really it was. I can't tell

you what a shock it was when Marc invited me over. Usually, he ignores Christmas completely. I've long given up trying to persuade him to do anything other than work. What have you done to him, Sophia?'

'I'd love to take the credit,' I say, 'but really I haven't done anything at all.'

'I think it must be your influence,' says Annabel, with a knowing smile. 'I've never seen my brother so head over heels. Before you came along, I never thought he'd settle down. Ever.'

Denise nods. 'Who'd have thought anyone would break down the Marc Blackwell wall?'

'Who'd have thought?' Annabel agrees. 'And yet, Sophia has.'

Dad comes over with a cup of tea for Annabel, so I slide onto the floor to let him take a seat.

'Age before beauty,' I say, and Dad playfully cuffs my head.

'How was hospital?' I ask Annabel, noticing a plastic medical cuff around her thin wrist.

'Hell at first,' says Annabel, creases appearing around her eyes as she tries for a smile. 'But, you know, it got better. Day by day. It's what I need. I know that. So I can bear it for a little longer. I have a good reason for bearing it.'

'Is there any news about your son?' I ask. 'About getting custody?'

'There might be. It's being looked into. If I can just stick with rehab this time, and stay away from my old friends … if I can do that, there's a chance Danny can come back to live with me.'

33

As I set the table for Christmas dinner, I feel Marc slide up behind me and slip his arms around my waist.

'Let me help you,' he says.

'Did you study the best waiters as well as the best chefs?' I squeeze a knife beside a paper napkin and a Christmas cracker. Our dining table is pretty small, but it's nice to be crowded in. It reminds me of when Mum was alive and Christmas dinner was all about knocking elbows and laughing.

'No,' says Marc. 'In fact, I could use a few pointers.'

We both pause as Marc squeezes my waist tight, and I give an involuntary gasp.

'Did you like your surprise?' Marc asks.

I turn to him, a bunch of cutlery still in my hand, and feel his cool fingers move around my waist. 'You know I did. I loved it. I think Denise was pretty surprised to be invited. She told me you don't usually bother with Christmas.'

'True. I need a pretty good reason to celebrate Christmas.' He moves his fingers up to run them through my hair, watching intently as strands move over his palms.

'And did you find a good reason this year?' I ask.

'The best reason.'

I feel a tug at my ankle, and look down to see Sammy trying to climb my leg. 'Sammy!' I dump the cutlery and duck down to scoop him up.

Sammy tries to grab at the cutlery on the table. 'You want to help lay the table?' I ask him.

'Looks like I have competition,' says Marc, smiling at Sammy. 'I'll lay out the starters.'

*****

Once the lobster plates are laid out, I pour champagne into a mixture of mugs, tumblers and the red wine goblets we used earlier, and everyone crowds around the table.

The lobster, of course, is delicious, and we all take huge forkfuls of seafood, swig champagne, pull crackers, put on silly hats and laugh as we bump elbows – just like we did years ago, when Mum was alive. Except of course in those days, we didn't have lobster or champagne.

I catch Marc's eye a few times, and just can't believe all of this. That Marc is here, with me, and so is his sister. That he looks so relaxed and content, sitting around my old dining table, drinking champagne from a football mug.

When the starter is finished, I take out the big, beautiful turkey from the oven, and Marc helps me carve it at the table. I lay out bowls of steaming roast potatoes, carrots and parsnips, cauliflower cheese for Sammy and sausages wrapped in bacon for my dad.

We eat, talk and laugh, and when we're stuffed with food I bring out the Christmas pudding and light it. After we've sung 'We Wish You a Merry Christmas', we eat huge slices of pudding with whipped cream.

As we're finishing up, Dad bangs a knife against his tumbler, clears his throat and stands up.

We all grow silent.

'Thank you, thank you everyone,' says Dad, adjusting his paper hat. 'This has been a wonderful day. And I'd particularly like to welcome all our guests.'

Dad is interrupted by a knock at the door, and we all turn to the hallway.

'It must be Jen,' I say, getting to my feet. 'She's kind of early though.'

Hurrying to the front door, I fling it open. 'Happy Christmas!' I call out. 'Oh!' I take a step back.

It's not Jen after all.

On the doorstep stands Genoveva.

34

Genoveva is wearing a lime green pashmina and matching trousers, and her hair has been blow dried so it hangs straight and shiny around her face. She's had more highlights done, I notice – she's much blonder than when I last saw her. It doesn't really suit her thick, dark eyebrows and tanned face.

'Genoveva,' I say, staring at her like an idiot.

'Is Mike home?' she asks, peering over my shoulder.

'Yes, I—' I turn around and see Dad has appeared behind my shoulder.

'Genny,' he says softly.

'I'm not stopping,' says Genoveva. 'But I had to do this in person. Mike, you have to stop harassing me. Every day, phone calls. And today, text messages too. It has to stop.'

'Harassing you?' Dad shakes his head. 'I never meant … I mean, I miss you. That's no secret. But today I was texting for Sammy's sake. He wants to see you—'

'I want a divorce,' Genoveva interrupts. 'I want to marry Patrick.'

Dad looks like he's been punched in the stomach. 'A divorce?'

'Patrick and I are in love. I'm moving on. You should too.'

'What about Sammy?' says Dad. 'Genny, please. This is all too quick. Take your time to think things over.'

'Patrick isn't keen on having Sammy living with us,' says Genoveva. 'He has children of his own. But we'll work something out. I'd like to see him Sammy, if he's here.'

Dad opens and closes his mouth. Then he stands back

to let Genoveva into the hallway. 'I won't stop you.'
*****

When Genoveva sees the dining table full of people, she looks annoyed.

'I didn't realise you'd have all these visitors,' she says accusingly, going to Sammy's high chair. She picks him up as though he's a bag of shopping, and pats him on the head like a puppy.

Sammy looks a little stunned at first. Then, as Genoveva tries to flatten his hair down, he starts to cry.

'He must be in a grizzly mood,' she announces, handing him to me. 'Too many people here, I imagine.' Her lips push into a little circle as she eyes up Denise and Annabel. 'Maybe it's best if he stays with you today, Mike. I don't want him if he's just going to cry all day. Who on earth dressed him this morning? That t-shirt doesn't go with those trousers.'

Genoveva slots Sammy back into the high chair. 'I'll come and see him next week, maybe. When he's a bit more settled.' She turns to Mike. 'Our solicitors will be in touch. Happy Christmas.'

With that, she waltzes out, slamming the front door behind her.

35

When Dad and I sit back down at the table, there's a stunned silence.

Denise has her hands covering her mouth. Marc is frowning. Annabel's blue eyes are wide and staring. Sammy is completely quiet, gripping his high-chair table and chewing his lip.

We're all watching Dad, but pretending not to watch, as he picks up his fork and pushes a potato around the plate.

After a moment, I say tentatively, 'Dad? Are you okay?'

'She's wants a divorce,' Dad says to no one in particular. 'A divorce. Sammy will grow up in a broken home.'

I risk a sideways glance at Marc. He looks serious and thoughtful.

Dad takes a swig of champagne from his mug. 'Sophia, let this be a lesson to you. Rushing into marriage causes nothing but heartache.'

'Dad, you're upset. Don't read too much into this right now. Maybe Genoveva—'

'No, I'm seeing sense for the first time in years,' Dad interrupts. 'You and Marc have known each other for five minutes. You're from completely different worlds. Just like Genoveva and I. I'm sorry, but I can't give my blessing for the two of you to marry. I just can't.'

I try not to get emotional. Dad's upset, I tell myself. He's just had some devastating news. He's not thinking straight.

'Dad, maybe you should take more time to think about things.'

'I don't need any more time. I've made my decision.'

'Dad, *please*—'

'I'm sorry, Sophia. I just can't see you get hurt the way I'm hurting.'

Denise leans over and puts a hand on Dad's arm. 'Mike. I'm so sorry you had that terrible news. We're all sorry. Truly. And I know you're coming from a good place, as far as Marc and Sophia are concerned.

'But how about rethinking your decision in a few month's time? Sophia's show will be finished in March – why don't you reconsider things then? I'm sure, once you've seen her do a whole West End show run, you'll understand what a grown-up young lady she is. And how well she and Marc fit together.'

Dad sighs. 'I know Sophia is mature for her age. She's had to be. But … I still think she's not seeing things clearly. Marc is a very forceful man. I don't think, with him around, Sophia is in charge of her own decisions.'

'I am,' I insist. 'Of course I am.'

'He's a very strong influence, Sophia. Perhaps you don't realise how strong. And then there's the over-protective thing – all these security guards prowling around the cottage. It doesn't seem healthy.'

I glance at Marc, my eyes silently pleading with him not to tell Dad why the security guards are here.

'Mike,' says Denise. 'Give them a few months to prove how well-suited they are. Don't make any hasty decisions just yet.'

Dad puts down his fork. 'Okay. Right. Fine. I'll re-think things in three month's time, when Sophia's show run is finished.'

I slide my hand into Marc's. 'Dad! Thank you—'

'Wait.' Dad holds up a hand. 'There's one condition.'

'A condition?'

'You and Marc have to spend those three months apart.'

'Three months *apart*?' I say.

'A few months not seeing Marc isn't going to hurt you,' says Dad. 'And it'll give you time to think. To consider life without Marc, and to understand there are other options for you.'

'Three months won't change my mind.'

I turn to Marc, and notice he's loosened his grip on my hand. He doesn't look angry. Actually, he looks thoughtful and that worries me.

'Marc.' I shake my head at him. 'You're not seriously considering this, are you?'

'I see the sense in what your father is saying. Taking a break will give you a chance to understand what you truly want in life. There may be someone out there who's better for you than me.'

'No.' I shake my head. 'Marc, I love you. Only you. You're all I want.' I feel tears coming and swipe at them, embarrassed to be making such a spectacle of myself. If Marc truly loves me, how could he stand all that time apart?

Marc gently wipes away my tears with his fingers. He puts an arm around my shoulder and his warmth comforts me a little. But not completely.

'I know how important it is for you to have the blessing of your family. And if separation means having your father's blessing, then I could bear it.' He turns to my father. 'But I have a condition too. I need to be able to see Sophia if her safety is ever compromised. And I need to be able to watch her via my security cameras. To make sure she's safe. But I'll give her space. I won't be a part of her life.'

'Agreed,' says Dad.

I shake my head. 'Dad, no! You don't have to put us through this. You could just understand that we're in love. That our love won't change.'

'I want you to be sure, before you commit to something that's for life. Forever.'

I hear the tone of Dad's words and see that practical look on his face – the one that says 'this has to be done'. I saw that look when we couldn't afford flowers for Mum's funeral and we had to cut down her favourite rose bush to decorate the coffin. He's not going to change his mind. He really thinks he's doing the right thing. That he's saving me from some terrible mistake.

I cling to Marc as reality sinks in. This is our choice. Three months apart, or Dad won't give us his blessing to marry.

I feel sympathetic looks from Annabel and Denise.

'Three months,' I murmur, feeling numb inside.

'Like Denise says, your play finishes in March,' Dad says. 'You'll have three months to focus on your career. Your future. And if the two of you still feel the same way after your play is finished, I'll think again about giving my blessing.'

'We will feel the same,' I say. 'Okay. Okay, fine. I agree. I agree because I want you to see what a good man Marc is. That he'll honour his promise to you. And that even after three months apart, we'll still be in love.'

36

Dad says that while we're separated, Marc and I can have one half hour phone call a week. That's it. Other than that, I'm not allowed to see Marc at all. And our separation begins from tonight.

As we head away from the dining table, I'm holding Marc's hand but I don't really feel him. I'm just in shock.

Marc is silent, deep in thought. I guess he's preparing himself.

'Are we really going to do this?' I whisper, as everyone takes seats in the lounge.

'It could be for the best,' says Marc. 'A break will help you think about your future. And whether or not I should be in it.'

'Of course you should be in it. Marc, I love you.'

Marc's jaw tightens, and at that moment all my worries about his love for me vanish. I know he's feeling this pain just as badly as I am. He's just coping with it in his own way – by trying to stay in control.

'I love you too,' Marc replies, as we sit next to each other on the sofa.

There's a knock at the front door.

I tense, wondering whether Genoveva has come back, but then the front door creaks open and I hear Jen call out, 'Well hell-oo everyone!'

Jen comes into the lounge, blowing a noisemaker. 'Happy Christmas!'

She's wearing a bright red dress with a white fur trim, and carrying a shopping bag full of presents and wine.

'Hey Jen.'

'What's up with everyone?' Jen says. 'It feels like I've

walked into a morgue. It must be present time, mustn't it? You've had your dinner.' She glances at the empty dining table, now strewn with empty Christmas pudding plates and cracker paper. 'Wow! Fabulous tree.' She drops her present bag under the branches.

'We hadn't got around to handing out presents yet,' I say.

Jen notices Annabel and Denise. 'You *must* be Marc's sister.' She totters over and gives Annabel a kiss on both cheeks. 'Nice to meet you. And I don't need to ask your name.' She gives Denise a kiss too. 'I saw you in *Les Miserables* years ago. You were amazing. And Soph says you're a fantastic teacher too.' She turns back to me. 'Is everything okay?'

'Not really,' I admit. 'Marc and I … Dad thinks it's best if Marc and I spend a little time apart.'

'Oh.' Jen looks from me, to Dad, and back again. 'Time apart?'

'Three months to be precise.'

'Why would you do that?'

'Because otherwise, Dad won't give us his blessing to get married.'

Jen's jaw drops open. 'You're kidding.'

'Nope.'

There's an awkward silence.

Jen plonks herself down on a sofa arm and turns to Dad. 'What's this all about then? Doesn't sound very Christmassy.'

'I don't mean to be the big, bad ogre,' says Dad. 'But if Sophia wants my blessing to get married, I think she and Marc should have some breathing space.'

Jen raises her eyebrow. 'Why can't you just trust Sophia's decision? She's in her twenties. It's not like she's a teenager.'

'I don't want her to get hurt,' says Dad. 'If the two of

them are meant to be, a break will do them no harm at all.'

'Don't hate me for saying this,' says Denise, leaning towards me. 'But I can see where your dad is coming from. Love when you're young isn't necessary the same as being married. You can fall in love many times when you're young, but a lifetime commitment is different.'

'I've only ever fallen in love once,' says Marc. 'With Sophia.'

'You might feel that way,' says Denise kindly. 'But what about Sophia? Mike's right, she hasn't seen nearly as much of the world as you have.'

'I'm aware of that,' says Marc. 'And I don't disagree with the decision either. I think it would be good for Sophia to have some time to consider what she's getting herself in to. There may be a better life out there for her – a life I can't provide.'

'Are you really going to do it?' Jen asks me. 'Spend all that time apart?'

'I don't want to,' I say. 'But … I don't see that we have much choice.'

Jen turns to my dad. 'Mike. Look, are you sure you're not letting other things cloud your judgement? I heard about Genoveva …'

Dad frowns. 'I think the Genoveva situation has made me see things clearer than ever. She came over earlier. And now I see a lot of things I didn't before.'

There's that awkward silence again.

I think of Genoveva's present, wrapped under the tree, and wonder why I ever held out hope that she'd act like a decent human being this Christmas.

Poor Sammy.

'Shall we open our presents?' I say, in a bid to change the subject. 'Annabel. Denise. I'm so sorry I don't have anything for you here.'

Annabel smiles and pulls a silver locket free of her jumper. 'I got your present in the post a few days ago. It's beautiful. Absolutely beautiful.' She clicks open the locket. 'How did you get the picture of Daniel?'

I smile at the child with blonde hair inside the locket. He looks a little like the childhood picture I saw of Marc. 'I asked Marc.'

'And thank you for my book,' says Denise. 'I love Robert Burns.'

'I noticed a few poetry books in your classroom and sort of guessed.'

I hand out presents to Jen, Dad and Sammy. Dad gets stuff for his car, and I give Jen some movies I know she likes and the tea set from Marc. Sammy gets a little plastic elastic man that folds in all sorts of directions. Then I give Marc his present.

'It's not much,' I say, embarrassed suddenly to have everyone watching. The gift is wrapped in black tissue paper and suddenly looks ridiculously small and humble.

Marc shakes his head and smiles. 'What happened to not getting me a gift?'

'I sort of ignored you.'

He gives that quirky grin of his. 'You sort of ignored me?'

'Yes. Well, I'd already made it for you when you said that. So ... open it.'

Marc pulls off the black paper.

'You made this?' he asks, pulling out a hand-woven wristband of black and silver silk. The band is woven with silver ivy leaves and has a little silver clasp to fasten it around the wrist.

'Yes,' I admit. 'It's really not much. But I enjoyed making it for you. I hope you like it.'

'I do,' says Marc, fastening it around his wrist.

God, I love his wrists. They're so strong, so dipped in light and shadow.

I blush. 'You don't have to wear it all the time or anything. I mean, it's nothing special.'

'It is to me,' says Marc. 'Time for your gift.' He goes to the tree and picks up a tiny, wafer thin square wrapped in gold and silver paper. There's a huge sprig of mistletoe decorating the corner.

'Nice wrapping,' I say, stroking the mistletoe. I'm relieved that the gift is small. I didn't want anything extravagant from Marc. It just would have made me feel uncomfortable. But then again, as Jen always says, big things come in small packages.

Carefully, I open the paper and stare at what's inside.

37

I turn to Marc. 'Is this … this isn't what I think it is, is it?'

'What do you think it is?'

I look down at what's lying within the folds of gift wrap. It's a photograph of a beautiful black horse with a white spot on its nose.

'It's a picture of a horse,' I say. But I know Marc better than that. He wouldn't just give me a picture of a horse as a present. Which means ...

'She's yours,' says Marc softly.

'You're kidding me.' I stare at the picture of the beautiful horse, with its shiny coat and beautiful black eyes. 'I … Marc I …' I shake my head. 'I don't know if I can accept this. I mean, I only got you a homemade bracelet, and this is …'

'She'll keep you company while you're away from me,' says Marc. 'Her name is Ebony. She's has a very good nature. I have people at my stable who'll take care of her. But you can see her, ride her, whenever you like.'

I get to my feet and throw my arms around Marc, hurling myself into his body. 'Thank you,' I whisper. 'This is … an amazing present.'

'I'll take you to see her today,' says Marc. 'She's an hour or so from here. On the farm we visited before.'

'*Your* farm,' I say.

'Our farm.'

I'm suddenly aware that there are other people around and peel myself away from Marc.

'We should … shall we all have a cup of tea?'

*****

Later that day, while the others are relaxing in the

lounge, Marc offers to take me to see Ebony.

'Will Keith drive us?' I ask.

Marc shakes his head. 'My Aston Martin was couriered over while we were preparing the dinner. I'm going to drive us.'

I smile. 'Sounds good.'

Jen and Annabel are having fun playing Scrabble, and Denise and my Dad are talking away, drinking tea and eating chocolate biscuits, so nobody misses us when we head out.

We drive to the farm in silence, happy to be together, but both lost in our own thoughts. There's a lot to think about after what Dad had to say.

When we arrive at the farm, I notice security guards surrounding the perimeter.

'Marc.' I turn to him as the car bumps over the muddy track towards the main house. 'You said you were going to tell me what's going on with all the security after Christmas. Well. I think my Christmas is pretty much over. So. Will you tell me?'

Marc pulls the car to a stop. 'Okay.' He stares out of the windscreen at the open countryside and I follow his gaze, seeing the bare trees sway in the icy wind. 'Maybe it'll help you understand why I'm not fighting your father's decision too much.'

A pause.

'Marc?'

'My legal team are taking care of Getty. You don't need to worry about him coming anywhere near you. But there's something else.'

'Okay.' I swallow.

'There are others.'

'Others? What do you mean?'

'Getty was part of an underground network. They're known as PAIN. They have clubs throughout London.

Few people know about them. But they're very protective of their members. Word has got out that Getty has been imprisoned. And so it looks like the leaders of this group want to take revenge on the people who put him behind bars.'

'They want to take revenge on us?'

'That's what it looks like.'

I feel sick. 'Do the police know about this group?'

'Not exactly.' Marc shakes his head. 'Not yet, anyway. That has to be handled very delicately. PAIN are clever. If we make the wrong accusations too soon, the police might not be able to prosecute them at all.'

Silence.

'Marc?'

'There's something else too.' Marc grips the steering wheel. 'Someone else, actually. Wrapped up in all this. Out for revenge.'

'Who?'

Marc turns to me. 'Cecile.'

38

'Cecile from Ivy College?' I ask.

'Yes. PAIN sought her out after Getty was taken into custody. She's been seen in their night clubs.'

'She's never liked me,' I say, feeling strangely numb inside. 'And now she has more reason to hate me than ever.'

'I don't know for certain how Cecile could be involved with them,' says Marc. 'But what I do know is that, right now, it's not safe for you to be at my townhouse.'

'That I don't understand,' I say. 'I thought your town-house was secure.'

'It is. Against almost everybody.'

'Almost everybody?'

'There's a woman. One of PAIN's leaders. Her name is Yasmina. She knows the townhouse inside and out. Security systems. Layout. Everything.'

My blood runs cold. 'How?'

'She worked for me. As my PA. Years ago. I hired her at Getty's suggestion. She was Getty's way of hooking into me. Of making sure he had a hold over me. She knows things about the townhouse. And about me. She's clever. Very, very clever. And ruthless. She and PAIN's other leader, Warren, have been accused of some fairly sickening crimes. But nothing has ever stuck.'

I nod slowly, feeling even sicker now. 'This Yasmina. Were the two of you …' I let the question trail away.

'No.' Marc shakes his head firmly. 'Never. She and I had different tastes in that department.'

'Oh. Right.'

'PAIN are clever,' says Marc. 'Discreet. I need to wait for them to make a move. But until then, I don't think it's such a bad thing that we're apart. I don't want you getting caught in the crossfire.'

'I don't want *you* in the crossfire either,' I say, sliding a shaking hand into his. 'Marc, I couldn't bear it if anything happened to you.'

'You needn't worry about me,' says Marc. 'I can look after myself. It's you we need to watch out for.'

'I guess I should warn Tom and Tanya. Cecile might try and cause trouble for them at college.'

'Cecile is no longer at Ivy College.'

'She isn't?'

'No. She's been asked to leave. It was clear she was having psychological difficulties, and I won't have anyone threatening one of my pupils. You or anyone else. She was offered the chance to get psychological treatment at our expense, but she refused. So right now she's on her own. But she's being watched. They're all being watched. I promise this will be handled.' He squeezes my hand. 'Let's go and see your horse.'

*****

As soon as I clap eyes on Ebony, it's love at first sight. She's absolutely beautiful, and a good size too – not huge like Taranu, but not too small either. Her coat shines like stars on a clear night.

Marc gives me some oatmeal to feed her, and after a few handfuls she whinnies, nuzzles my hand and lets me stroke her flank.

'Do you want to ride her?' Marc asks.

'I'd love to,' I say. 'But I can't leave Sammy with Dad for too long. I'll come back when Christmas is over. She'll help me, I think. When I'm missing you.'

*****

The rest of Christmas day feels a little subdued. We eat cheese and biscuits for tea, drink champagne and play more games, but every moment is blackened by knowing that before long Marc and I will be forced apart. How am I going to stand it?

We squeeze each other's hands every so often, telling each other, wordlessly, how much we love each other. But when I look at Marc, I can tell he's deep in thought, trying to get his feelings under control about what lies ahead.

When late evening comes, Denise, Annabel and Jen say their goodbyes and Dad stumbles up to bed. With Sammy already fast asleep, Marc and I head out to the garden to be alone together.

We stand by the tall trees looking up into the black sky, knowing we don't have long before Marc has to leave.

I can feel Marc's warmth against my face and neck. Having him beside me is both beautiful and heartbreaking.

Eventually, I say, 'How was your Christmas?'

'Not quite what I had planned. But I'm still glad I got to spend the day with you.'

'Me too. It really was the best Christmas, if only for that reason.'

I watch a squirrel run up into bare tree branches.

'I guess I should go,' says Marc. 'It's nearly time.'

'I guess it is.' I swallow, trying to be hard and practical like Marc. Trying not to let thoughts of our separation overwhelm me. But I can't. My face crumples.

'I hate to see you hurting,' says Marc through gritted teeth.

'And here I was trying to be strong,' I try to laugh, but the laugh gets all choked up with tears. I let out a long breath. 'It's only three months. Not an eternity. And we can still speak to each other once a week.' I place both palms flat on his chest. 'And when it's done, we can be together. Forever.'

Marc's lips quirk up at the corners. 'Does that mean you're accepting my proposal, Sophia Rose?'

'You'll have to ask me again, if you want an answer to that question.'

'I intend to.'

39

I sit in the dark lounge, watching as Marc's car pulls away. Wheels crunch over gravel, and then he's gone.

And I'm all alone. In the dark.

A low, flat mood overtakes me.

I sit, staring at the place where Marc's car was parked. Then I climb the stairs and throw myself into bed.

I sleep like the dead, and don't wake until late the next morning.

*****

'Hey pretty lady. Penny for your thoughts?' Leo Falkirk walks onto the stage wearing nothing but skin-tight y-fronts, emblazoned with the Texan flag. His body is lethally toned and tanned, and blond hair falls across his muscled chest.

I'm on stage in leggings and a long, loose t-shirt, staring wide-eyed at Leo's choice of costume.

'Please don't tell me that's what you're planning on wearing for the show tonight,' I say.

'These are for rehearsals and your eyes only,' Leo replies with a boyish grin. 'I thought they might cheer you up. Get you out of your slump.'

Leo and I don't really have to rehearse anymore, since the show is doing really well. But we're both committed to performing as best as we possibly can, so we practise between shows, feeding on reviews and audience reaction.

'I haven't been in a slump,' I counter.

'Not during the shows maybe, but ooo-eee! You haven't been much fun the rest of the time.'

'Sorry Leo. I just can't make myself feel excited about much right now. Everything feels like an endurance.'

I take a seat on a purple couch, which looks soft, but is actually stuffed with cardboard. The set has been laid out for the scene in Beast's house, when Beauty reads Beast poetry.

'I know, I know,' says Leo, swaggering towards me. 'Because of M.A.R.C and the star crossed lovers being cruelly torn apart. My heart goes out for you. It does.' He thumps his chest and pretends to swoon. 'But you know – you two did always seem kind of intense to me. A break might do you good. Help you see that there are other men out there besides Marc Blackwell.'

'Did you pick those up from a souvenir shop back home?' I say, nodding at his underpants.

'Nope.' Leo takes a seat on the couch beside me and slings a bare arm around my shoulder. 'Christmas gift. From my mom.'

'Nice the two of you get on so well.'

'She has a sense of humour, my mom,' says Leo. 'Maybe you should try it. You've been sour faced for weeks now. Ever since Boxing Day. Here. This might cheer you up too.' He bounds off stage and returns with a tabloid newspaper, which he throws into my lap.

My mouth drops open as I read the headline.

Getty Gets Life

40

I look up at Leo. Does he know? Does he know what happened to me?

'Leo, how did you—'

'He's one of the paps who was bothering you, right?' says Leo. 'The one who was behind all those bad stories?'

'That's him,' I say slowly, my eyes scanning down to the article.

'I thought you might be happy to hear he's gone to jail.'

I nod, reading the article. It doesn't mention my name at all – only that Getty was involved in a kidnapping and sado masochistic sex ring, and that he's been sentenced to life in prison.

There are pictures of Getty being taken into a police van in handcuffs. He looks pale and old, and his trademark sideburns have grown straggly and out of shape.

'Oh my god,' I say, reading more text. 'It mentions Cecile.'

'Who's Cecile?' asks Leo.

'She's ... a girl from my college.'

The newspaper doesn't say that Cecile used to date Getty. It just calls her a 'friend', and quotes her as saying:

'It's a sad day for British justice when the innocent go to prison and the guilty walk free. I won't let Giles's imprisonment go unpunished. I have powerful friends, and we intend to make sure the person truly responsible for this crime feels pain.'

PAIN.

A sickly shiver goes through me.

'Are you okay, Soph?' says Leo, taking the limp paper from my hands. 'You've gone kind of pale.'

'Fine.' I try to slap a smile onto my face.

'You're not fooling me,' says Leo.

'Okay, fine.' I let the smile slide away. 'Better?'

'More honest, at least. I'd have thought you'd be happy today. Friday, right? Isn't this the day you're allowed to call Prince Charming? Your weekly phone call? Do you have a warden standing beside you while you make it?'

'No. Marc's going to call me after the show.'

'Uh oh,' says Leo.

'Uh oh?'

'Does that mean you're going to spend the whole of tonight's show wrapped up in thoughts of Marc Blackwell, forgetting your lines, missing your cues ...'

'Of course not,' I say. 'Since when have I ever done that? Performing is the only time I forget about Marc.'

'What about when we rehearse?'

'Maybe a little. Sometimes.'

'Just a little?'

We're interrupted by Davina, storming along the rows of seats, her red fingernails gripping a rolled-up newspaper.

'Hey Davina,' says Leo, standing tall so she can get the full view of his underpants. 'How's it shaking?'

Davina doesn't seem to notice what Leo's wearing. 'We got THIS review today,' she says, waving the paper around. 'Sophia, you need to do better. Try harder.'

I stand up. 'Can I see the review?'

'Here.' Davina reaches the stage and throws the newspaper at my feet. I flick to the review pages and begin to read. Leo reads over my shoulder.

'Davina, this review isn't so bad,' he says.

'It's terrible,' says Davina. 'Didn't you see what it said, about taking a chance hiring an unknown, inexperienced actress?'

'Yes, but Leo's right,' I say. 'That's about as bad as it gets. Other than that, it's not bad at all. Okay, not great. But definitely not terrible. There's stuff here we can work on.'

Leo nods. 'I agree with Sophia. Anyway, the audiences are loving the show. We're getting great blog and online reviews.'

Davina looks at me. 'It was always going to be a gamble hiring you. We were bound to get some bad reviews.'

'Davina, this isn't a bad review,' I say, beginning to feel annoyed. I thought she'd got over her problem with me after all the great audience feedback we've been getting. But I guess not.

'It could be better.'

'And it could be worse,' I say, hearing volume and colour in my voice. 'Much worse. Like Leo said, the audiences are loving the show. And we're working our arses off to improve all the time. When are you going to give me a break?'

'A break?' Davina blinks at me.

'Ever since we started this show, Leo's been your hero and I've been your villain. But the show's doing well. Really well. Much better than expected. All the newspapers are saying so.' I wave the paper at her. 'Even this review says that ticket sales are strong. What on earth is your problem?'

Davina takes a step back, and stumbles a little on her high heels. 'Well … if you feel so strongly … I suppose maybe I picked a bad time …'

'There's never a good time,' I say. 'You always think

the worse of me. When's it going to stop? Do I need to be a big Hollywood star before you'll accept that I add value to the show?'

Davina looks at the ground. 'Maybe I've been coming across wrong ... I apologise if anything was misinter-preted ...' She lifts her head and pastes on a smile. 'Let's start again. Okay? I'll try harder to see things from your point of view.'

'Thank you,' I say, tired suddenly. 'Let's try and start again.'

'Great!' says Davina brightly. 'Well. I'll let you two rehearse while I grab a coffee. Can't wait to see the show tonight.' She suddenly notices Leo's underpants. 'And for goodness sake Leo, put some clothes on. You're not a Chippendale.'

Leo lets out a spurt of laughter as Davina walks away. 'About time you told her off. I was wondering when you'd snap.'

'I just wanted to get things straight. I've got too much on my mind right now to deal with Davina's hate campaign.'

'Like Marc Blackwell?' says Leo, raising an eyebrow.

'More than that,' I say. 'Security stuff.'

'I know I can't compete with Mr Perfect,' says Leo, 'but I just want you to know, while you and Marc are apart, I'll look after you. Okay? I care about you. I don't want anything bad happening to my co-star.'

'Thanks Leo. That's very sweet.'

Leo laughs. 'That's something I've never been called before.'

41

That night, the show is great and the audience is great, but as Keith and I drive towards Dad's cottage, I realise my phone reception is *not* great. And it's getting worse. I don't want to risk Marc not being able to get through.

'Change of plan,' I tell Keith. 'I'm going to stay at Ivy College tonight. Can you turn the car around? I need somewhere with good phone signal.'

'No problem,' says Keith, indicating and pulling over.

*****

After Keith drops me off at the college gates, I call Dad to let him know I'll be back first thing in the morning. Then I walk through the beautiful college grounds, eyes glued to my phone, waiting for Marc's call.

At exactly midnight, Marc's number flashes up.

I smile. Trust Marc to be exactly on time.

'Sophia.' Marc's voice is rich and dark, and I instantly think of his strong arms and broad chest.

God, my body aches to be near him. I've been carrying a hole in my heart since Christmas, but that hole has just turned into a chasm. To know he's nearby, in London, but that I can't be with him … touch him … it's agony.

'Hi,' I say, my voice strangely light and unfamiliar.

'Where are you?' Marc asks.

'At Ivy College. There's better reception here. I didn't want to miss your call.'

A pause.

'Good.' His voice is so deep. 'It makes sense to break up your location. It means people can't guess where you might be.'

'Uh huh.' I grip the phone tighter.

'I miss you,' says Marc softly, his words making my stomach flip over.

'I miss you too.' A whole tsunami of feelings rush forwards. 'I miss you so much Marc. Sometimes I'm not sure if I can stand it. How am I ever going to do three months? It's only been a few weeks so far, and I'm in agony.' I try to think happy thoughts, and manage to get my voice to level out. 'Are you okay?'

'Without you, I'm never okay,' says Marc. 'I'm very, very far from okay. But I'm coping.'

'Same here,' I say, heading away from the central buildings and towards the accommodation block. 'Coping. But far from okay.'

'There aren't many moments when I'm not thinking of you,' says Marc.

'Me too.' I let myself into the accommodation building and head towards the stairs.

'I hate knowing that you're with Leo every day.' Marc's voice grows tight. 'Knowing he can talk to you. Touch you. And I can't.'

'I know I keep telling you not to be jealous,' I say, climbing the stairs to my old room, 'but I'd probably feel the same if I were you.' I reach my old bedroom door and unlock it. 'If you were with some other woman while I couldn't be with you ... I'd find it hard.'

'A part of me thinks he could be the better man for you,' says Marc. 'When your father spoke of separation, Leo came to mind. He can give you things I can't. A normal relationship. No dark undercurrents.'

'I don't want normal.' I take a step into my old room, smelling dust and soap. It's a little cold, so I throw coal and paper into the grate and light a fire one-handed. 'And I like dark undercurrents.'

'Your father would certainly be much happier if you were with a man like Leo.'

'But I wouldn't be.'

'You know that for certain?'

'Yes.'

A pause. 'Are you in your bedroom?'

'Yes. How did you know that?'

'I heard you climbing the stairs. Close the bedroom door.'

I snap the bedroom door closed and sit on the edge of the bed.

'Take your jeans off.'

'How do you know I'm wearing jeans?'

'Aside from the fact you almost always wear them? I know because my security team take hourly video footage of you. And I study it closely.'

'You've seen video footage of me since I left the theatre?'

'Of course I have.'

I feel myself smiling. 'Doesn't that go against the rules? We're not supposed to see each other.'

'Correction. We agreed that *you* wouldn't see me. And that I could see for security purposes. But since you're in an obedient frame of mind, I have a few more rules for you to follow. Go to your wardrobe and take out a scarf – the softest, thinnest one you have.'

'Why?'

'Don't ask questions.'

I do as Marc asks, and find a long black scarf with white skulls on it – a birthday present from Jen last year.

'Now tie it around your mouth.'

'What?'

'I told you. Tie it around your mouth. No arguing.'

'You want me to tie this scarf around my mouth? Like a gag?'

'Correct.'

'But then I won't be able to talk to you.'

'Also correct. At least, not until I say so.'

'But I've waited all week to speak to you—'

'Sometimes listening can be better than talking.'

I look at the scarf, then back at the phone. 'Marc, I'll feel stupid sitting here with a scarf tied around my mouth.'

'You won't for long. I've spent a good deal of this week thinking about how I'm going to make you come. And gagging you is one of the few ways I can dominate you from a distance.'

'Dominate me?' I smile. 'Is that what you call it?'

'One of the many things.' I hear Marc's smile down the phone. 'Tie the scarf around your mouth.'

Reluctantly, I take the scarf and feed it behind my head, pulling it tight across my lips so it slides between my teeth. The cotton dries up my tongue and makes it difficult to swallow, let alone talk. It's not uncomfortable exactly, but not my every day choice of how to wear a scarf.

'Sophia?'

'Mmmph,' I mumble down the phone.

'I'm going to fuck you now.'

Instinctively I look at the door, expecting Marc to walk into my bedroom. But I know he'd never go against the agreement we have with my father. He'd never break his word.

I try to say 'How?', but all that comes out is a mumble.

'You haven't taken your jeans off yet. Take them off now.'

I do, sliding my boots off first, and then pulling my tight blue jeans from my legs.

My skin is pale in the bright light of my bedroom.

There are a few bumps and bruises from being lifted around by Leo during our performances.

'Now your panties.'

42

I climb out of my underwear – a plain white set of knickers from Marks and Spencer. I'm glad Marc can't see them. They're hopelessly plain and virginal. Not sexy at all. At least, they don't look sexy to me.

Now I'm sitting in just my sweater, with my mouth gagged. Part of me is tempted to untie the scarf and tell Marc I'm not up for playing this game right now – not when I haven't spoken to him all week. But the gentle warmth that's building between my legs stops me.

'Roll onto your stomach and put me on speakerphone.'

I jab the speakerphone button, place the phone on the duvet and roll onto my stomach, feeling soft cotton against my bare legs.

'Spread your legs.'

I do, feeling cool air between them.

'I want you to imagine that I'm standing behind you.'

I think of Marc, so tall and sexy and intense, and shiver at the thought of him between my legs. If I concentrate hard, I can pretend he's here in the room with me, waiting to touch me.

'I'm going to pull you down the bed by your ankles,' Marc says. 'I want you to slide down the bed.'

I wriggle down the bed, shimmying left and right until I feel nothing but air under my ankles and shins.

'Now I'm going to bend you over the bed. I want you with your backside in the air, legs apart, waiting for me to fuck you.'

Oh god.

I slide further down the bed until my legs drop over the end. I wait there, naked from the waist down, rear end in the air, just like he instructed.

I wiggle my legs apart.

It's so hard not to speak. I reach forwards and pull the phone towards me so it's right by my ear.

God, I feel so turned on. Gagged and following Marc's instructions ... wanting him to touch me so badly, but only having my imagination to play with.

What I wouldn't give to feel his fingers grabbing my backside, his body pressed between my legs.

'Spread your legs wider.'

I do, and feel electric shocks running up and down my thighs. I moan into the gag, and hear Marc breathing faster down the phone.

'I'm not going to fuck you yet,' says Marc, his voice thick. 'I'm going to leave you waiting. Wanting. And when I'm ready to have you, I will. But only when I'm ready.'

I moan harder into the gag, wiggling against the bed, rubbing myself against the hard frame.

'Don't move,' Marc barks down the phone. 'I can hear you moving. Don't move until I tell you to.'

I stop moving.

Silence.

I wait. And wait. And the more I wait, the hotter I feel and the more desperate I am to hear Marc's voice. I try to call his name through the gag, but all that comes out is a muffled moan.

I want more. More instructions. More of Marc's voice. More of *him*.

Just when I don't think I can bear it any more – when I'm about to rip the gag out of my mouth and call Marc's name – I hear his deep voice down the phone.

'Do you know how hard I am, thinking about you bent over the bed, gagged and ready for me?'

I moan into the gag again. 'Mmmph.'

'*God.*' I sense Marc is losing control now, and I am

too. This is almost unbearable.

I rub myself against the bed frame, up down, up down, pushing myself forward and back as I imagine Marc behind me, slamming between my legs.

'I told you not to move,' Marc warns.

I moan into the gag, and I hear Marc's breathing get even heavier. I try to stop myself moving, but it's tough to stay still. I'm getting so, so hot.

'Because you moved when I told you not to,' says Marc, 'I'm going to spank you hard, three times.'

Oh *god*. I give a long moan into the gag. 'Mmmmm.'

'One.' I hear a 'smack!' down the phone, and guess Marc must have hit something with his palm.

I imagine the sting on my buttocks.

'Two.' Another smack.

If the gag wasn't in my mouth I'd be gasping right now as I imagine Marc's palm.

'Three.' Another smack.

Oh god, oh god. I'm desperate to move. Desperate to rub myself forward and back, to pretend Marc is fucking me.

'I'm running my knuckles over the nice red colour on your backside.' Marc's voice is much lower than usual now, and I sense him coming undone. 'And now, because seeing you red like that has made me so hard, I'm pushing myself between your legs, sliding inside you, all the way inside.'

I moan into the gag again, and now I just can't help myself. I push up and down against the bed, rubbing and rubbing as I imagine Marc inside of me. God, I wish he was. There's an aching, stinging red-hot feeling where I want him to be.

I move my fingers between my legs and rub in circles, moaning and moaning into the gag, wanting Marc so, so badly, and hearing his deep breathing down the phone.

It's too much, and I can't hold on any longer.

'*Mmmm.*'

I come, trying to shout Marc's name into the gag, but the only sound I manage is a high-pitched noise that makes Marc's breathing grow hard and heavy.

'I love hearing you come,' Marc groans.

Shudders ripple up and down my legs, over my breasts and up my neck. I fall limply against the bed as pleasure washes over me and cool air strokes my bare skin.

'Get into bed now,' says Marc. 'You can take the gag off.'

I untie the scarf and climb up onto the bed, taking the phone with me. I fall exhausted against my pillow, lying the phone by my side.

'I love you, Marc. I miss you so much.'

'I love you too,' says Marc softly. 'Take your sweater off and pull the duvet over yourself.'

I do, feeling my eyes begin to close.

'Goodnight Sophia. I'll speak to you next week.'

43

The next morning, I wake up feeling happy and rested. And a little frustrated. Marc's voice on the telephone was better than nothing, but it doesn't compare to him in person. And of course, now I have the agony of another week's wait to hear his voice again.

I dress quickly and head back to the cottage, where I find Dad giving Sammy a breakfast of honey straight from the jar.

'Let me get him some porridge to go with that honey,' I say, inwardly sighing at the state of the house. I don't know how my dad does it, but since I left last night the house looks like someone has shaken it upside-down.

'Thanks love,' says Dad. 'Do you want breakfast?'

I throw myself onto a chair at the table and pull a silly face for Sammy. 'I'll get it. Aren't you supposed to be starting work again today?' I eye my dad's stained t-shirt and boxer shorts.

'In an hour or so. At least, that's the idea. But I'm happy to stay here and help out. I mean, you had your show last night. I don't want you tiring yourself out.'

I laugh. 'It's easier to look after the house without you in it, Dad. You should know that by now.'

'You *do* look a little tired, love.'

'A little.' I yawn.

'I can always get that girl from the village to come. Charlene.'

Sammy begins to wail. 'No, no, *nooooo*.'

I shake my head. 'Sammy doesn't like her. And you can't ask Charlene to tidy up, which is what this place needs. You go to work. It'll be good for you to start having a normal life again.'

'I'll be back by tea time. Call me if you need me to come home before then.'

'I will,' I say.

When Dad leaves, I take the honey away from Sammy, clean him up, make him breakfast and tidy the house. Somehow, Dad has managed to get honey on the cupboards as well as Sammy, so I wipe all that off and change Sammy's clothes.

Then I set to work learning new lines Leo and I have rewritten for one of the scenes. Some of the reviews said that Leo's character was too mean at times, so we've rethought some of the dialogue.

Sammy tugs at my leg while I'm trying to learn the lines, and I soon realise how hopeless it is trying to memorise stuff while he's here, crawling around, chattering for attention. Also, Sammy hasn't left the house yet. He needs fresh air.

'You win, Sammy.' I close my notepad. 'Come on. Let's take you to the park.'

44

By tea time, I've got the house back in shape and Sammy is all tired out, thanks to plenty of time in the sandpit and on the swings. I drink strong coffee and summon the last of my energy to make spaghetti with pesto – one of Sammy's favourites.

I like to make spaghetti by hand, like my mum used to, but I don't today. The thought of rolling the dough while Sammy is crawling around is way too tiring.

Sammy and I are just sitting down to eat, when I hear the front door click.

I stop grating cheddar over Sammy's spaghetti and call out, 'Did you have a good day back at work?', as I hear Dad throw his money belt down by the boots and shoes.

But I realise I can hear two pairs of shoes clumping around in the hallway, and a voice that isn't Dad's.

'Great place you've got here, Mr Rose.'

I'd recognise that voice anywhere.

Leo Falkirk.

I jump up out of my chair as Dad and Leo walk into the kitchen area.

Leo is all bundled up in his duffle coat, his tanned face and perfect white teeth looking out of place in our humble little cottage.

I'm so surprised to see him that I nearly drop the cheese grater. 'Leo.' I look from Leo to Dad, and back again. 'What are you doing here?'

'Pleased to see you too, Sophia,' says Leo, lighting up the room with his huge white grin.

Sammy picks up a spoon and bangs it hard on the table, excited to see a guest.

Leo ducks down to dodge a wooden beam, and takes a seat at the dining table as if it's the most natural thing in the world for him to be here. 'What's for dinner?' He raises a cheeky eyebrow. 'Smells good.'

I look up at Dad, my face questioning.

'Leo was outside the house as I was pulling up,' says Dad. 'So I invited him in to eat with us.'

'Thought I'd call round and see how you were doing,' says Leo, scooping one of Sammy's toy cars from the floor and spinning the wheels. 'I've never seen your family home before. And I thought, maybe I could come visit, then take you to the show tonight.'

My mouth opens and closes as Leo leans forwards and smells the huge pan of spaghetti and pesto I've placed in the middle of the table.

'Can't wait for dinner.'

I stare at him, unsure whether to be angry or pleased. It's good to see him, but I'm pretty sure Marc wouldn't be happy about him just dropping by like this.

In the end, I don't get a chance to be angry. Leo picks up two forks and makes them do a little dance on the table for Sammy.

Seeing Leo Falkirk, with his action-man square jaw and huge muscles, being silly with cutlery just hits my funny bone.

I giggle, along with Sammy. 'Good to see you Leo,'

'I know I'm no Marc Blackwell,' says Leo, dropping the cutlery and putting his large elbows on the table. 'But since he can't come visit you, I'll just have to do.'

'I guess you will.'

Dad takes a seat at the table. 'It's good for you to have friends, other than Marc,' he tells me. 'I'm glad Leo came by.'

'Why thank you Mr Rose. I think it's good for Sophia to have me as a friend too.'

'Call me Mike.'

I'm shaking my head as I serve Dad and Leo spaghetti. 'Well. Nice of you two to decide these things for me. I mean, it's not as if I know my own mind or anything.'

The portions aren't very big, since I didn't know Leo was coming, but there's still enough food. Just about. I grate cheese over the plates to make the meal larger.

'Looks great,' says Leo, picking up a fork and sticking it right into the middle of the spaghetti. He lifts a massive pile, spins it around to make a ball, then crams the whole lot in his mouth.

'Delicious,' he mumbles.

'It's okay,' I say. 'I didn't make the spaghetti myself or anything. But then again, I didn't know you were coming.'

'And here I was thinking, as your co-star, I'd be welcome at your home,' Leo says, through chews of pasta.

'You are,' I say. 'I just ... it was a surprise, that's all.'

'A good surprise?'

'A surprise. I don't know how happy Marc will be to know you're here.'

'You can't let your life be ruled by Marc,' says Dad, loading spaghetti onto his fork.

'I don't,' I say. 'If I did, I would have asked Leo to leave. But I do love Marc, Dad. I respect his feelings. And that won't change.'

Dad looks down at his meal. 'Things *do* change sometimes, love. And if they do, you could do a lot worse than young Leo here.'

I turn scarlet. '*Dad!*'

Leo grins from ear to ear. 'It's okay Mike. Sophia and I have a love hate relationship. She hates to love me. But I know deep down she's crazy about me.'

'God.' I shake my head at Leo, but I can't help smiling. 'I'm crazy about you as a friend and nothing more.'

Leo clicks his fingers. 'So you *are* crazy about me? That sounds like progress.'

I raise an eyebrow at him. 'Don't hold your breath.'

I'm about to take a mouthful of spaghetti when a shadow flashes past the window.

I drop my fork.

'What was that?' I leap to my feet, almost choking on a piece of pasta.

45

Leo and Dad both turn to the window.

'Sophia?' says Leo.

'Did you see it?' I point at where the dark shadow was. But of course, it's gone now. 'It was ... there was a shadow. It was there. In the garden.' I go to the window and look out onto the green lawn. But there's nobody there.

'Are you sure?' Leo asks.

I nod, running to the backdoor and yanking it open. Sharp winter air stings my cheeks as I head out into the garden.

I stand on the lawn and turn in a circle. Then I check the bushes and around the trees at the sides of the garden, but there's nothing.

'Are you okay?'

I turn to see Leo beside me.

'There was someone there,' I say. 'I'm sure of it.'

'Hey. I believe you. You want me to check around the cottage?'

'Would you?'

'Sure.'

Leo bounds over the little garden gate, and I hear him crunching around in the undergrowth.

'Love?' I turn to see Dad. 'Is everything okay?'

'Fine. It's fine Dad. Just ... seeing shadows that's all. Leo is checking it out.' I put my fingers to my temple. 'Nothing to worry about.'

Dad shakes his head. 'Who wouldn't see shadows with all this security around?'

'The security is here to keep me safe,' I say.

'Seems like overkill to me, says Dad, heading inside.

As the back door closes, I notice something – a white thing fluttering in a shrub. I walk over to it, thinking maybe it's a stray piece of litter or something. But when I get close, I see it's a piece of paper with red biro scrawled on it.

'PAIN will have its revenge. '

I take a step back, dropping the note on the lawn. The breeze picks it up, and pulls it higher and higher, up and over the trees, then the cottage roof, and away.

I watch it drift away, my heart thumping harder and harder.

PAIN will have its revenge.

Oh my god. They were here. In our garden.

Leo bounds back over the fence. 'Couldn't see anyone. Hey, are you okay? You look like you've seen a ghost.'

'There was a note,' I say, my voice all shaky. 'We should go inside.'

46

'Dad. DAD!' I call, as I come in from the garden. 'I need to call Marc.'

'Why?' Dad asks.

I hesitate. I don't want to tell Dad about the note. That would involve a lot of explaining.

'To tell him I saw something in the garden,' I say.

'It was just a shadow, love.'

'I need to tell him.'

'How about *I* call and tell him? Then you'll still be keeping to our agreement.'

'Okay, fine. Yes, you tell him. Say we need more security. Right away.'

*****

During the show that night, I'm jumping at shadows. Any movement in the wings or the audience makes me flinch and forget my lines, and Leo keeps having to rescue me from stumbled phrases and missed cues.

When Leo and I are doing our final number, I swear I see Cecile in the front row and I start singing the first verse all over again.

Leo, true professional that he is, goes back to the first verse too, and we eventually get through the song. By the time we're finished, I realise the person I thought was Cecile looks nothing like her.

I'm seeing things.

'Tough night,' says Leo, as we head off stage. He puts a gentlemanly arm around my shoulder and steers me through the backstage area. 'Hey. I know why you were jumpy. It's okay.'

'I'm so sorry Leo.' I look up at him, embarrassed. 'You deserve better. Someone more professional.'

'Hey, hey.' Leo turns me to him, his large, heavy hands on my shoulders. 'Like I said. We all have bad nights. You wouldn't be human if you didn't let personal things get to you sometimes. It happens to all of us.'

'It hasn't happened to you yet,' I say, seeing Davina heading towards us.

'Sure it has,' says Leo. 'Plenty of times. When Sigourney dumped me for that French guy, I messed up my lines for weeks. The movie I was shooting took twice as long to wrap up.'

My face softens. 'A big tough guy like you? Getting all messed up over a girl?'

'A big tough guy like me. I used to fall in love every other week, back in the day. And I thought Sigourney was the love of my life. She was so sophisticated. Classy. Everything I wasn't. But we weren't right together. The supermodel and the surf bum. Not the best combination. And she wasn't real. She looked totally different without all the clothes and hair and makeup. Not like you. You're beautiful all the time.'

I blush. 'Oh come on. No one's knocking at *my* door asking me to pose for Vogue or do a Chanel commercial.'

'They should be.'

'Isn't Sigourney Seymour married now?' I blurt out, in an effort to change the subject.

Very tactful, Sophia.

Luckily, Leo doesn't look hurt or offended.

'Oh, yeah. To the guy she dumped me for. Louis Dupois.'

This I already know. Jen makes it her business to find out *all* the celebrity gossip, and she shares it with me, whether I'm interested or not.

It's weird be talking about someone as famous as Sigourney Seymour, as if she's just some girl Leo knows. But then Leo's a huge star too. Sometimes I forget, because he's so down to earth.

'Sophia. Leo.' Davina comes clicking towards us, and I brace myself for a telling off.

I have no defence. I deserve some harsh words this evening. But it's not me Davina seems to be angry with.

'The box office haven't been reselling cancelled seats. Can you believe it? We could have been selling twenty extra tickets a night.'

'Twenty's no big deal, Davina,' says Leo. 'Don't sweat it.'

'I will sweat it. I'll be having words with them tomorrow.' Davina uncrosses her arms. 'You two were great, as per. Loved that re-jig of the last number.'

'It wasn't a re-jig,' I admit. 'I messed up.'

'Well it sounded great,' says Davina. 'It's good to keep a show organic. After all, why pay for the theatre if you're going to see exactly the same thing every night? I liked that you shook things up. Is everything okay?' Her sharp eyes prickle with something that I think is concern. But I can't be sure. Davina's face doesn't really suit caring expressions.

'I will be,' I say, turning to Leo. 'I had a bit of a shock today, that's all.'

'You look exhausted.'

As soon as she says that, I realise I am. My whole body feels tired, from my eyes right down to my toes. I could lie down on the floor right now and fall asleep. I'm sure my eyes must have huge dark circles under them.

'Yes,' I say. 'I should get home. I have an early start tomorrow.'

'Early start?' Davina blinks. 'Days should be for sleeping when you do these sorts of shows. Mornings at least.'

'I know. But my family need me right now.'

'Well. Try and get someone else to help. This show needs you too.'

47

After I get changed, Leo and I head out to the foyer to sign autographs. I should be pleased that there are fans waiting for us, but all I can think about is sleeping. Still, I paste on my best smile. With Leo beside me, it's okay. And I really do feel honoured to be signing autographs.

Just as I'm reaching out to sign theatre tickets for a smiling family, Leo nudges me and holds up his phone.

'Hey. I got a text message. Guess who from?'

'No idea,' I say, turning back to the family and thanking them as I sign.

'Marc Blackwell,' says Leo.

'Marc?' My pen stops dead on the last ticket, but I catch myself and finish my signature. Then I shake hands with the family and wish them a safe journey. I turn to Leo. 'Marc texted you?'

'Yep. He's asked me to give you a message.'

'What's the message?' I ask.

'He says security has doubled around the cottage. And he wants me to tell you to go home. He says you're too tired to be signing autographs.'

'How does he even know I'm signing autographs?' I whirl around, looking for Marc in the crowd.

'All the security Marc has around the place. They have their eyes on you.'

I give a tired laugh. 'I can't believe it was you he texted. He must have been really desperate to get that message to me. He ...' I cut myself off.

'No, you can say it,' says Leo. 'He hates me. Right?'

'I wouldn't go that far,' I say. 'He's just very protective, that's all. A little jealous. Who wouldn't be? He can't see me, and you can.'

'I get it,' says Leo. 'I wouldn't like me much if I were him, either. But he's right – you should go home. You look like you're about to fall down.'

'I can't leave,' I say. 'All these people have waited. There's no way I'm just going to walk off without giving them an autograph.'

'You're going to wear yourself out,' says Leo. 'You do know that, don't you?'

'Probably,' I say. 'But I just don't see any way out of that right now.'

*****

I'm so tired I can barely stand by the time I reach the cottage. I've got a spare key, but as I try to weave it into the lock my eyes go in and out of focus.

I'm about to kneel down so I can be eye level with the door lock when I sense someone beside me.

The hairs on my neck stand up.

I should feel afraid, but I'm not. I'm totally calm, because I know who it is.

'Marc.'

48

'Don't turn around.' Marc's voice is full of authority and depth, and it does things to me, just like always.

'I mean it, Sophia. Keep looking straight ahead. We agreed we wouldn't see each other, and I intend to keep to my word.'

My hand begins to shake at the lock. 'You don't think this is breaking the rules? You speaking to me outside of our weekly phone conversation?' My voice has gone all tight and high. God, having him right there, behind me … my body starts to feel warm, even though the air is freezing.

'No.' I sense Marc's large body coming closer and feel his warmth. '*You* agreed not to see *me*. But I can see you, if it's in the interests of your safety.' I feel a smile in his voice. 'So we're not breaking the rules. You can't see me, can you?'

'No.'

'Good. I needed to be here tonight. After the note in the garden.'

'How do you know about that?'

'Security footage. I'm always around. Watching over you. Even if you don't know it. When I saw footage of you at the theatre earlier, you looked like you were falling down with tiredness.' A pause. 'Sophia, I can see right now that you're not okay. You're burning yourself out.'

'I'm tired,' I say. 'But my only real problem is that I miss you. Desperately.'

'Desperate isn't the word for the way I feel right now.' Marc's voice runs through me, and it's all I can do not to whirl around and throw myself against him. To press myself against his lips and feel his arms around me.

The key shakes in my hand, and I move my other hand to steady it.

'Tomorrow I want you to go back to Ivy College,' says Marc. 'To rest there. Looking after your father and doing this show at the same time is proving too much. I'll have help sent.'

I shake my head. 'Sammy doesn't take well to strangers. And Dad needs me. His daughter. Someone who cares about him. I couldn't possibly leave him.'

There's a very long pause, and I hear Marc's beautiful breathing.

'Okay. Stay then. But I'm having help sent, whether you agree to it or not. I have to go now.' Marc's voice grows deeper. 'Being close to you like this ... I'm struggling to control myself.'

'Don't go.' The words tumble out, full of emotion. Having him here, so close to me, is like someone holding out a cold glass of water in the desert.

'I have to. You know I do.'

'Yes.' My stomach flips over and I swallow hard. 'I ... yes. This is hard. So, so hard. We still have months to go.'

'*Christ*. I have to leave right now, or things are going to get out of hand. Go inside now and get straight into bed, Sophia. And tomorrow, I want you to sleep in until noon.'

'Noon?' I say. 'Sammy wakes up at six.' I check my watch. It's nearly one am, meaning I'll get approximately five hours sleep before I have to wake up.

'You needn't worry about that. Someone will be here to take care of Sammy tomorrow. And to take care of the housework.'

'Dad won't like that,' I say. 'He's still a little fragile.'

'He understands. It's all arranged. I spoke to him

earlier today. We settled on a plan B, in case you were falling down with exhaustion this evening.' Marc gives a little laugh. 'Your father and I both agree on one thing at least – that you come first.'

'Sammy doesn't take too well to strangers—'

'The person coming tomorrow isn't a stranger. Now go inside and get some rest. No arguing.'

'Marc—'

'I said no arguing. I'm glad Leo was here earlier.'

'I … he came over unannounced.'

'I heard what he did. The shadow in the garden. How he sprang to your defence.' I hear a little bit of anger in those last words, and I realise how hard it must be for Marc to know Leo took his place earlier. My insides twist a little.

'I appreciated it,' I say.

'So do I. Maybe he's grown up more than I realised. He wants to protect you. And that's what you need right now.'

'The only person I want to protect me is you.'

'But if I can't be there with you all the time, then I'm glad Leo can be.'

I hear him take a step back. Every fibre in my body wants to turn around. But I don't.

'Leo has a high profile. He's a star.' I hear the hardness in Marc's voice. 'But unlike me, he's well liked. Loved, even. He's Hollywood's golden boy. PAIN can paint me as a villain, but they won't touch a hair on Leo's golden head. If they do anything to him, there'd be a backlash. He's a good protector for you and your family.'

I can feel Marc's hurt. His pain and frustration. How hard he's working to overcome his jealousy and let another man take over his role. 'Marc?'

'Yes Sophia?'

'That you're willing to put your feelings aside like

that ... for our safety ... I think you're amazing.'

'I'm struggling, believe me. Now go inside, Sophia. You need to sleep. And I'm on the border line of breaking the rules right now.'

49

The next morning, I wake to the sounds of vacuuming and the smell fresh coffee drifting up the stairs. I sit bolt upright, listening out for Sammy, but hear nothing.

I check my watch.

It's 9am.

Wow. I really did sleep last night. But my heart starts beating fast when I realise Sammy didn't wake me. God, I hope he's okay.

I leap out of bed and run into his bedroom, but he's not in his cot. My heart beating even faster now, I run downstairs in my pyjamas and nearly bump into Rodney, who has a vacuum cleaner in one hand and Shake and Vac in the other.

'Oh!' I give a startled yelp. 'Rodney. You must be ... Marc said ... where's Sammy?'

'He's in the living area,' says Rodney. 'Playing.'

I tear into the lounge and find Sammy clambering over another house guest. A very familiar one.

I break into a huge smile.

'Jen.'

'Soph.' Jen smiles back. She's sitting on the sofa, helping Sammy climb over her legs. She's dressed in what counts for her as casual attire – her shiny hair is pulled back in a sleek, sophisticated bun and her tight black jeans fit her perfectly. 'Marc called me in as the emergency babysitter. Said you could use a little help. I wish you'd called me. I would have been here days ago.'

I take a seat beside her and help Sammy climb onto my lap. 'I thought you'd be working. I didn't want to—'

'Bother me. Yes, yes, I've known you long enough.

You don't want anyone else put out on your account. But you know, sometimes Soph, you've just got to reach out. Or you'll fall apart and then you'll be no good to anyone.'

'It's great to see you,' I say. 'Really great.'

'You too. I feel like I've lost my best friend this last month. A show every single night? Who works seven days a week? Even God gets a day off a week.'

'It's only until March.'

'I know, I know. And then you'll have a big white wedding and live happily ever after.'

'Hope so.' An uneasy feeling works its way up my spine as I think about that note in the garden last night.

'Are you okay?' Jen cocks her head. 'You just shivered.'

'I'm probably just cold.'

'Then go upstairs and put some clothes on, for god's sake.' Jen smiles at me. 'It's winter. You didn't need to come charging downstairs like a mad woman. Sammy's fine with me. Honest.'

'I know he is.' I kiss Sammy's head. 'He loves you almost as much as I do.'

'Oh, you.' Jen play slaps my arm.

'How'd you get time off work?' I ask. 'Are you sure your company are okay with you leaving them in the lurch like this?'

'Oh, they're fine,' says Jen. 'Absolutely fine.'

'But they're usually so strict.'

'I know. But I don't pay any attention right now. You know why?'

'Why?'

'Because as of yesterday, I don't work for them any more.'

My eyes widen. 'You don't?' A crazy thought enters my head.

'Jen, you didn't quit to come help me out did you?'

'No. I mean, you know I'd do anything for you, but as it happens, this was just the right time to leave.'

'Is everything okay?' I ask. 'You didn't get sacked, did you?' I know Jen. She's not afraid to speak her mind and sometimes it gets her into trouble.

'No.' Jen laughs. 'I'm setting up my own business. You know. The one I've been talking about since I left school. My own PR firm.'

'Wow. That's amazing. But shouldn't you be in front of a computer somewhere, looking for clients or something?'

'I've got a bit of breathing space, actually. On account of the fact I've already got an amazing client.'

'Wow! Already? Who is it? Anyone I've heard of?'

'Oh, I think you've heard of him. His name is Marc Blackwell.'

50

I stare at Jen. 'Marc Blackwell is your first PR client?'

'Yep. I'm going to do an amazing job for him. And for you. You're part of his business, in case you didn't know. Damage limitation. I have to protect your reputation at all times.'

I laugh. 'Wow. That's weird. But ... I guess good weird. I mean, are you happy about it?'

'I'm bloody ecstatic. My first client, a Hollywood star. It's amazing. Thank you so much Soph, for introducing me to him. I can't wait to start work.'

'Oh, I don't think I did all that much,' I say. 'I mean, he wouldn't have hired you unless he thought you were good. And we both know you're more than just good.'

'Flattery, flattery.'

'But if Marc's your client, shouldn't you be working for him right now?'

'Well, like I said, I have a bit of breathing space. On account of the fact he asked me to come over and help you for a few weeks. And he's paying me a retainer while I'm here. Nice guy, isn't he?'

'A little too nice,' I say. 'I don't want anyone put out for me. You or him, or anyone. But … it's good to have you here.'

'I know. We'll have fun, won't we?'

'We always do.'

*****

Later that afternoon, I get another surprise. Marc has arranged for Denise to come over and give me singing lessons at the cottage.

When she arrives, the house is sparkling clean thanks to Rodney. Sammy is sleeping soundly upstairs and Jen is flicking through *Heat* magazine. Rodney is in the garden, scrubbing the patio with bleach. Dad is upstairs making a pile of old clothes for the charity shop.

'Denise.' I throw my arms around her. 'Good to see you.'

'Can't let my favourite pupil get behind on her studies.' Denise ambles into the cottage and puts her huge handbag on the floor by piles of muddy trainers and wellies.

'Oh, I'm sure you have lots of favourite pupils,' I say, leading her into the lounge area.

'True. But that doesn't mean I don't love them all very, very much.'

'Come on through.'

In the lounge, Jen's head snaps up. 'Hi Denise. How are you doing?'

'Fine, fine. And you?'

'Great.'

I hear a thumping sound as someone runs down the stairs. It's Dad, of course. No one else can make a noise like that just by moving around. He comes spilling into the lounge area, looking a little out of breath.

His face lights up when he sees Denise. 'I thought I heard your voice.'

Denise smiles back at him. 'Good to see you Mike.'

'Tea?' Dad asks.

'Lovely,' says Denise.

'I can make it,' I say, spying the now tidy kitchen. If I let Dad loose in there, there'll be milk all over the counter and sugar on the floor.

'No, *I'll* make it,' says Rodney, coming in from the garden with yellow rubber gloves on and a bucket of black water hanging from his fingers. 'You, Sophia Rose, are supposed to be taking it easy today.'

'I slept in until nine,' I counter.

'It should have been until noon,' says Rodney. 'And don't think I didn't catch you trying to tidy the kitchen today.'

'I was just doing the cupboards—'

Rodney wags a finger at me. 'No more! That's my department. Now you sit down and I'll bring in the tea.'

51

Before the lesson starts, Denise and I have a catch up about Ivy College. Tom and Tanya are looking very much in love these days, apparently. Which makes me smile a lot. I feel bad, though, about not having seen them since before Christmas.

Wendy is on a much deserved holiday, so the admin side of college life is a bit of a mess.

Marc still teaches classes, and the students are all learning plenty. Hearing that makes me pine, not only for Marc, but for his lessons. I learned so much from him in such a short space of time. When he taught me for a week, after the Giles Getty incident, I felt like I really grew.

After a general catch up, Denise hits me with the bombshell.

'I'm sure you're aware that Cecile was asked to leave the college,' Denise says, stirring sugar into her tea.

'I was aware.'

'Her friend Ryan isn't very happy about it. But he hasn't had the courage to complain. He just walks around the place with a scowl on his face.'

'I imagine leaving the college must have been devastating for her,' I say.

'Indeed. The plan was to let her get the help she needed, and then she could come back when she was well again. But … oh the poor girl. Her family won't have anything to do with her now, what with her leaving the college and being pregnant. So … she's taken a turn for the worse. And from what I hear, she isn't getting any help at all.'

I chew a thumb nail. 'That's … bad news,' I say. 'To

be pregnant and all alone. It must be terrible.'

'Yes. It must be. But she was offered help. She didn't take it. She's chosen to go in another direction.'

'Another direction?'

Denise nods. 'She's been seen around certain underground clubs.'

'Oh. I heard that too,' I say, chewing so hard that a strip of fingernail comes free.

'From Marc?' asks Denise, raising an eyebrow.

'Yes.'

'He's keeping an eye on her. We all are. But I'm sure everything will work out just fine.'

'Yes,' I say, uncertainly.

'Shall we get on with the lesson?'

*****

It feels weird singing at full volume in my dad's cottage, especially since I know Dad, Jen, Sammy and Rodney are around the place. But once I get over the embarrassment, Denise and I have a great lesson.

By the time we've finished, I'm reaching notes I've never reached before and my voice sounds clearer than ever.

Rodney brings us an afternoon tea of freshly baked scones, homemade jam and farmyard butter when the lesson is over, and Jen, Dad, Denise and I sit in the lounge, feeding Sammy spoons of jam, eating scones and drinking loose leaf tea.

It doesn't take long before Dad starts chatting to Denise about 1960s music, and soon they're both lost in a world of psychedelic tunes and childhood memories, while the rest of us play with Sammy.

Seeing my Dad talking to Denise, I realise it's the first time I've seen him properly smile since Christmas morning The two of them are really making each other laugh.

When we finish our scones, Dad asks Denise if she'd like to stay for the afternoon and a spot of dinner later, and Denise agrees.

'Don't you have classes to teach at the college?' I ask.

'Not this afternoon,' says Denise. 'You don't mind me staying, do you Sophia? You can say if you do. I'll understand. I know I came for Christmas, but a weekday social visit from your teacher might be a step too far.'

Jen gives a snort of laughter. 'She's done much more than that with her teacher.'

'Jen!'

'Sorry. Easy line.'

'I don't see you as a teacher anyway,' I tell Denise. 'You're a friend.'

'I'm pleased to hear it,' says Denise. 'Because you're a friend too.'

'I'm glad,' I say. Then I have an idea. 'Dad, if Denise is staying for the rest of the afternoon and Jen is watching Sammy, how would you feel if I went to visit Marc's sister before my show? She's back in hospital now and she must be pretty lonely.'

I don't add that with Denise here, I'm no longer needed to keep Dad company.

Dad frowns a little. 'Sophia, the whole point of not seeing Marc is so you can do your own thing. Be your own person. Get some distance.'

'It's not Annabel's fault that you've put me in this position,' I say. 'Don't keep her from having visitors, just because you're not sure about Marc.'

Dad sighs. 'Point taken. Okay. Fine.'

'I'll be back in time to cook dinner.'

'Oh no you won't.' Rodney picks up cups and saucers and loads them onto a tray. 'Marc's orders. You're to take it easy, and focus on the show.'

'For once, Marc and I agree on something,' says Dad.

52

The hospital isn't at all what I expect. For a start, it doesn't look like a hospital. It's more like a stately home with red brick walls, big chimney stacks and acres of green lawn and fir trees all around.

Annabel is staying in West London, not far from where Marc took me when Ryan drugged my drink. It takes me a full five minutes to walk up the long stone path to the grand pillared entrance of the hospital.

I push through a heavy black door into a light, airy reception area with thick carpet, and smell lemon fragrance and camomile tea.

Waiting on a beige-leather sofa by the reception desk is Annabel.

'Sophia.' She leaps up and throws her arms around me in a bony hug. 'I'm so, so glad you came. It's … I've had a bad day today.'

'Then I'm extra glad I came,' I say. 'I brought you scones. Tell me about your bad day.'

I hand her a wicker basket, covered with a red checked cloth.

'Did you make these?' says Annabel, pulling back the cloth. 'They smell delicious.'

'I should have,' I say. 'But no. Rodney did. Next time I'll bake you something myself.'

'Don't be silly. Having you here is more than enough. You don't need to bring anything other than yourself. It's such a relief that I can have visitors now. Before Christmas, I was so, so lonely.'

'You're looking really well,' I say. 'I'm sorry to hear today hasn't been great.'

Annabel nods and puts the scone basket down on a

coffee table. 'Shall we go for a walk?'

*****

As Annabel and I stroll through the green grounds, it's great to smell the soil and see the bare branches overhead. Sometimes, when I'm at the theatre, I feel like concrete is caving in on me. It's nice to know there are parts of London, aside from Ivy College, that are green and natural.

We walk for a while in silence. Then Annabel tells me why she's had a bad day.

'This morning, I found out that getting my son back isn't as straightforward as I thought,' she says. 'There are lots of assessments. Paperwork. Things I have to prove that I just can't prove. That I'll provide a stable home. That there'll be friends around to support me. That I can earn an income. I … everything just feels impossible right now.'

Her bony face sags and I notice how much older she looks now we're in the daylight. I slide an arm through hers.

'I can help you,' I say. 'I had to fill out lots of those sorts of forms for Dad when I was younger. Some of the neighbours thought he wasn't a fit parent. So we had people coming to check on us all the time.'

'I'm surprised to hear you had those sorts of troubles,' says Annabel.

'We're a close family,' I say. 'But we've had hard times, too. It wasn't anyone's fault. Dad had just lost his wife when all that stuff happened. He was grieving. But anyway, enough about me. Marc and I will help you get everything you need to get your son back.'

'But Marc has already done so much for me. And you have too. The whole point of getting well is so I can stand on my own two feet. I need to stop taking from people and start living.'

'Annabel. You're beating a major drug addition. Now is exactly the time you need help from other people. Get well first, then you can start giving to others.'

'I don't know, Sophia. Everything just feels a little hopeless right now. I don't deserve Daniel. That little boy needs a better mum than me.'

I shake my head. 'Annabel, no little boy should grow up in care. You're a good person. You've just had a tough life, that's all.' I slide my arm free from hers and put my hands firmly on her shoulders. 'If you can beat heroin then you can do anything – including being a good mother. And Marc and I will help you every step of the way.'

53

I visit Annabel a few more times during the week, and she has good days and bad days. When I see the forms she has to fill in, I get more and more desperate to talk to Marc. I've seen those forms before, and I know it's really important that Annabel has her own place if she's going to get her son back. So I need to ask Marc if he can help.

When Friday comes around, I spend most of the day doing internet research at the cottage. I need to know all the laws and regulations about adoption and custody, so I can tell Marc exactly what Annabel needs. It's important that I don't leave out any detail. We have to get everything right if Annabel stands a chance of getting her son back.

By evening time, I've got together a long list for Marc and I'm feeling really positive about Annabel's future.

Rodney cooks us all a delicious lasagne for dinner, and after we've eaten I soak in a hot bath while Sammy sleeps. Jen has already driven back to her apartment and Dad is at work, so the house is nice and quiet – except for the sounds of Rodney tidying the kitchen.

I'm just towelling myself dry when I hear the doorbell downstairs.

'I'll get it,' Rodney calls.

I hear the clump of heavy feet and Leo's voice in our hallway.

'Just coming,' I call out, running out of the bathroom in my towel, and heading to the guest bedroom.

Typical Leo – he's standing at the bottom of the staircase as I run past, so he gets a full-length view of me bound up in a white towel, my hair soaking wet.

'Nice outfit,' he calls up. 'I thought you might like some company on the way to the show again.'

'Wait in the lounge. I'll be right down.'

After I've dressed in leggings, Ugg boots and a huge pink sweater, I head downstairs, still towelling my hair.

Leo is lounging on the sofa wearing ripped jeans and a sweatshirt with a picture of a pastel sunset on it.

'Ah, my favourite co-star. All dressed up and ready to go,' says Leo. 'I thought I'd pick you up tonight. You don't mind, do you?'

'No,' I say, truthfully. 'It'll be nice to have the company in the limo.'

'Hey, what are those yellow flowers in your front garden called? They're awesome.'

'Daffodils,' I say. 'They always come up early around here. I have no idea why.'

'Daff-o-dils,' says Leo. 'I should write that down. I want to tell my mom about them. She loves yellow flowers.'

'They're really easy to grow,' I say. 'Just put the bulbs in the ground and that's it. They come up every year. If you like the front garden, you should see the back. It's covered in them right now.'

'Wow. Can I see?'

'Sure.'

Leo follows me outside, and I point out the bright daffodils sprouting from every flowerbed. They make a blanket of yellow petals around the lawn.

'Pretty,' says Leo.

'Aren't they?'

'You know, I'm sure gonna miss you. When the show finishes.'

'We've got *ages* before the show finishes,' I protest. 'We're only half way through the run.'

'I guess maybe time is going slower for you than it

is for me,' says Leo, throwing me a wonky grin. 'But you're having fun, right? At least some of the time?'

I smile. 'Yes. It's fun. Working with you is fun. And performing is fun too. I just wish I didn't miss Marc so much.'

'Still miss him, huh?' says Leo.

I nod. 'More than ever.'

'Shame. But if you ever get lonely in the night, you know where I am.'

I laugh.

'Hey, laugh all you like, but if it wasn't for Marc Blackwell you might just have given me a shot by now. We could be living happily ever after.'

'You're not my type. And you're only interested in *me* because you can't have me.'

'*So* untrue,' says Leo. 'Well. Maybe a little bit true. But how do you know I'm not your type?'

'I just know.'

'I always thought I'd hate frozen yoghurt. And then I tried it. And now I love the stuff.'

'Trust me. I don't need to try you out to know you're not my type.'

'Are you sure about that?' Leo drops his face so our noses are almost touching. He rests a hand on my shoulder. 'You could be missing out on something incredible.'

Before I know what's happening, his lips touch mine and his arms come around my body, pulling me close.

54

It feels like so long since I've been held or kissed. So very, very long. And as Leo's lips press harder against mine and begin moving softly, I don't pull away. I let it happen, because I've missed this – being close to someone. Feeling someone's hand stroke my hair. Strong arms around my body.

Leo's lips work back and forth, opening and exploring. His hand slides around my hair and his chest presses tight against mine. I have to admit, it feels good. But it's Marc I've missed kissing. I don't want to kiss anyone else.

I pull away, feeling a shame I've never known before. My skin is sticky with guilt.

I step back, shaking my head. 'Oh god. Leo I didn't mean for that to happen -'

Leo runs his fingers through his thick, blond hair. 'Actually, I didn't either. Guess I just had to try it out.'

'You did that all right,' I whisper, feeling guilt, shame and embarrassment tumbling around in one awful sickly spin cycle. 'God, why did I let that happen? Why? I love Marc.'

I look away from Leo, feeling tears come.

'Hey.' Leo puts steadying hands on my shoulders. 'It wasn't your fault. I kissed you, remember? And you've been away from your boyfriend for over a month. Don't be too hard on yourself. Be hard on me instead. It was my fault. I should have realised how vulnerable you were.'

Tears slide down my cheeks. 'I have to tell Marc what happened.'

Leo shakes his head. 'No you don't. It was an accident,

that's all. And it wasn't your fault. I should have known better. We're friends and nothing more. I should know that by now. You've told me often enough.'

'I can't keep it a secret,' I say, close to tears.

'Who would you tell him for? Him or yourself?'

'He'll find out, Leo. Whether I tell him or not. There are cameras out here.' I feel sick. 'I don't want to risk him finding out second-hand. It has to come from me.'

'I don't see why it's such a big deal,' says Leo. 'It was just a friendly kiss, that's all. We kiss on stage every night.'

I chew at my thumbnail. 'I shouldn't have let it happen.'

'Then at least tell him it was my fault. I mean, it *was* my fault.'

I shake my head. 'I should have pulled away sooner.'

'Hey, you're only human.'

'Please don't joke.'

'Sorry. But seriously, that kiss was nothing. I could tell you weren't into it. It was a stupid thing to do. I'm an idiot.'

'You and me both,' I say, feeling the nausea wrap itself around my waist. 'I need to find him. Right now.'

'But what about the show?'

I hesitate.

'Are you going to just disappear and let down all those people?' Leo asks.

'I …'

'Come on, Sophia. You know as well as I do that your audience can't wait. They've paid to see you tonight.'

I find my eyes drifting to the pink patio stones under my feet.

'Don't you have your weekly phone call with Marc tonight?' Leo asks.

I nod.

'So. Call him after the show,' says Leo. 'He probably doesn't even know what just happened. Maybe he won't care. I mean, it's no big deal. I kissed you and you pulled away.'

'Okay,' I say, the sinking feeling reaching my toes. 'Yes, you're right. The audience can't wait.'

55

All through the show I feel sick. I perform okay – I'm kind of on automatic pilot, reading my lines and singing my songs like a robot. But the whole time I'm driving myself crazy, wondering what's going to happen when I tell Marc.

When the curtain falls, I'm just a mess. I don't know what to feel or think.

What if Marc leaves me? *What if he leaves me*? God, I can't even bear to think that …

I run straight to my dressing room and grab my phone. But of course, there's no reception down there, so I change and head up to the street.

I'm buffeted around by the theatre crowds on the street as I dial Marc's number again, and to my relief the call connects first time.

'Sophia?' Marc's voice is low. 'Where are you? You're supposed to get straight in the limo after the show.'

'I needed to speak to you,' I blurt out, my voice shaky. 'Marc, something happened. Something bad. I need to see you.'

'Sophia, calm down. Tell me what's wrong. Are you okay? Are you hurt.'

'No, nothing like that.'

'Good.' I hear the relief in Marc's voice. 'Get in the limo. Keith will drive you to Ivy College. I'll meet you there.'

*****

As Keith and I drive through London, it begins to rain. Lightly at first, and then in big heavy drops that splatter on the windscreen and cover the glass with water. By the time we reach Ivy College, a full on storm is underway. The sky tumbles with grey clouds, and sparks of lightning flash around the college turrets.

I run through the grounds of Ivy College in the rain, and by the time I reach my bedroom I'm soaked. I sit on my bed, shivering and dialling Marc's number.

'Sophia.'

'It's me.'

'Have you changed out of your wet clothes?'

'How did you know my clothes were wet?'

'The college security cameras filmed you running across the grounds, covering your head with your coat. When you reached the accommodation block, you were soaked through.'

'Marc, there's something I need to tell you.'

'Promise me you're not hurt.'

'I'm not hurt.'

'Then what is it?'

'It's about Leo.'

Silence.

'Marc?'

'I'm listening.'

'We … Leo and I kissed.'

More silence.

'It didn't mean anything,' I say, my words garbled and fast. 'Truly it didn't. We were just joking around and he kissed me, and then I pulled away. It meant absolutely nothing to me. I was just missing you, missing being near you, and I think it made me all confused. I should have pulled away sooner, but … I didn't. I feel so awful about it. So terrible. Marc, I love you. I love you so much.'

'Leo kissed you?' says Marc, his words slow.

'And I let him.'

Marc let's out a long sigh. 'Sophia, I understand.'

'You do?'

'Yes. This was … my plan, in a way. When your father suggested time apart, I wanted you to spend time with Leo. To see if he was the right man for you after all. The better man. The man who can give you a better life – no press controversy, no dark sides. So I understand. And I love you enough to let you go.'

I shake my head at the phone. 'Please Marc … *please*. Listen to me. I love you. I don't love Leo. I don't feel that way about him at all. I didn't need to kiss him to know that – I knew before. Forgive me Marc, please. I love you so much.'

'I forgive you,' says Marc. 'Forgiveness isn't the issue. The issue is who the right man is for you. And the right man could be Leo.'

'No. He isn't. Leo's my friend. Nothing more.'

A long pause.

'You have to believe me,' I say. 'Please. It's you. It's only ever been you.'

'I'm coming to see you.'

My throat goes tight. 'Marc?'

But the line has already gone dead.

I call Marc straight back and he picks up after two rings. That's two rings slower than usual.

'Marc—'

'Sophia, I told you. I'm coming over. You don't need to know any more than that.'

'Marc, please don't break up with me.'

'Sophia, calm down,' Marc replies softly. 'I'll be there soon.'

The line clicks off again, and I'm left staring at my phone.

I sit on my bed and wait, watching the door and jumping like a crazy woman at the slightest sound. When half an hour has passed, I hear a knock.

I know it's Marc – not just because of the sharpness of the knock, but also because whoever is outside climbed the stairs so stealthily that I didn't hear them.

I climb off the bed.

'Wait. Don't open the door.' It's Marc's voice.

I hesitate. 'Wait here?'

'Yes.'

I hear something – a slight skidding sound like a t-shirt being taken off – and see a dark, thin object slide under the door.

I lean forwards.

'What's that?' I ask.

'A blindfold. Get off the bed and put it on.'

I'm totally confused now. 'A blindfold? But … why?'

'Because we have an agreement with your father. You're not allowed to see me. And I intend to stick to that agreement.'

'Oh.'

Sliding off the bed, I pick up the blindfold, feeling its silky fabric stroke my fingers.

'Put on the blindfold. Then open the door.'

56

I swallow, lifting the blindfold to my eyes, my hands trembling a little.

I tie the blindfold behind my hair and instantly the world goes dark. I can hear my own breathing and feel the silky fabric against my fluttering eyelids, but other than that I'm not aware of much at all, except blackness.

Carefully, I take little steps towards the door and feel around for the handle. I wonder what on earth I must look like, hands outstretched, hair pulled down under the blindfold, stumbling around like a drunk woman.

My heart thumps faster and faster as I feel the cool wood of the door under my fingertips.

'Marc?' I call out, placing my palm flat against the wood.

'I'm right here. Are you blindfolded?' Marc asks.

'Yes,' I reply, clicking open the lock and fumbling for the door handle.

I pull the door open and step back.

There's a moment of stillness as I feel cool air against my face. And then I hear the slap of Marc's leather shoes as he walks into the room and feel his hands take mine and lead me to the bed.

It's all I can do not to hurl myself at him. I want to feel his arms around me. To be safe and warm against his chest. But I don't know what he's feeling right now. Or why he's here. God, please don't let him break up with me. Please.

Once he's sat me down, I hear him return to the door and close it.

Silence.

'Marc?'

'You should change out of those wet clothes,' Marc says from some unknown part of the bedroom.

I hear him walking around, circling the bed. Then I hear a crumpling sound, and feel the breeze of something falling beside me. I reach out and find my dressing gown.

'Put this on.'

'Marc, I'm sorry. I'm so, so sorry—'

'*Now*, Sophia,' Marc interrupts. 'You'll get ill if you stay in those wet things.'

I do, struggling out of my clothes and sliding the warm towelling robe over my arms.

'Did you come here to break up with me?' I ask.

'No. If I had, I wouldn't make you wear a blindfold. Our agreement wouldn't mean much if we weren't together.'

My heart lifts.

'When you phoned earlier … I just couldn't get it out of my head that something terrible had happened. That your safety had been compromised. So I needed to see you. To make sure you were safe.'

'Something terrible did happen,' I whisper. 'Marc, I'm sorry. I'm so, so sorry.'

'You don't need to be sorry. I saw the footage. In the garden. I saw how it happened. He kissed you and you pulled away.'

'I was missing you so much,' I say, starting to cry. 'That's why I didn't stop that kiss sooner. But I'm so ashamed of myself. So, so ashamed.'

'Don't be.' Marc's voice is tender.

'Please forgive me.'

'I told you. There's nothing to forgive. It's Leo who should be asking my forgiveness.'

'Don't hate Leo. He was only messing around.'

'With my future wife.'

'I know, but he didn't mean anything by it.'

'If it wasn't for the fact he looked after you when there was an intruder in the garden, I'd have beaten the living daylights out of him by now,' Marc growls.

'Marc—'

I sense him behind me and hear his breathing getting closer. The hairs on my neck stand up as I feel his weight on the bed. Then his fingers feel their way under my hair, stroking up from the nape of my neck to my damp hairline, and I let out a long, low moan.

'But as long as you're safe,' says Marc, 'that's all that matters to me. And I can see that. I should go now. I don't want to break our agreement.'

I'm trying to hold it all together, trying not to go crazy at the sound of him. I can smell his delicious woody, soapy smell, and feel the warmth of his body behind me.

'Yes.' My voice is wobbling and so are my intentions. I don't want him to leave. Every bit of my body is crying out for him.

Marc leans closer, so close that I can almost feel his lips touching my neck. 'Stay strong, Sophia. We'll be together again soon.'

Marc's breathing is sharp, and I know he's trying to hold it together too.

'You test my self control to the very limits, do you know that Sophia Rose?'

I feel his weight leave the bed and hear his shoes make contact with the floor.

'I don't want you to be self controlled right now,' I say, knowing I sound out of breath. 'God, I don't. Truly.'

'I never break my promises. To anyone.'

I laugh, and it releases the tension a little. 'I know. You're a good man. No matter how much you try to deny it. Thank you. Thank you for forgiving me.'

'I already told you. There's nothing to forgive.'

'Marc?'

'Yes Sophia?'

'I won't choose Leo. You do know that, don't you?'

'Most of the time.' I feel a smile in his voice. 'Just don't make a habit of seducing any more Hollywood stars while I'm not around.'

'I didn't seduce Leo.'

'Not intentionally. You didn't seduce me intentionally either. But it happened.'

'I seduced you?' I say.

'More or less.'

I know Marc is teasing me, but I can't resist playing along.

'Funny. I always thought it was a little more mutual than that.'

'Mutual? I tried to walk away, if you remember.'

'I remember. But I wouldn't say that I seduced you.'

'No. Seduced is totally the wrong word. Bewitched is better.'

I grab a pillow and throw it at empty air.

Marc laughs. 'Not a bad shot. Well, what other word would you use? I fell under your spell.'

'My *spell*?' Now it's my turn to laugh. 'Watch out I don't fall off that pedestal you've put me on, Marc Blackwell. It's mighty high.'

'Not high enough.' Marc pauses, and even though I'm blindfold, I can feel him looking at me.

'I wish you could kiss me,' I blurt out.

'So do I,' Marc growls. 'I need to leave. Before things get any harder.'

'Bad choice of words.' I say.

I hear my bedroom door creak.

'I'm leaving,' Marc says. 'Before I rip that dressing gown off you, tie the cord around your ankles, bend you over the bed and fuck you.'

I swallow. '*Why* did you have to say that?'

'Why do *you* have to be so irresistible?'

A weird noise from outside makes my head snap up, and I turn towards the balcony.

'What was that?' I say.

The noise changes from a breaking sound into a strange, cat-like screeching that echoes across the campus.

'Stay where you are,' Marc says. I feel the air turn as he stalks past me, back through the bedroom.

'Marc?' I call. 'What is it?' The noise outside sounds like some sort of animal, but the sick feeling in my stomach tells me it's something else ... something human.

There's a dull thud on the window, and every instinct tells me to rip the blindfold off. I reach my fingers up.

'Keep that blindfold on,' Marc snaps. 'Sophia, stay where you are.' His voice is blunt and serious. 'Exactly where you are.'

'Marc, what's going on?' I say, my voice turning to a whisper.

I hear curtains swishing closed.

'You'll be fine in this room. But right now, I need to go downstairs and deal with something.'

I hear him stride across the bedroom and the next moment, the bedroom door bangs closed behind him.

I yank the blindfold off, my chest heaving. The bedroom is still warm from Marc, and I smell that beautiful woody spicy smell that comes from his body. But something is badly wrong, and I need to know what.

I'm not nosy by nature. But the sight of the closed curtains awakens something in me beyond curiosity.

I have to see what Marc wants to shield me from.

I go to the window and pull the curtains aside.

When I see the window, my body turns very, very cold.

57

Running down the glass, I see bright red streaks.

Oh my god. Although I want to turn away, I find myself looking closer, examining the long smears running down the windowpane.

Blood. I'm pretty sure of it. The way it moves down the glass and turns thick at the bottom ... it couldn't be anything else.

There's a sort of streaky splatter, then three long trickles running down the glass like rain drops.

As my gaze falls to the balcony outside the window, I jump back in shock. There's something red and meaty looking out there, glistening in the moonlight.

I put a hand to my chest to steady my heart, and it's then I hear the noises again – the strange, screeching sounds cutting through the still night air.

As I listen to the sounds, they become words.

'You're dead, Sophia Rose. D.E.A.D, dead.'

It's Cecile.

Perhaps not the Cecile I remember from Ivy College. She's more than just angry and hate-filled. And she's shrieking like an insane person.

My heart is beating even faster now. How did she get into the college?

I hear the ground floor accommodation door slam and Marc's clipped footsteps head out into the night.

The shrieking stops and turns into crying. I think I hear Marc's voice, followed by the voices of other men – Marc's security team I think. And then, silence.

As I try to make sense of what I've just heard, my eyes grow used to the dark, and I focus once again on the meaty thing on my patio.

Suddenly, I know what it is.

I've seen something like it before in the village butcher's shop, but I've never bought one. It's a pig's heart – huge and bloody. Cecile must have hurled it at the window. How on earth did she throw it so high?

I shiver, and the shiver turns into a shake that just won't stop, even when I wrap the duvet around myself.

Cecile really has flipped. She could do someone some harm right now.

Thank god Marc was here.

My phone rings.

I see Marc's number on the screen and snatch it up.

'Marc?'

'Sophia.' His voice calms me a little. 'Are you still in the bedroom?'

'Yes. Are you okay?'

'You needn't ever worry about me. It's you and your safety that are important.'

'Your safety is important too.'

'I can take care of myself.' He pauses. 'Cecile was here.'

'I know. I heard her. How did she get in?'

'Someone must have given her a key. My guess is Ryan. But I don't want you to worry. You're safe here. The security team would never have let her get into the accommodation block. There are cameras everywhere.

'Security were well on their way to intercepting her before I even got downstairs. She's in a much more fragile state of mind than any of us thought. I should have known. I should have guessed.'

'How could you have?' I say. 'Who'd have thought she'd have gone this crazy? To turn up in the dead of night, hurling meat at windows …' I catch myself.

'You've seen the balcony then,' says Marc.

'Yes,' I admit.

'I told you not to open the curtains.'

'I know. I don't know why I opened the curtains. Something just came over me. How did she throw it all the way up here?'

'She used a catapult. Someone will come clean the mess up first thing tomorrow.'

'Do you think this counts as breaching our one weekly phone call? Since this is our fourth call of the day?'

'We haven't spoken for more than half an hour. This all counts as part of the same call. Now. Listen carefully. I've given the security team a new password. Ask them for it before you speak to any of them or let them in your room.' A pause. 'The password is ivy.'

My body feels all shaky and scared. 'I'll remember it.'

'I hate to leave you alone up there. I *hate* it.' I feel Marc's frustration down the phone. 'But I'll be on campus all night. Seconds away if you need me. Sophia …'

'Yes Marc?'

'There'll be some press about this tomorrow.'

'About what?'

'About Cecile. When we took her to the entrance gate, there were paparazzi outside. She went straight to them. They got a picture of me standing next to her. Talking to her. Chances are they'll make some story out of it.'

'Oh.' I hate the thought of Marc being lied about in the newspapers, especially when those lies involve Cecile. But there are worse things that could happen. I mean, at least Marc wasn't hurt. 'Well, I guess we'll just have to weather that storm when it comes.'

'Go to bed now, Sophia. I'll be watching over you.'

'I know.'

58

The next day, Keith drives me back to the cottage first thing.

I'm sitting in the cottage garden reading my lines, when Jen comes hurrying outside with a wodge of newspapers.

'Sophia, did you know about this?'

I look up from my crumpled script. It's cold outside and I'm huddled in the coat Marc gave me and wearing thick wool gloves.

I see a dark, grainy picture of Marc and Cecile, blown up big on a front page.

'Sort of,' I say. 'I mean, I knew they got a picture of Marc and Cecile last night. She broke into the college, and Marc and his team escorted her out.'

'But these articles …' She fans the papers out for me.

I scan the headlines. 'Oh my god.'

Blackwell Love Child
Marc Beds Student No.2
Love Rat Blackwell

'Can I see the articles?' I take the clump of news-papers from Jen's manicured nails and dump them on the garden table. Then I take off my gloves and flick through the papers.

The articles are all about Marc fathering Cecile's unborn child.

Cecile is quoted in all of them – she must have run to every newspaper in London.

'She's totally flipped,' I say. 'I mean, she's lied to the papers before, but this is different. These articles are complete fantasy land.'

'I wish someone had told me,' says Jen. 'How can I stop the two of you getting bad press if I'm not told when these sorts of pictures are taken?'

'I'd never have guessed the stories would be this bad,' I say.

'They've been clever,' says Jen, wrapping her arms around herself and shivering in her thin blouse. 'It's all allegedly this and allegedly that. Nothing we can sue for. But I'm going to make sure a counter story is run, showing that Cecile refused a paternity test.'

'She refused a paternity test?'

'Not yet. But she will when I get Marc's lawyers to demand she take one. I've got work to do.'

'But you haven't started working for Marc, yet,' I say. 'You're on babysitting duty. Jen, this isn't your problem.'

'Of course it is. You're my friend. Which makes your boyfriend my top priority. I'm not going to let someone badmouth him. I have a few hours here and there. Right now, Sammy's sleeping. That gives me most of the afternoon to try some damage limitation.'

'Has Dad seen these?' I ask, nodding at the papers.

'Not these exact ones,' says Jen. 'But he's bound to pass a newsstand at some point. We should probably go talk to him before he does. So you can tell him what really happened, before he gets the wrong idea.'

'Okay.' I get up out of the wiry garden chair, scooping the newspapers under my arm. 'Let's go talk to him.'

We find Dad by the front door, strapping on his money belt ready for work.

'You're going to work already?' I ask, pleased that Dad is getting back to his old routine. It didn't suit him, moping around the house.

'I'm trying to get as many hours in as I can before

next weekend.'

'Why's that?' I ask.

Dad suddenly becomes very interested in his money belt. 'Oh, just that I was hoping to take Saturday night off. So I could take Denise out.'

'Denise? As in, Denise from Ivy College?'

Dad coughs and doesn't meet my eye. 'Yes. I mean, it's no big deal. Just two friends going out to dinner.'

'You two are going out to dinner?' I say. 'Like a date?'

'I wouldn't call it a date exactly,' says Dad, his cheeks flushing. 'There's this 1950s diner Denise read about in Soho, so ... we thought we'd check it out.'

'That's great, Dad.'

'It's just a dinner. That's all.'

'Denise is a lovely lady,' says Jen. 'And very attractive too, don't you think, Sophia?'

'Yes,' I say, catching Jen's tone. 'A very attractive lady.'

Dad scratches his ear. 'All I know is that she's a very warm and friendly person. And I enjoy spending time with her.'

'Well you enjoy away,' I say. 'You deserve a nice night out.'

'See you girls later.'

'Hang on a minute, Dad,' I say. 'Can I talk to you? The newspapers are running a story today. About Marc. And before you hear about it from someone else, I just wanted to tell you that it's total rubbish. All made up.'

'What story?'

I look at Jen and she looks at me.

'You may as well see for yourself,' I say, handing him a newspaper.

Dad unfurls the paper and scans left and right. He's never been the fastest of readers, so it takes a few moments before his eyes widen, and he starts shaking his head.

'I'm so sorry, love.'

'Dad, it's okay. Really. These articles don't bother me. I know they're all lies. But I just wanted to make sure you knew the truth before you read them on some newsstand somewhere.'

Dad frowns. 'Soph, love. Are you sure they're lies? I mean, you haven't seen Marc for a while. And he's photographed right next to this girl.'

'They took that picture at Ivy College last night,' I say. 'I was there. Cecile broke in and threw a pig's heart at my window. And Marc went down and escorted her out of the building, with his security team. That's when the picture was taken. Look, you can see them in the background.' I point to two men in black uniforms.

'She threw a pig's heart at your window?' Jen asks, her eyes widening.

'I know. She really has flipped.'

'So this Cecile girl was at your college last night?' Dad asks.

I nod.

'And Marc was there too?' Dad says the words slowly.

'Yes.'

'And so were you?'

'Yes.' My stomach drops as I begin to realise what Dad is thinking.

59

'The two of you are supposed to be separated,' says Dad. 'That was our agreement.'

'We have been,' I say. 'But … something happened last night, and Marc came over to check that I was okay. He was about to leave when Cecile turned up. I didn't even see him—'

Dad's lips go all thin and white.

'Honestly, Dad. We were keeping to your rules. We've been apart this whole time. Just phone calls. That's kind of what last night was. An extended phone call. Like I said, I couldn't see him—'

'Well then,' says Dad. 'There's an easy solution, isn't there? No more weekly phone calls.'

'But Dad—'

'Do you want to stick to this agreement or don't you?'

'If it means you giving us your blessing to marry, then of course I do.'

'Then from now on, no phone calls. There are only a few weeks left before you can see him again. I'm sure you'll manage.'

I feel sick to the stomach.

'*Please*, Dad. There are things I need to tell him. About Annabel. She needs our help. Dad, wait.' I put a hand on his arm. 'Can you at least let me call him today? To tell him what's happening?'

Dad frowns. 'You can *email* today. To let him know the new arrangement. But after today, that's it. No more contact until the three months are up.' With that, he storms out the door.

'You'll be all right,' says Jen. 'You're tougher than you look.'

'That's what you think.'

'That's what I know. You've already toughed out over two months. And at least you can email Marc today. That's better than nothing, isn't it?'

I find myself nodding at that little bit of light at the end of the tunnel. 'Yes,' I say. 'I guess that's better than nothing.'

From: SophiaR
To: MarcBlackwell

Dear Marc,
I don't know how to start this email. But here goes.
I love you.
I love you so much it hurts. In fact, everything hurts right now. Being away from you hurts, not hearing your voice hurts, thinking about you hurts.
I have some bad news. Dad has read the newspapers and found out that you were at Ivy College last night. And now he says we can't phone each other any more. We can only talk by email, and only today. After that, nothing until this last month is up.
I need to tell you about Annabel. I was looking over the forms she has to fill in, and what she has to do to get her son back. She needs somewhere to live. And I thought, could she live near us? Could you get her a place? That way, I could help her with her son.
I'm typing this in the garden, wearing the coat you gave me.
Leo thinks that—

I pause, my cold fingers hovering over my iPhone keypad. No. Better not talk about Leo. Delete, delete, delete.

Some people think that space can be healthy. But to me, it feels like I might just die during these last weeks. Our weekly calls were what got me through the days, but now we don't have them I'm lost. Totally, utterly lost. Please write back quickly.

I love you,
Sophia.

My thumbs ache because I typed so fast. It's cold out here, but I'm understanding now what Marc means about liking the cold. It's helping me feel something, because otherwise I'd be numb.

I sit staring at my phone, waiting, waiting for a reply. After twenty minutes, I realise that the email is still waiting in my inbox and my signal bar is low.

I head into the house, but the signal is no better in there. Jen is playing with Sammy in the lounge area, and she looks up as I come in.

'Did you send him the email?'

'No reception.' I wave my phone at her. 'I'm going to head to Ivy College. The phone reception around this village is too hit and miss.'

'How are you going to get there? Didn't you say Keith had the morning off?'

'Bus and train. Just like the old days.'

60

As I walk through the little cobbled streets of our village, past greengrocers and butchers, I finally get phone reception and the email leaves my inbox.

I watch my phone anxiously as I walk, waiting for Marc's reply. It comes within five minutes.

Sophia.
Let me speak to your father and try to explain. And apologise.
And I've been trying to persuade Annabel to move to Richmond for years. I'd buy her anywhere she wanted. The problem is, a part of her is still attached to Daniel's father and her old friends.
I love you too.
Marc.

I hurriedly write a reply, tripping over a cobblestone in my rush to respond.

No, no, don't! You don't know Dad like I do. He's angry about us seeing each other last night, so he won't change his mind. This is just how it has to be.
And I don't think Annabel wants that life any more. But she's feeling a little depressed about having to lean on people. She wants to be independent. We need to find a way to give her a place without her feeling like she's taking charity.

Within moments, Marc fires back:

Re: your father, I've never been good at accepting

things. But for you, I can accept anything. If this is how it has to be, then we'll get through it.

Tell Annabel to find somewhere suitable, and I'll buy it for her. She can choose the place. And then, when she gets back on her feet, she can pay me a monthly rent until the place is paid off. She won't be leaning on anyone. Just taking out a loan.

You never cease to amaze me. I bring in Jen and Rodney to make sure you're not overstretching yourself. And then you go and make my sister into your new project. Don't tire yourself out.

I'll be watching over you. Keeping you safe.

I love you,

Marc.

I spend the whole bus and train journey emailing Marc and reading his replies. We write about how much we love and miss each other, and we talk about the wedding – and what we're going to do on our honeymoon.

I get pretty hot reading and writing the honeymoon emails, and hope the other train passengers can't see the blush spreading up my neck. When I tell Marc I'm on my way to Ivy College, I receive the quickest response ever.

Not alone you're not. I'll send a driver to wherever you are. Keith isn't working this morning, but I have a replacement.

I message back:

Too late. I'm already at Liverpool Street. I have to get the tube now, so no reception. Don't worry – I'm in public the whole time.

Before I hop on the Central Line tube train, I receive a reply:

Did I ever tell you how much I both love and hate your independent side, Miss Rose? It gets in the way of keeping you safe. I'll have security sent to watch you, and no arguments.

I smile as I read that last message. When I get off the tube at Oxford Street, I see Marc has already sent me another email:

Sophia,
Where are you now?

I reply:

Walking to Ivy College. It's okay. I'll be there in twenty minutes.

Marc replies:

You'd better be. Or I'm coming looking for you. Since we at least have a day where we can email each other, I've arranged to have something waiting for you in your room at Ivy College. Because you like surprises.

I smile at that message too, and nearly walk out into a line of traffic. I catch myself on the pavement and wait for the green man. Then I reply:

Depends on the surprise, Mr Blackwell, but so far your surprises have all been pretty good.

Marc replies:

Message me when you get to your bedroom.

Intrigued, I slip the phone into my pocket and head through the London crowds to Ivy College.

61

When I open my bedroom door at Ivy College, I see a large black box on my bed, tied with a bright pink ribbon. The window has all been cleaned up, and a huge bouquet of fresh white roses sits on my bedside table. They're just like the roses at the fancy London hotel Marc and I stayed at.

I sit on the bed and message Marc to tell him I've arrived. Then I take the box, pull at the ribbon and carefully lift the lid.

The cardboard is that thick, expensive kind that squeaks.

My heart begins to flutter as I see what's inside the box.

Laying on swirls of soft pink silk is a length of chain and a pair of panties with some sort of hard, plastic object sewn into the crotch area.

What is all this?

I pick up the chain and panties, holding them up to the window, and begin to get an idea of what Marc has in mind.

My phone bleeps and I hurriedly jab at it so I can read Marc's email.

Take off your clothes. All your clothes. Put on the panties. Then sit on the bed and wait for my instructions.

I look at the panties. What on earth is that plastic thing inside the underwear all about? I guess I'm about to find out.

I strip off my coat and clothing, socks, shoes, panties, everything and climb into the panties.

Now I'm pretty much naked. As I move, the panties rub up against me.

I sit on the bed and feel the cool, hard plastic press between my legs. It feels pretty good.

Marc sends another message.

Wrap the chain around your ankles. I don't want you running away.

I get a little burn of pleasure between my legs as I eye up the chain lying on the soft silk. I reach towards it, but then I hesitate. Can I really do this without Marc being here? The heat that's creeping up my thighs tells me I can.

Reaching for the chain, I bind it around my ankles, hearing the links clank together and feeling the cool metal against my skin. My phone bleeps again.

Lift the silk out of the box. There are things underneath.

62

I reach into the box and lift out the length of pink silk. Underneath it is stiff black velvet with lengths of chain and a little black wooden pole lying on it.

As I lift the objects out of the box, I realise there's more to this bunch of chain and wood than meets the eye.

For a start, there are two objects. One is mainly chain, with two small silver ivy leaves at each end. The metal leaves are beautiful, but I swallow hard when I see they're actually little clamps.

The other length of chain has a rolled piece of black wood in the middle of it, and a clasp at each end of the chain.

My phone bleeps again, and I reach towards it.

I want you to clamp the ivy leaves onto your breasts. Then take the wooden mouthpiece and bite down on it. Secure the clasp behind your head.

I message back:

You certainly know how to treat a girl.

Marc replies:

Don't talk back.

My hands shaking a little, I secure one of the ivy clasps to my breast, just like Marc said. It burns a little, but gets more bearable as the seconds pass.

Then, gingerly, I take the other clasp and do the same.

Ouch. Ouch, ouch, ouch.

That one hurts. As the stinging makes my eyes water, I pick up the wooden mouthpiece, place it between my teeth and secure the clasp behind my head. Biting down on the wood helps take my mind off the stinging a little, but not much.

There's another bleep and another message:

Go look at yourself in the mirror. Then sit down on the bed again and wait.

I stand up carefully and shuffle towards the mirror with the chain around my ankles. I try not to let my breasts move, but of course they do – and they burn with each jolt.

Heading towards my wardrobe, I open it and take a look at myself in the full-length mirror. I get a throb of pleasure between my legs when I see myself. I have to admit, it's sexy being all gagged and trussed up like this.

I return to the bed, knowing wetness is building.

My phone bleeps and I read Marc's new message:

I'm going to go down on you now. My tongue will be just gentle enough to make it unbearable. You'll be screaming for me to go harder, but I won't. Do NOT touch yourself. Doing so will result in punishment.

Just as those words sink in, I feel a buzzing between my legs. The hard plastic of the panties is vibrating against me, and I nearly jump in shock. It takes a moment to realise that Marc must be operating the panties by remote control.

I moan as the vibrations roll around, up, down, making me hotter and hotter. But Marc's email was right – it's all too soft and gentle. I want more, just like he said. I want it harder. Stronger.

The phone bleeps again:

I want you to squeeze the clamps hard against your breasts.

Oh boy. Can I really hurt myself like that? I reach up to my breasts, putting my hand onto the left ivy leaf. I hold it there for a few moments, working up the courage. The clamp is already painful, and I think squeezing it might tip me over the pleasure/pain boundary right into pain.

Okay. Okay, just do it Sophia. Marc likes to test you.

I squeeze, just a little, and feel a hot burn of pain.

Ouch.

But it's a good ouch, and mixed up with the vibrations between my legs, it drives me a little crazy.

I nearly drop the phone.

'Oh god,' I hear myself say, as the pain subsides and I'm left with the gentle vibrations between my legs. 'Oh Marc, I can't bear it. Please. I need more.'

My eyes are a little out of focus as Marc's next message comes through.

Are you begging me for more? I hope so. Because I've had my fun torturing you, and now I'm going to make you come.

Suddenly, the vibrations in my panties get strong and hard. So much so that I begin leaping and twitching against the bed, shouting and yelping and moaning.

'Oh god, oh god. Yes. Yes, yes.'

Another message:

Roll over onto the bed and press your breasts hard into the mattress so they burn. Now you have my permission to touch yourself.

I moan again, rolling onto my belly and feeling the clamps push hard into my flesh. They dig right into the breasts, causing a delicious burning, pulling sensation that makes me roll back and forth so I can feel more of it.

I grab at the panties and push them hard between my legs, right into me, so the vibrations are as strong as they can be. Heat ripples up and up and over me, until the pleasure becomes unbearably good and I feel dark waves start to flow down my stomach and thighs. I can't hold on any longer.

'Oh god,' I moan, pushing my breasts harder against the mattress to feel the sting. 'Oh god, I'm coming. I'm coming.'

And I do. Hard. Feeling bright, bruisey tingles zoom across my breasts and nipples and pleasure and warmth spread over my body.

I lay on the bed for a moment, letting the good feelings overtake me. Then the phone beeps again, and I reach for it, turning my head to read the screen.

I wish I was with you.

I struggle to focus. To make my fingers work. Somehow I manage to tap out a reply.

You have no idea.

63

Marc and I send messages back and forth until midnight. Some of them make me smile. And some of them make me ache for him so badly that I can hardly stand it.

At midnight, we both know we have to say goodbye. No more messages. No more phone calls. Nothing. But there are only a few more weeks to go now. And then we can be together.

*****

After our day of emailing, time drags along. Hours and, eventually, days pass.

The aching feeling in my chest and stomach begins to lessen as March rolls along, but I'm still not eating or sleeping well.

Performances go by in a sort of daze as I do show after show, and then sleep in the cottage all morning and hang out with Jen and Sammy in the afternoon.

All I can think about is Marc, Marc, Marc. I should be feeling happier as each day passes, but the closer I get to the end of our separation, the slower time seems to move. It's like the days are tied to my ankles and I'm dragging them along.

Jen does all sorts of things to try and cheer me up. She takes Sammy and I out to see farm animals, or to the organic market to buy ingredients for pasta sauce. But all I can think about is Marc.

The only time the darkness really lifts is when I ride Ebony.

She's such a beautiful horse, and the more she gets used to me, the more excited she is to see me. I talk to her about anything and everything – missing Marc, the show, things happening in the village. Ebony let's me rattle on, and just bows her beautiful black head and nuzzles against my hand.

Some days, I ride her. Other times, I walk her around the field, feeling her warmth beside me and sharing a quiet moment.

Seeing Marc's sister feels good too. Annabel is getting closer to winning custody of her son, and watching her get stronger and happier really lifts my spirits.

I visit her whenever I can – at least a couple of times a week, sometimes more.

One morning, I'm at the cottage, packing a bag with fresh bread and homemade soup for my visit with Annabel, when I get a call from her rehab hospital in West London.

It's pouring with rain outside, and for some weird reason the weather tells me that bad news is coming.

'Miss Sophia Rose?' says a young lady, when I pick up the phone.

'Yes,' I reply. 'How can I help?'

'I'm calling from Tower Clinic. I understand you're scheduled to see Ms Blackwell today.'

'Yes,' I say. 'I was just leaving now, as a matter of fact.' I glance out of the window and see the limo perched on the pavement outside our cottage. Rain beats on its shiny black roof and rushes down its tinted windows. 'Is everything okay?'

There's a pause.

'Ms Blackwell left the clinic a few hours ago. I thought I should let you know. To save you a wasted journey.'

'She left the clinic? But ... why?'

'She had some bad news this morning. About her custody situation. And she left.' Another pause. 'Sometimes, addiction is just too strong. Around half our patients leave and return to their old lives.'

I shake my head at the phone. 'But she's been doing so well. I honestly don't think she'd give up. Even after bad news. Are you absolutely sure she's left the premises?'

'We've checked her room. And the refectory and the recreation rooms,' says the woman.

I grab my bag. 'Has anyone checked the grounds?'

'It seems unlikely she'd be out there in this weather.'

I hear the rain hammering against the window, and think about Annabel. I know she's relapsed many, many times before. Maybe I'm just being naïve, but I honestly don't think she'd give up now. My gut tells me she's still at the hospital. Somewhere. Unhappy and alone.

'I'm coming down there,' I tell the woman, grabbing my coat and pulling the front door open.

'Soph, are you off to see Annabel?' Jen calls out from the sitting area.

'Yes,' I call back. 'See you soon.'

'Did you want some breakfast before you go? Rodney's making pancakes.'

'No time,' I call back, heading out into the storm. 'Maybe I'll eat at the hospital. Back later.'

64

When I arrive at the hospital, I check Annabel's room, just in case. She's not there, so I head out to the grounds and begin hunting around the woodlands.

It's still absolutely pouring with rain, and I get soaked within minutes. But I don't care. All I care about is finding Annabel.

After searching the east side of the building, I head west, my ankle boots squelching in the mud as I weave through fir and oak trees.

Annabel and I have walked around these grounds many times so I know them well, but finding someone out here is a different story, especially in this weather.

There are acres and acres to cover, and the thick evergreen trees mean I can't see more than a few metres ahead.

Eventually, I stumble upon a huge, craggy grey rock under a feathery fir tree. The rock is sheltered from the rain, thanks to the thick branches and leaves above, and I take a seat, realising for the first time since I arrived that I'm actually pretty faint with hunger.

I hear my own laboured breathing fade into silence.

As my ears become accustomed to the pouring rain, a sound carries on the breeze. A choked-up, desperate crying sound.

I sit up straight.

It's Annabel. I'm sure of it.

Jumping to my feet, I splatter through the mud towards the sound, stopping every so often to listen.

After five more minutes of walking I find her, hunched over in a ball under a huge oak tree. She's soaked to the skin and weeping as the rain splashes down.

I crouch beside her and rest a hand on her back.

'Annabel, it's me. Sophia.'

The weeping dies down a little, and Annabel's head turns to the side. 'Sophia,' she says softly. 'How did you find me here?'

'I looked.'

'You're soaked,' says Annabel. 'Please go inside. I'm no good to anyone right now.'

'I'm not going anywhere without you,' I say. 'Will you tell me what happened?'

Annabel starts to sob again. She cries hard for a few minutes, her whole body shaking. I let her get it all out.

Then I ask again, gently, 'What happened?'

'They say I can't have Daniel,' Annabel sobs. 'Even if I have a home and support. They say he's going to be adopted. His last name will be changed. I'm not even allowed to know what he'll be called.' She breaks down again, clutching her knees to her chest and sobbing.

'Who says he's going to be adopted?' I ask.

'A social worker called me this morning.'

'Has he been adopted already?'

'Not yet. But he will be.'

I stand up and pull her to her feet. '*Going* to be adopted is not the same as *being* adopted. You won't help anyone or anything sitting out here in the rain. We're going back to the main building so we can make some calls.'

'But it's so hopeless,' say Annabel, swaying a little as she tries to get her footing on the mud.

'Annabel. You're a mother. You have to find hope. You have to look for it. Always. You can't ever give in. Daniel needs you to be strong. Come on. Let's go inside.'

65

I get Annabel up to her room and make her change into some dry clothes. Meanwhile, I take off my soaking wet coat and hang it on the radiator. My jeans are drenched too, and they stick to my legs as I get Annabel a dressing gown and help her into it.

'You need to change your clothes too,' says Annabel. 'I have some pyjamas. Here.' She hands me a pair of hospital-green pyjamas with a long drawstring.

As I change into them, I realise I'm feeling a little hot and shivery. Oh no. I can't get sick. I have the show tonight. And tomorrow night. And the night after. There's barely two weeks left now, and then we'll have finished.

'Do you have the number of the social worker who called this morning?' I ask, trying to ignore the pounding feeling in my head.

'Yes,' says Annabel, picking up a 'Tower Clinic' notebook with a phone number and the name, 'Mandy Reynolds' pencilled onto it. 'She told me to call when I had a place sorted. She said maybe we could set up some sort of visitation, if the new parents agree.'

'Is it okay if I call her?' I ask. 'You'll have to speak to her too. To give permission for us to discuss your personal circumstances.'

'Of course,' says Annabel.

'I don't think they can go ahead and have Daniel adopted if you're still willing to take custody of him,' I say. 'Unless the rules have changed majorly from when Dad and I lived together, I'm pretty sure a lot of time has to go by, and you can still go to court and appeal.'

'You really think so?'

'Yes,' I say, taking the paper and punching the number

into my phone.

A nasal voice comes on the line. 'Hello, Mandy Reynolds.'

I clear my throat. 'Oh, hello. Good morning. I'm Sophia Rose. I'm a close friend of Annabel Blackwell's. She's here with me now. She's given me permission to speak about her circumstances – would you like to confirm that with her?'

'If she's there with you, it's fine,' says Mandy.

My neck prickles. Mandy should definitely be checking that Annabel has given permission for me to speak about her case. After all, I could be anyone.

'You're phoning about Daniel, I imagine?' says Mandy.

'Yes,' I say. 'Annabel is worried that you want to have him adopted.'

'It's the next step, given Ms Blackwell's current location and situation.'

'But she has a lot of support right now,' I say. 'Myself and her brother will be there to look after her and Daniel.'

'Her brother, the famous Marc Blackwell,' says Mandy. 'Yes, I've read all about him. It sounds like he has childcare issues of his own. Hardly a stable influence.'

'You can't make a judgement based on something you've read in the papers,' I say. 'They fabricate things all the time. Anyway, as far as I was aware, Daniel can't be adopted yet. Annabel has to permanently give up custody of him, or have it legally taken away from her. Which as far as I'm aware, hasn't happened yet.'

'She put him into our care—'

'That's not the same as giving up custody permanently,' I point out. 'Care was supposed to be temporary.'

'I wasn't aware ... as far as I knew, Ms Blackwell had

given up custody.' I hear papers shuffling.

'Did she sign a P12?' I'm crossing my fingers that Annabel didn't accidentally sign the permanent custody form.

'Mmm,' says Mandy. 'I don't see that form here, but ...' There's silence, then more shuffling. 'As far as I was aware ... I was told ... hang on a minute.' The phone clunks down on a table.

More papers shuffle, and then I hear Mandy's voice again. 'I do apologise. There's been an error. You're quite right, we don't have a P12. Yes, Daniel can't be adopted as yet. He needs to be fostered first. If Ms Blackwell can prove she has a stable home and environment, then it's possible that the boy may be returned to her.'

I feel a smile growing on my face. 'She will have a stable home. I promise. Very, very soon. Thank you.'

'Okay. Well, goodbye now.'

The line goes dead.

I turn to Annabel. I mean to give her a hug, but something happens to my knees. It feels like they're made of jelly. And my head starts to spin.

The next moment, everything goes black.

66

I wake up in the guest bed at Dad's cottage. The sky is growing dark outside. My throat feels croaky and sticky, and my head is pounding.

I sit up, wondering how on earth I got here, and pull back the bedclothes to see I'm dressed in my own pyjamas.

As I pull myself upright, the room begins to sway and my head pounds harder. I feel hot and feverish, and there's a weird metal taste in my mouth.

The bedroom door opens and I see Jen, holding Sammy.

'Thought I heard you waking up,' she says. 'Are you trying to get out of bed, Sophia Rose?'

'I was—'

'Oh no you don't.' Jen puts a firm hand on my shoulder and pushes me back onto the pillow. 'Bed rest for you. You've caught a fever. Overwork, the doctor says.'

'How did I get here?' I ask. 'I was with Annabel.'

'You fainted. Marc called an ambulance for you. But they said it was just a fever, so the doctors thought a home environment was best. You were brought here to be looked after.'

'Marc was at Tower Clinic?' I ask, rubbing my eyes.

'No. But Annabel called him when you fainted, and he called the ambulance. He's worried sick about you. He calls every half hour.'

'How did I get into my pyjamas?'

'You put them on when you got here. Don't you remember?'

I shake my head. 'I guess I really do have a fever.'

'That's what the doctors think too. But nothing too

bad. Nothing that can't be treated with good food and bed rest.'

'What doctors?' I ask.

'Well, you have two private doctors looking after you right now,' says Jen. 'Doctor Holmes, Marc's private doctor. And Doctor Freeman. A friend of Leo Falkirk's.'

'Leo?' Now I'm really confused.

Jen nods. 'Leo was at the cottage when the ambulance brought you here.'

'He was?'

'Yep. He was coming by to visit you. And then you showed up in an ambulance and scared us all to death. Oh my god, Leo is … there are just no words for what he looks like in real life. I nearly passed out when he turned up on the doorstep.' She smiles at the memory.

'I'm so sorry to worry everyone,' I say.

Jen shakes her head. 'Don't you even think about any of us. Just rest and focus on getting better.'

'Where's Marc now?' I ask.

'You two have an arrangement, remember? He didn't want to break it. I think he would have done, if your condition was more serious, but … he's holding out. It was clearly torture for him, not being able to see you before. He wanted to fill this whole room with flowers, but the doctor thought best not. Just in case part of your flu was caused by early hay fever.'

I laugh. 'Me, with hay fever?'

'I know. Anyway, Leo recommended a load of healthy food instead of flowers. So the whole kitchen is full of it. Deli soups. Organic vegetables. Fresh brown bread. Squeezed orange juice. Lots of nourishing stuff. I think Marc was pretty impressed.'

'Marc impressed with Leo?' I raise an eyebrow. 'That would be a pretty big turnaround.'

'I think Marc understands that he and Leo are on the

same page, when it comes to looking after you.'

'Wait.' I try to sit up again, but one look from Jen sends me lying back down on the pillow. 'Were they both here?'

'Yep.' Jen shifts Sammy from one hip to the other. 'Both of them. Marc was going out of his mind with worry. I think he nearly broke your agreement, to be honest. But he stayed strong. And Leo ... well, he was emailing homeopaths and acupuncture people and just trying to find out things that might help you get better. He's such a sweet guy. A *really* sweet guy.'

'Yes he ... Jen? You've gone all gushing all of a sudden.'

'Have I? Well ... Leo and I were talking for ages, and we really got along ...'

'That doesn't surprise me,' I say with a smile. 'Does Dad know that Marc called an ambulance for me? And that he had me sent here?'

'Yes.' Jen pauses. 'I think it helped your Dad's view of Marc. To see how much he cares.'

I sit up, suddenly. 'Oh my god, what time is it? I have a show tonight.'

'It's okay, Sophia. Davina knows you're sick. The show can afford to lose a few nights.'

'But—'

'No arguments. It's doctor's orders that you rest in bed for a few days. If you don't, you'll just get sicker and probably end up not being able to finish the show run at all.'

'I hate letting people down.'

'I know. But there's not much you can do, right now. Everyone understands.' She hoists Sammy a little higher. 'I'm going to take Sammy out for a quick walk before bed. He's getting fidgety. Rodney's here. And your dad's here too. He'll be happy to know you're awake again.'

I yawn. 'Jen, what time is it?'

'Six o'clock. Are you hungry? There's loads of food downstairs.'

'It's okay, I'll get it—'

'No you won't.' Jen shakes her head. 'I'll have Rodney bring you something up.'

67

I spend the next few days in bed, watching spring appear through the bedroom window. It feels so strange, doing nothing but resting. I'm not sure I've ever done it before. But the doctors and everyone else are insisting, so I'm trying very hard to listen – even though sometimes I'm dying to go downstairs and play with Sammy or cook a meal.

By the afternoon of day two, I come downstairs on wobbly legs and head to the kitchen.

Jen's out with Sammy and Dad is working, so it's just Rodney and I in the cottage.

'How's the patient?' Rodney asks.

'Okay, I just … I wish I could speak to Marc. Tell him I'm getting better.' I pad over the lino in bare feet.

'How's the separation going?' Rodney asks.

'Awful,' I say with a smile, going to the kettle. 'But not long to go now. Tea?'

'You, Sophia Rose, will sit down while *I* make the tea.'

'Okay.' I sigh, and reluctantly take a seat at the kitchen table.

'So,' says Rodney, filling up the kettle. 'What is it … a week now until you can see Marc again?'

'About that,' I say.

'He misses you,' says Rodney.

'I hope so.'

'I've never seen Marc like this.' Rodney gives me a kind smile. 'You've changed him. For the better. But he's suffering for it.'

'I don't want him to suffer.' I watch Rodney pour hot water into mugs and add teabags.

'No. Of course you don't.'

I smile. 'I wish I could be with him.'

'You will be soon,' says Rodney. 'This last few week will fly by.'

'I hope so.'

*****

Time doesn't fly by, but little by little it moves. Or rather, trudges its weary feet.

After three days, the doctor says I'm well enough to get back to the show, and it feels good to be back on stage with Leo. I love performing again, and the show is as popular as ever. But these last few days are still passing slowly, especially at night.

I think of Marc constantly, and stay awake until the early hours, thinking of him and wishing he was with me.

During the daytime, I do everything I can to distract myself.

Ebony and I go riding in newly spring green fields, and I also spend a lot of time with Annabel, viewing apartments and townhouses, and helping her think about her future.

Annabel is really keen to work and pay her way, but she's never had a job, so writing her CV is tough. A few museums and art galleries have offered her unpaid placements, though, and she decides to take one at the Tate Modern. It's a start.

Day by day, I see Annabel growing stronger and brighter. I know she'll be a good mother. And Marc and I will support her every step of the way. And day by day, I get closer to being with Marc again.

68

For some reason, the weather goes crazy warm the night before the show finishes, and Leo wants me to check out the roof garden at his favourite Mexican restaurant.

'You'll love it, Sophia,' he tells me. 'The garden has straw donkeys and red chilli fairy lights all over the place. And the best view of the London sunset ever. Oh, and did I mention it serves awesome margaritas?'

'Several times,' I say.

'Come on. You must have run out of excuses by now. Can't a friend take another friend out to eat?'

'After what happened … that kiss … I don't want to be disrespectful to Marc,' I say.

'Marc and I had a good talk when you were ill. I told him what an idiot I was. And how much I value your friendship. And I think … maybe he'll never be totally cool with me, but he doesn't want you to lose a good friend, either. He can tell that I care about you. And he doesn't want that gone from your life.'

'He said that?'

'Words to that effect. Anyway, I think when he saw how well I was getting on with your friend Jen, he stopped being worried about me moving in on his territory.'

'Jen said the two of you talked.'

'She did?' Leo smiles. 'I *really* like her. I might even stay in London a little longer, if she agrees to go out with me. She's worth putting up with bad English food for. Speaking of food … are you coming to dinner or not?'

'You really think Marc is okay with us being friends?'

'Yes. I really do. I mean, he said so.'

'Okay. I guess I have run out of excuses. And actually, it'll be good to have a distraction today. Time is moving SO slowly. I just can't wait for it to be tomorrow. One more show to do, and then I get to see Marc.'

*****

Within half an hour, I find myself on a higgledy piggledy roof terrace of Mexican hats and cactus plants, drinking a frozen margarita and watching the sunset with Leo Falkirk.

It would be stupid not to admit how good looking Leo is. I mean, every woman in the restaurant is following him with his eyes.

'Great margaritas, huh?' says Leo, taking a swig from a bubbly tumbler of green slush.

'Really good,' I agree, taking a sip of my own.

'Am I helping you pass the time?'

'God, I'm terrible aren't I?' I say. 'How do you put up with me?'

'Well. The fact you're super pretty helps.'

I blush. 'Oh. I'm sure you've known plenty of girls prettier than me.'

'Nope. You're pretty inside and out. You don't get many girls like that around. Marc's a lucky guy.'

'I've been so mopey these last few months. I'm really sorry.'

'You haven't been so bad,' says Leo, accepting a bowl of handmade nachos from a waitress. 'But promise me after this show, you'll stay in touch. Even if it's only so I can see that cute friend of yours.'

'Why wouldn't I stay in touch?'

Leo grins. 'Us actors go with the tides. You make the best, most amazing friendships, and then poof! The film wraps up, the show finishes, and you drift apart.'

'I don't want that to happen to us,' I say. 'And it won't.

You're a good friend.'

Leo puts his large elbow on the table and waggles his little finger. 'Okay. Pinkie promise. We'll stay in touch.'

I laugh and hold out my little finger too, linking it with Leo's. 'Pinkie promise.'

69

That night after the last-but-one show, I don't fall asleep until 5am. Thoughts of Marc are running so quickly through my mind that it's impossible to shut down. But finally, *finally*, morning comes. And after three long months of waiting, the day arrives when I can see Marc again.

When I go downstairs, I hear Jen in the garden.

I head outside to find her at our little umbrella table, peeling open a red Baby Belle cheese for Sammy.

'Morning Soph,' she says. 'So. Last day, huh?'

'Fourteen more hours,' I say, taking a seat and watching Sammy playing on the grass. It's a warm spring day and the daffodils are still filling the beds with sunshine yellow petals. 'And I'm going to feel every second of them today.'

Jen smiles. 'You put Romeo and Juliet to shame. How are you and Marc going to meet up tonight? Is he going to blast fireworks over the Thames at the stroke of midnight?'

I laugh. 'I don't know. We're not allowed to speak, remember? But I'm hoping Marc will come to the theatre and see me after the show.'

'Does that bother you? Not knowing how and when you're going to see him?'

'No. That part doesn't bother me at all. It's just getting through these last hours – that's the problem.'

'You were singing to yourself when you came out,' says Jen. 'Just like you used to. Am I getting my old, happy Sophia back?'

'Hope so.'

Rodney pokes his head out of the back door. 'Sophia.

Can I get you breakfast?'

*****

I spend the rest of the day riding Ebony and hanging out with Jen and Sammy. And the day passes.

After dinner that night, I'm having my usual fight with Rodney over who will do the clearing up, when there's a knock at the door.

'I'll get it,' I say, drying my hands on a tea towel and heading out of the kitchen. 'Dad will have forgotten his wallet or something.'

Dad is taking Denise out tonight. Again. The two of them are really getting along. It's good for Dad to have someone kind and caring in his life. I thoroughly approve. Although I do feel sad for him about Genoveva and how things ended.

The village rumour mill says that Genoveva and her doctor boyfriend are having problems, and that she's staying in a hotel right now. But since she hasn't been in touch, and doesn't take any of Dad's calls, there's no way of knowing.

I have to admit, I'm glad Genoveva hasn't come back. She's shown her true colours, and if she doesn't care enough about Sammy to come visit, then good riddance. I'll always be here for him, and so will Jen, Dad and Denise.

Jen is upstairs giving Sammy his bath, so I shout up, 'I've got it Jen!' as I pull open the front door.

On the doorstep is Leo, wearing a tight white t-shirt and ripped jeans.

'Hey leading lady,' says Leo. 'Since it's our last show together, I thought I'd pick you up one last time.' He looks over my shoulder. 'Is Jen here?'

I smile. 'Yes. She is. You weren't expecting dinner, where you? We just finished.'

Leo shakes his head. 'Nope. Just the pleasure of your

company. And maybe Jen's company.'

My smile turns into a grin. 'Come on in. Keith will be here in half an hour. So you and Jen will have all that time to enjoy the pleasure of each other's company. I think I might have some things to do in the garden ...'

70

By the time Keith arrives, I have to practically drag Leo away from Jen. But not before he gets her number and she agrees to go out with him.

When I finally get Leo into the limo, all he talks about is Jen, from the cottage to the theatre, and I have the pleasure of agreeing that she really is the most wonderful girl.

Our last performance together goes really well. I have to keep reminding myself how special it is that this is the end of my very first West End Show run. But I don't forget for one moment that in a few hours time, I'll be seeing Marc again.

When the curtain falls to thunderous applause, I head backstage and find Jen and Dad waiting.

'Soph!' says Jen. 'We have a surprise for you.'

'How come you two are back stage?' I ask. 'And what are you both smiling about?'

'We have a note,' says Jen. 'From Marc.'

'You do?'

'Yes.' Jen reaches in her handbag and pulls out an envelope. It's plain brown, with the words, *'For Sophia, to be opened immediately after your last show'* written on it.

I frown. Mmm. That doesn't sound like something Marc would write, but … I guess he likes surprising me.

'Thanks,' I say, taking the envelope and ripping it open, tugging out the white paper inside. The note has been typed on a computer in a heavy, blocky font.

When I read the words, my stomach drops and my mouth falls open.

Time for revenge, Sophia Rose.
Tonight, we snatched your brother, Samuel.
We will hurt him unless you do as we say.
DO NOT TALK TO ANYONE.
Go straight to Marc Blackwell's house in Richmond.
We will meet you there.
PAIN.

'Where did you get this note?' I ask Jen, trying to stop my hands from shaking.

'It arrived at the cottage just after you left,' says Jen. 'Is everything okay?'

'Yes, fine,' I say, trying to hold my voice steady. 'Absolutely fine. Marc just wants me to meet him, that's all.'

'He's not coming here?' says Jen. 'It'll be midnight soon.'

'He's … I'm going to meet him somewhere else, okay?' I wave the note. 'Back soon.'

71

My huge Belle dress buffets around my legs as I head out of the theatre.

I run out into the street crowd, heading towards Tottenham Court Road tube station.

Everyone stares at me as I rattle along on the tube train to Richmond. But I don't care. I have to get to Marc's townhouse. I have to get to Sammy.

*****

When I arrive in West London, the night feels very still and there are clouds overhead. I can't see the stars or the moon.

I reach the gates, unsure of my next plan. Should I ring the buzzer? Or shout over the gates? But before I can make any decisions, I see something that makes my stomach pull tight.

There are objects tied onto the black railings.

As I get closer, I see one of the objects is a baby doll – the kind that closes its eyes when you lie it down. It's been stripped of all its clothing, so its body is nothing more than white cotton with little plastic legs and arms attached. It's been tied to the railing by the ankle, so it hangs upside down.

Next to the baby is what used to be a rose, except there's only a thorny stem left now – all the petals have been plucked off. There's also a pair of handcuffs chained to the gate and a toy knife.

I look over the dark townhouse and see no lights on. No one is home. Maybe this is all a hoax. A horrible joke from PAIN to frighten me, but nothing more.

I'm about to try the buzzer, when I feel something hard bash my hand.

I turn around, but before I know what's going on, something grabs my hair and throws me to the ground. A clawed hand comes at my face, slapping and scratching, and as I shield myself with my arm, I see Cecile kneeling over me, her face scrunched up in anger.

'You bitch,' she screeches. 'It's time you paid for what you did.'

I fend off her blows as best I can, but I'm not going to try and hurt a pregnant woman. I just can't do it.

'Cecile,' I say, as I slap at her hands and try to push her back. 'This is crazy. You need help.'

'I don't need help,' Cecile screams. 'Why does everyone keep saying that?'

I manage to push her back a little, and now I've gotten over the shock of being knocked down, I begin to notice things about Cecile – the slimness of her face and body, and the tight-fitting black cashmere jumper she wears.

If she's pregnant, where is the baby? Because there's certainly no bump on that flat stomach of hers.

I scrabble to my feet. 'You're not pregnant.'

Cecile gets up too. 'I got rid of it. When they started asking me for all those tests.'

'Did you write that note? Where's Sammy?'

'PAIN have him. If you want to see him again, you'd better come with me.'

My stomach pushes up into my throat and I feel myself heave. I put a hand to my mouth. 'Oh my god,' I say through my fingers.

'I'm serious.'

It's too much. Before I can stop myself, I turn and vomit onto the pavement.

I feel like someone has put my chest in a big metal vice and squeezed all the air out of it.

'Please don't hurt him. I'll go anywhere you want.'

'The car's over here.'

72

Cecile pulls me towards a black car, waiting under a bright yellow streetlight. It looks pretty battered and bruised, and when she opens the back door I let out a little scream.

Waiting on the back seat is the creepiest looking man I've ever seen. He's completely bald, with a huge beefy body and big broad shoulders. He's wearing little round glasses that make his eyes seem tiny and insect-like, and one of those leather jackets that looks like a blazer.

He reaches out a hand to me. 'Warren. Head of PAIN. Good to meet you at last.'

I shrink back from his hand.

In the front seat I see the back of a woman's head. She has platinum blonde hair, and when I catch a glimpse of her eyes in the rear-view mirror, they're black like coal. She has spidery eyelashes and blood red lips.

'And Yasmina you've probably heard of,' says Warren, nodding to the front seat. 'My co-leader. And a good friend of Marc Blackwell's.'

The car smells like ... I don't know. Unwashed bodies and something chemical. I put a finger to my nose and take a step back.

'Nice of you to dress up for us,' Warren continues, nodding at my dress. 'Very pretty.'

'Where's Sammy?' I ask.

'Come with us and we'll show you.'

'Please. You haven't hurt him, have you? Is he okay?'

'He will be,' says Warren. 'As long as you get in the car right now.'

I nod and climb into the car, leaning as far away from Warren as I can. In response, he leans closer to me.

'I don't bite,' he breathes, and I realise he's like Getty – he gets excited when women are scared. 'At least, not yet.'

I sit up straight and stop leaning away from him. Instead, I try to look as relaxed as possible. Which is hard, considering my heart is beating so fast in my chest that I feel like it's going to break out and fly away.

Cecile walks around the car and jumps into the front seat.

'Well done Cecile,' says Yasmina. Her voice is low and throaty. 'Good work.'

'Thank you Yasmina,' says Cecile, all sickly and sucky up. 'I told you it would be me who got her.'

The car starts.

I feel sick and lonely as we pull away from Marc's house.

The platinum blonde woman turns to me as we wait at a junction.

'We're going to have a lot of fun with you.' Her dark red lips move in the mirror. She has very pale skin, made more pale by white makeup. 'You deserve a little pain, don't you think? After what you've done.'

'What I've done?'

'To Giles Getty. He was one of our most loyal members.'

I shake my head.

'Getty kidnapped me. I did nothing to him. Nothing at all.'

'He's in prison now, because of you. And our organisation is being investigated. We're being forced into the shadows.'

'Look, just tell me that Sammy's okay.'

'Don't speak anymore. We don't answer to you. You answer to us.'

The car drives on into the night.

73

We drive from West to East London, and I watch all the grand, beautiful buildings transform into tower blocks, narrow roads and the shells of market stalls.

The car comes to a stop outside a seven-storey building that looks like it's been bombed. There's no glass in the windows – it's little more than a blackened, concrete carcass.

Yasmina gets out of the car and pulls open the back door beside me. Now I can see all of her, I notice her face is scarred quite badly under the white makeup.

The tiny black flecks of her eyes and the dark red of her lips are the only other colour to her.

She's wearing black tapered trousers that finish at strappy high heels, and a black-leather waist cincher over a black blouse. The cincher pulls her waist in so tight that she looks like a wasp.

'Out,' she barks, grabbing my arm and pulling me onto the crunchy cement. I fling my hands forward as I go flying towards the ground, then pick myself up and stand tall.

'Where's Sammy?'

'In there,' says Yasmina, pointing to the tower block. 'Follow us.'

Oh god, I feel sick. To think of little Sammy, somewhere in that building ... I want to throw up again, but I manage to hold it in. They're monsters, these people. Absolute monsters. And Cecile has become a monster too.

'Is someone with him? Is he alone?'

'No more questions.'

I follow Yasmina, Cecile and Warren across the

concrete, and into the shadowy depths of the tower block.

Dimly, I notice that Warren is carrying a large briefcase.

We walk up crumbling cement stairs that were maybe once carpeted, but are now nothing more than concrete built around iron bars.

Although it's shadowy in the tower block, some light comes from the bright orange streetlights outside. They shine through big square holes that used to be windows.

The second floor looks empty, except for a weird sort of makeshift bar in the corner, made of wooden planks and stocked with whisky bottles.

I'm about to ask where Sammy is again, when I notice manacles screwed into the wall ahead.

My stomach pulls itself into a tight ball.

'Where's Sammy?' I cry out, unable to hold back the tears any longer. 'Please. Is he here? You have to tell me where he is.'

Yasmina and Warren laugh.

'You really think we took him?' says Yasmina. 'How could we, with all the security around your cottage?'

Security. Of course. God, I'm an idiot.

Although I still feel sick and frightened, part of me is sagging with relief. Oh thank God Sammy isn't here. Thank god.

'Will you do the honours, Yasmina, or shall I?' asks Warren, holding up his briefcase. He takes his leather jacket off, revealing a white, short-sleeved shirt with sweat around the armpits. There's something really icky about his skin. It glistens like it's wet.

'I think Cecile should do it, don't you?' Yasmina replies, grabbing my wrist. I struggle, knowing I have nothing to lose now, and pull away from her.

I turn and run towards the concrete steps, but before

I can reach them, Warren chases after me and throws himself at my back. He falls on top of me, and I go smashing into the floor.

I feel my body smack onto the hard concrete.

Ouch.

Something in my wrist makes a cracking sound, and I feel a throb of pain run down my arm.

Warren climbs roughly off me, then grabs me by the ankles. He drags me back over the concrete floor, so my whole body is pulled over the snaggy stones sealed in the cement. I hear my Belle dress ripping and tearing.

The next moment, I'm hauled to my feet and my wrists are snapped into a pair of rusty manacles.

The pain that runs up my left arm is unbelievable as my wrists are held up high. I struggle against the chains, and tears of pain sting my eyes.

Yasmina comes closer to me, her sharp heels clicking over the floor. I look right into her eyes, determined not to show fear.

'It's not the first time we've gotten rid of young girls,' she says, taking the briefcase that Warren is handing to her. 'We like to do it in our own special way. And out of respect to Giles Getty, we've brought one of our favourite torture devices this evening. To make sure your death is as unpleasant and drawn out as possible.'

The briefcase is clearly heavy, because Yasmina's shoulders pull downwards as she takes it from Warren.

She comes closer – so close that I can see the zigzag pattern of the scars under her makeup. Then she opens the briefcase.

As the brown leather lid opens, I can't suppress a horrified gasp.

Oh my god. I will not break down. I will not. I will not show them fear.

Warren and Yasmina are both transfixed by what's

inside the case. Their eyes are wide and glistening, their lips curve into smiles.

Lying on brushed felt is a large wrought-iron ring, about the size of a dinner plate. It looks rusty and black, like an antique, and there are huge tapered spikes on the inside. I feel like I've seen it before, and then I remember.

Years ago, my class went on a school trip to the local castle. We were shown down to the castle dungeon and allowed to see all the old torture devices. Racks. Leg irons. Saws. And something that looked a lot like this ring.

Jen and the rest of the class were fascinated, but I felt really sick, thinking of how awful human beings could be to one another. I didn't want to hear about how bodies had been stretched and ripped apart. In the end, I pretended I needed the toilet so I could leave the dungeon early.

As I look at the wrought iron ring, my stomach beats so hard that I'm sure I'm going to throw up.

'Beautiful when she's frightened, isn't she?' says Yasmina, holding out the suitcase to Warren.

'Isn't she?' Warren uses both hands to lift out the large spiked metal ring. It's obviously heavy, and he takes a few steps back and forth to get his balance.

'We call this device Svetlana,' says Yasmina, running her grey fingernails over the ring. 'She's from Russia. A KGB torture device. One of our greatest prizes. She's a very clever piece. Svetlana can be fitted almost any-where on the body – leg, chest, head. And then tightened with this side screw.'

She smiles, her breathing quickening. 'We tighten. And tighten. Until we see blood. And then we let our unfortunate guest bleed to death.'

Yasmina and Warren share a look, and I shudder.

'Svetlana is the only girl I never get bored of,' says Warren. He moves closer to me.

I try to hold my body firm, despite the pain in my wrist and arm.

I know Warren will get off on me being afraid, and I refuse to give him the satisfaction. At the same time, though, the thought of his horrible moist fingers touching me makes me absolutely want to vomit, and it takes everything in my power not to shrink away from him as he comes closer.

Warren opens up the spiked ring and holds it at my waist. I can smell his awful stench – like rotten meat and disinfectant.

Fear climbs up my throat.

I try not to look, but my eyes keep flicking down to the device. Although it's made of old, blackened metal, the ends of the spikes have clearly been sharpened and are silver and lethal. It won't take much pressure to pierce my skin.

'Smile, darling,' says Warren, feeding the ring around my waist. 'You never know. You might enjoy this.' His hands are trembling with excitement, and sweat glows on his forehead. 'My favourite part is when I tighten so hard that we snap bones.' His shoulders give a little shiver.

I'm beginning to lose it, my breathing running away from me. I know my eyes are wide with fear as Warren clamps Svetlana loosely in place. I feel the spikes pierce the fabric of my dress and press lightly against my skin.

Oh my god, oh my god.

It won't take much tightening before those spikes

start piercing me deeply. So deeply that they'll cause permanent damage. And fatal injuries.

I blink away tears. I know it's no good to beg. That's exactly what they want.

'After you, we get Marc,' says Yasmina. 'Of course, we'll let him suffer for a few weeks first, not knowing where his beloved disappeared to.'

The thought of them hurting Marc is unbearable.

'There's no need to hurt Marc,' I say, my eyes darting to Cecile. 'He hates that Getty's in prison. Getty is … a friend of his.'

Cecile's gaze snaps away from the window hole.

'Marc always talks about you, Cecile,' I continue, catching her eye. 'I've always wondered whether secretly he might prefer you to me.'

Cecile's eyes widen. 'He talks about me?'

'I think he knows he made a mistake. That you're the one for him, after all.'

'She's stalling,' says Warren, his whole body beginning to twitch with excitement. 'We have her here now. Let me play with her.'

'Wait.' Cecile walks towards me. 'Marc talks about me?'

'All the time. Maybe the two of you can be together after all. Why not just take your revenge out on me? You don't need to hurt Marc. He … he always wanted to be friends with Getty again. Marc is innocent in this. What happened to Getty was all down to me.'

Yasmina laughs. Then she fixes me with her black eyes. 'You really are quite an incredible actress. I would believe every word you just said, if I didn't know better. Marc hates Getty. He's turned his whole security team over to protecting you from him.'

I shake my head. 'No. He wishes Getty wasn't in prison—'

Yasmina puts a grey fingernail to my lips. 'You're lying. After we've killed you, Marc will be next.'

Cecile shakes her head. 'Yasmina, what if she's telling the truth? If Marc is innocent in all this, he and I could be together ... I could have money again ...'

Yasmina rolls her eyes. 'Sophia is lying. Marc doesn't care about you at all. But I'm sure after a few minutes in Svetlana, we can find out for certain.' She turns to Warren. 'Take Sophia to the brink – just far enough to make her tell Cecile the truth. But don't go too far. We don't want anything to be over too quickly. It's a slow, painful death for her. Getty deserves nothing less.'

A horrible dark look falls over Warren's face. 'Play time.'

He turns the screw at the clasp of the device so it locks tighter around my waist.

The spikes drive further through my dress, and I can feel them poke my skin like a ring of needles.

I suck in my breath, feeling dizzy. Sick. Faint.

'Tighten it again,' says Yasmina. 'When she sees blood, she'll tell Cecile the truth.'

I see Warren's glistening bald head bob down to tighten the screw.

Oh my god, oh my god. I breathe in as tightly as I can, trying to hold myself away from the sharp spikes. But as Warren tightens, I feel stabs of pain all around my waist and cool metal drives into my body.

Warren steps back, his eyes fixed on my face, his chest thumping with excitement.

I daren't move. I daren't talk. I daren't look down at the damage.

Fear comes over me in one great rush.

I know now, beyond a doubt, that Warren is capable of killing me. But I won't tell them what they want to hear. Not if there's still a chance I can stop them hurting

Marc.

'I'm not lying,' I manage to say, all in a rush of breath. The spikes dig into me, and I quickly suck in my breath once more. 'He and Cecile should be together. I'm the only one who should get hurt.'

Yasmina and Warren look at each other.

'Hurt her more,' says Yasmina.

'Oh yes,' says Warren. 'Not a problem.'

I summon all my strength.

'Do whatever you have to do,' I say. 'I won't tell you anything different. It's the truth.'

Warren takes a step back, cocking his head to watch my face.

'It looks like you'll have to work a little harder,' says Yasmina.

Warren bobs down and tightens the screw again.

The spikes go further through my skin this time, and it's all I can do not to scream. It feels like someone has just run a burning knife around my waist.

I can't help looking down, and when I do I see blooding seeping out onto my dress in a ring of red dots.

'Anything you want to tell us?' Yasmina asks.

I shake my head.

'I believe her, Yasmina,' says Cecile.

'You're either with us or against us, Cecile,' says Yasmina. 'We're going to punish Marc for what he did to Getty. You'd better work out which side you're on. And quickly. Because PAIN have no time for cowards.'

Cecile turns away from Yasmina, looking at the night sky through a huge square hole in the wall. 'Fine,' she whispers. 'Okay. I'm with you.'

'Good girl,' says Yasmina. She nods at Warren. 'Time to leave.'

'But—'

'No Warren. Any more and she'll be dead too quickly.

For Getty's sake it should be slow. Painful.'

Warren doesn't seem to hear Yasmina at all. He's staring at my waist.

'*Warren,*' Yasmina snaps.

Warren's eyes become more focused, but he's still looking at the blood on my dress.

'We've done what we need to do,' says Yasmina. 'She'll survive a few days. In constant pain. Pretty soon, she'll be begging to die.'

Warren's eyes glisten. '*Begging.*'

Yasmina moves closer to me. 'And then on Sunday, we'll come and collect the body.'

75

After PAIN leave, I begin to scream. Weakly at first, and then as loud as I can.

'*HELP ME PLEASE! HEELLLPP!*'

But no one comes.

When I'm all screamed out, the panic of being totally alone hits me. Shackled to the wall like this, with no food or water, blood running freely from my waist, I'll die within days.

Outside, it seems like the night is getting darker and darker. I feel like I'm being choked by blackness. It crawls down my dry throat and dances around the spikes in my waist.

Hours pass, but I have no way of knowing what the time is.

At some point in the night I must pass out, because I open crusty eyelids to see the dawn rising, and feel an odd sense of hope as the sky turns dusky grey.

My wrist is totally numb now. It must be broken, but I think some sort of natural painkiller has kicked in.

The blood around my waist keeps coming, though. Every time I breathe, the spikes pierce my skin and keep the wounds open.

I feel vomit heave into my mouth and swallow it down. My mouth is so dry.

I watch the sun rise from a far window and see the black dots of birds fly past.

'Help,' I croak again. 'HELP! HELP! *HEELP MEEE PLEEEASE!*'

But no one comes. Way up here in this abandoned tower block, there's no one to hear me.

After a while I smell petrol fumes and realise the daily

traffic must have started. The sun climbs higher in the sky, until it disappears over the tower block and I can't see it anymore.

I keep screaming, 'HELP! HELP!' until my voice is hoarse, but still nobody comes.

I think of Marc and my family. I love them all so much. I'd gladly sacrifice myself for any one of them. But I ache to think of how my disappearance must be hurting them, scaring them, right now. And the thought of never coming back to them, to Marc ... it's unbearable.

I pull at the manacles, but only succeed in creating a fresh ring of pain around my waist and a new flow of blood.

I'm trapped. Totally and utterly trapped. And nobody knows where I am.

I must fall asleep again somewhere around midday, because for one glorious moment I think I hear Marc whispering in my ear, telling me everything is going to be okay. But when I open my eyes, I'm still alone, shackled and getting dizzier with every breath.

The sun begins to set once more, and I think about Marc. My time with him was so beautiful. So very beautiful.

76

As dusk falls, I look down at the torture device, then up at my hands. There must be something, something I can do to get out of here.

I give a few more weak shouts, but my voice is so wrecked that I can barely hear myself, let alone get someone else's attention.

I can move my legs, but not without causing a great deal of pain around my waist.

Holding my breath, I bring my knee up as hard and high as I can towards the torture device, thinking maybe I can knock a hinge out of place or something.

The spikes press right into my flesh, digging in deeper than they ever have before, and the air is knocked out of me as fresh blood pours down my skirt.

I'm dizzy for a moment, trying to focus.

My knee didn't even make contact with the metal. It came nowhere near.

As I'm wondering whether to try again, I hear the echo of shoes hitting the concrete stairwell, and my breathing goes from fast to turbo.

Oh my god. Someone is coming. Someone is coming!

'Help,' I croak. 'Please help me.'

A shadow appears at the top of the stairwell, and gets bigger and longer.

For a glorious moment, hope lifts me and I feel light and free of pain. Then I see who it is.

Oh my god, oh my god.

It's Warren, his face drenched in sweat.

He has a crowbar in his hand, and his low voice echoes around the empty tower block.

'I think it's time for you and I to play, don't you?'

'Weren't you supposed to leave me to die?' I croak.

'The thought of you, all bloody and begging,' says Warren. 'I couldn't stay away.'

'Where are the others?'

Warren frowns. 'They've got other things to worry about right now.'

'I won't scream,' I tell him. 'And I won't beg.'

'We'll see about that. I'm very good. Very, very good. Just you wait and see.'

My vision starts going hazy as Warren comes closer, but through the blur and black spots I see something – another shadow on the stairwell.

Perhaps Yasmina and Cecile are coming after all. Maybe they're angry with Warren for coming here without them.

The shadow keeps growing. Getting longer and taller, and I see ... I see ...

It can't be.

I shake my head.

Marc.

He can't be real. I must have passed out again. This is a dream. But then I hear his voice, firm and deep.

'Move away from her, Warren. Right now.'

Warren's shoulders shoot up in shock. He turns, and stumbles a little when he sees Marc coming up the staircase.

Marc's eyes burn into mine. 'Sophia, he won't touch you. You have my word. I'll kill him first.' He turns to Warren. 'You must have known it would be a risk coming back here.'

'I couldn't stay away.' Warren slaps the crowbar into his palm and takes a few steps forwards. 'The risk was worth it for her.'

'You won't get anywhere near her.'

'I can try.'

Marc strides towards Warren, and like lightning his fist connects with Warren's jaw.

Warren stumbles back. He looks dazed, and puts a hand to his face.

Then he lunges forwards, swinging the crowbar at Marc.

The crowbar connects with Marc's shoulder, and Marc's face registers pain, but he doesn't stumble or stoop. Instead, he punches Warren squarely on the hand so the crowbar goes spinning to the ground.

The next punch Marc delivers is so fast that I don't even see it. I only see Warren stumble backwards, throwing hands to his chest, his face white and afraid as he goes sprawling towards a gaping hole that used to be a window.

At first, I think Warren is going to catch himself before he falls. But he's just a little too late to find his footing, and his heavy, lumpy body topples backwards, out and down.

I look away, hearing the sickly crashing sound of Warren hitting the floor outside.

And then silence.

'Sophia.' Marc is by my side now. I don't know how he reached me so fast.

'Is he dead?' I whisper.

'Probably.'

'Is it really you?' I say, as Marc unfastens the screw from the torture device. 'I'm not dreaming again, am I?'

'If this were a dream,' says Marc, 'I would have been here sooner. I need to get you to a hospital.' He pulls the ring free from my waist, and I wince in pain.

A fresh flurry of blood flows as the spikes come free of my flesh, and Marc catches me as I fall forwards.

Dropping the torture device and holding me with one hand, Marc reaches up and unscrews the manacles.

With a clank, the right one comes free and my arm falls down. It's totally numb and white and empty of blood, and I can't feel it at all.

'How did you find me?' I whisper, as Marc goes to work on the left manacle.

'Cecile came to see me. It seems you put on a very convincing show of pretending I might be in love with her. After her visit, we used CCTV to track her movements. One camera at a time. We found Yasmina that way. Then Warren.'

'CCTV?'

'MET security streams. They have cameras all around London. I had temporary access. A rare privilege, and one I will be eternally grateful for.'

I flinch as Marc loosens the screw on the left manacle. As my arm falls away, a shudder of pain shoots into my wrist and hand.

Marc catches my arm and holds my cold wrist to his lips. Then he scoops me up. 'Yasmina and Cecile are in custody. But Warren got away from us. We tracked footage of him coming here.'

I see blue police lights flashing outside.

'Let's get you out of here.'

77

When Marc carries me out into the open air, I'm not prepared for the flurry of activity that explodes around me.

Police and ambulance people rush forwards. A stretcher bed is raced over the craggy ground.

Before I know what's happening, Marc lifts me onto the stretcher and helps the paramedics strap me down.

'Marc—'

'It's okay,' Marc whispers. 'I'm right beside you. Now and always.'

As I'm wheeled into the ambulance, Marc stays by my side, gripping my good hand like he's afraid I might slip away.

The journey through London in the ambulance is a blur, but on the way, a drip is put into my arm.

At the hospital, I'm tested for all sorts of things, but in the end, all the doctors diagnose is dehydration and loss of blood.

My injuries aren't bad. There was superficial damage to my intestines, but nothing that won't heal. My wrist bone was cracked, and needs some time in plaster. I've been lucky, everyone tells me, over and over again.

Yes, I tell them.

I know.

*****

As I stand outside Marc's farmhouse, watching two delivery men hulk a very familiar sofa towards the front door, I thank god for how very, very lucky and blessed I am.

PAIN have been sentenced to life in prison for attempted murder, with the exception of Cecile. She was given a lighter sentence on medical grounds, and will be given psychological help in prison. But she'll be locked away for a long time.

Apart from a ring of scars around my waist, my injuries have totally healed. And Marc and I have moved into the farmhouse together.

We're so in love, it's crazy. And after what happened, well ... let's just say we're both determined to make every day count. You never know what's around the corner.

My family don't know too much about the night the show finished, but they know I went missing, and that Marc turned over the whole city to find me. And that without Marc, I could have been badly hurt.

Needless to say, Dad realises that any man who could tap into the MET security streams to find his daughter is a man who will take care of me. Now and always.

'Hi.' I wave at the delivery men. 'Let me show you the way.'

The sofa is a soft beige colour, and hand-embroidered with tiny bells and crosses.

My mother did the embroidery before she died, and the sofa was in the annex with me for a long time before the new tenants moved in. I stored it at Jen's house while I was at Ivy College, but as soon as I told Marc about it, he decided we should bring it here so I could see it every day.

Marc's put me in charge of decorating our new home. He's taken me to countless designer home stores, but I never quite see anything that feels right, so I've mostly made things myself, or bought furniture from thrift stores and fixed it up. It feels more personal that way.

The result is that our home is a little bit of a mishmash, but it feels really warm and friendly.

Marc comes to stand beside me as I watch the two

men lumber towards the house. He slides his hand into mine, and I feel those familiar tingles in my stomach.

'It's arrived then,' he says.

'Yes. And I promise after this, they'll only be a few more deliveries. We're nearly done.'

'You can have as many deliveries as you want.' He kisses me on the head and squeezes a thumb into my palm. Then he stands back to let the delivery men into the house. 'I love watching you home-making.'

We follow the men inside.

'Where would you like this, sir?' one of the men asks Marc, nodding at the sofa.

Marc turns to me and gives me that mesmerising smile of his. 'Would the lady of the house care to answer that?'

My insides go all soft. 'Over there please, just by that plant.'

The house, of course, is full of plants now. I did warn Marc that I can go a little plant crazy. I'm always seeing sad brown-leaved plants by skips, or on 'last chance' sale in the plant centre, and I just have to rescue them and bring them back to life.

Marc understands.

After Marc has tipped the delivery men and they've jumped into their van, we stand in the living room, looking at Mum's sofa.

'Thank you,' I say, feeling love well up in my chest. 'It's so good to have this back with me.'

'It looks very much at home,' says Marc.

I squeeze his hand. 'I wish you could have met my mum. She would have loved you.'

'I wish I could have met her too.'

I sit on the sofa, pulling Marc down with me. 'Comfy, isn't it?'

He laughs. 'Very. And I'm glad you're sitting down. Because I think this is the perfect place to ask you something that's been on my mind for a while.'

'Oh?'

Marc lifts himself from the sofa, then bends down on one knee.

He takes a box from his pocket.

78

I put a hand to my mouth, and feel silly tears leaking from my eyes. 'Oh my god. Marc? Is this—'

He nods. 'Sophia Rose, will you marry me?'

He opens the box, and I see the ring – the beautiful antique diamond ring that Marc presented me with all those months ago.

My lips are all soft under my fingers, and I feel myself nodding hard.

'Yes,' I splutter, offering my tear-covered hand forwards. 'Yes, of course I'll marry you.'

Marc lips lift into the most beautiful smile. He slides the ring onto my finger, kisses my knuckles, then sweeps me into his arms.

I'm weeping and spluttering, unable to put words together for a little while. Finally, I manage to mumble into Marc's shoulder, 'I should phone Jen. Tell her the good news.'

'You might want to hold off on that,' says Marc, 'until you see your visitors.'

'Visitors?' I wipe tears away. I'm a mess of red eyes and tear-stained cheeks.

Marc smiles. 'I think you'll be pretty familiar with them.'

As if on cue, the doorbell rings

'Perhaps the lady of the house should answer that,' says Marc.

I throw him a curious sideways smile and go the door. When I pull it open, my smile gets so big that it practically reaches my ears.

There, on the doorstep, are Jen, Dad, Sammy, Denise, Tom, Tanya and Annabel.

'Oh my ... wow!' I say. 'Did Marc ... do you all know about ...?'

Everyone's vigorous nodding cuts me off.

'We know,' says Jen, throwing her arms around my neck and covering me in perfume. 'Marc made extra sure he had all the right approvals this time. Congratulations.'

'And you all gave the okay?' I ask.

'Everyone one of us,' says Dad. 'The two of you have our complete blessing. I couldn't wish for a better man to take care of my daughter.'

'Thanks Dad.' I throw my arms around him. He hugs me, and when I step back I see tears in his eyes. 'Are you okay, Dad?'

Dad nods, looking away and dabbing at his eyes. 'Fine, fine. Just ... my little girl, getting married. All grown up.'

'You should come inside,' I say, shepherding everyone into the house. 'Tom. Tanya. I can't believe it's been so long. What with the show, and then recovering, and home-making and everything, I—'

'We know,' says Tanya, giving me a hug. 'Don't worry. We understand.'

Tom wheels up to pat my shoulder. 'We've missed you.'

'I've missed you guys too,' I say. 'But I'm so happy for you both. Denise tells me you're still very much in love.'

Tanya turns scarlet.

Tom grins from ear to ear. '*Very* much in love. And hope to be for the rest of our lives.'

'Really? Does that mean you might be getting—'

'No,' Tanya interrupts. 'No need to rush into anything. We'll finish college before we start thinking about anything like that.'

'Promise you'll invite me when you finally *do* decide to get married,' I say, with a teasing smile.

'Of course!' says Tom.

Tanya rolls her eyes. 'Thanks for that. He'll be looking at wedding suits before you know it.'

'Speaking of weddings,' I say. 'Jen and Tanya, would you do me the honour of being my bridesmaids?'

'As if you even need to ask,' says Jen.

Tanya grins. 'Of course, Soph!'

'And Tom, I'd like you to be my bridesmaid too,' I add.

Tom laughs. 'Sophia, perhaps you're a little confused. It may not be obvious to everyone, considering my flamboyant choice of outfits, but I'm a man.'

Tanya and I laugh.

'I know,' I say. 'But I think we can break with tradition for your sake.'

'I'd be delighted to be your bridesmaid,' says Tom. 'But I have another idea. How about I conduct the ceremony? I did it for my cousin last year, so I'm very familiar with the procedure. I'd be delighted to stand before you and Marc and help you say your vows.'

I smile. 'I can't think of anything more perfect.'

'Who would have thought it?' says Tom. 'Sophia Rose marrying Marc Blackwell. And living happily ever after.'

Once we're inside the house, we all sit on Mum's sofa and the collection of thrift-store armchairs I've reupholstered. Marc and I are squeezed onto an armchair, me on his lap, our fingers woven tightly together.

Rodney brings in a tray of tea and freshly baked shortbread biscuits.

'Soph?' Jen asks. 'Will you be inviting Leo to the wedding?'

'I hadn't even thought about who I was going to invite,' I admit. 'But ... yes, of course I'll invite Leo. He's my friend. A good friend. And that's exactly who I want at the wedding. Good friends.' I turn to Marc. 'Are you okay with that?'

'I'm okay with that,' says Marc, his blue eyes flashing me a beautifully intense look.

'Honestly?'

'Honestly. The more friends you have, the more people are around to take care of you.'

I turn back to Jen. 'So there you go. You can bring your date along.'

We smile at each other, both knowing that Leo is much more than Jen's date these days. The two of them can't stay away from each other. Leo has bought an apartment in London, and Jen spends almost every night there.

As we're all chatting and catching up, I notice Annabel is a little quiet – but happy quiet. She's had a smile on her face since she arrived on the doorstep.

Eventually, my curiosity gets the better of me. 'Annabel?' I ask. 'Social services were going to give you an update this week. Have they called you?'

'Yes.'

'And?'

'It's good news. But I'll tell you another time. This is your big moment.'

'Don't be silly,' I say. 'Just tell me your news.'

Annabel's smile grows, and for the first time since I've met her, I see teeth appear from behind her lips. They're white and straight like Marc's.

'I'm getting Daniel back.'

I screech and throw my hand to my mouth. 'Oh my GOD! Annabel, that's wonderful. So, so wonderful.'

I head towards her and give her a big hug. She starts crying, and I feel warm tears on my own cheeks too.

'It was all thanks to you,' Annabel whispers, her voice croaky with tears.

'No,' I insist. 'You've beaten a drug that kills most people. And you've proven you're strong enough to be a mother. I'm so happy for you.'

79

A few weeks later, my head is swimming with wedding plans. I never knew there was so much to organise.

I'm so grateful Jen is my friend. She's good at all the things I'm really bad at, like planning and organisation, and she knows all the things that are needed at weddings, like cake and photographers and invitations.

I've tried to keep everything as simple as possible, but there's still a lot to do. I never realised a wedding was so much work.

Jen has been going on and on at me about choosing a venue, and over the weekend I finally worked out the perfect place. The only place, in fact, where I could imagine marrying Marc.

'Are you absolutely sure about this?' Jen asks, her high heels stumbling over the muddy ground. 'This is where you want your wedding? Your once in a lifetime, big show off party?'

'Positive,' I say, linking arms with her. 'Wait until you see exactly where I want the ceremony. You'll love it too.'

I lead her along the woodland path, past bright green feathering ferns and under towering trees.

Jen sighs. 'You and your trees, Sophia Rose. You could get married anywhere. Anywhere in the world. Your boyfriend is a billionaire. And where do you choose? The woods behind Ivy College.'

I smile. 'I know. Isn't it perfect? Come on.' I lead Jen further into the woods. 'I can't wait for you to see the spot.'

Jen folds up her linen suit trousers, rolls her eyes good-naturedly and follows me along the path.

The path weaves around a huge sycamore tree, then opens out into the most amazing circular space, under a beautiful canopy of trees.

'This is it,' I say, standing back so Jen can see the space. 'This is where I want to get married.

My mum used to call spaces like these 'fairy circles'. They're natural round clearings in the woods, and they're always surrounded by wild flowers and green shoots of grass.

Birds twitter and hop among the branches overhead, and a squirrel scurries up a tree as we approach.

We both stand for a moment under the bright green leaves, listening to bird song and smelling leaves and fresh soil.

'Soph,' Jen breathes. 'It's absolutely perfect. So beautiful.'

'I thought we could marry in the woods,' I say, 'and then have a picnic on the lawns around the college. It's the summer holidays, so the college is empty. All the guests can stay in the visitor accommodation block.'

'Oh Soph, that sounds brilliant,' says Jen. 'Truly. Of course, we'll have to have marquees on standby in case it rains. And some sort of contingency plan in case the paths here get too muddy—'

'It won't rain,' I say. 'I know it won't.'

80

When it comes to the night before the wedding, I don't want to be separated from Marc until the last possible moment.

I'm booked into the Ambassador Room at Ivy College so I won't have to travel on my wedding day, but Marc is staying there with me until midnight. We've had enough separation this year to last a lifetime.

When Marc and I arrive at the room, I'm blown away. It's a huge ground floor suite that overlooks the lawns and woodlands, and it has 'his and her' bathrooms and a huge Jacuzzi pool.

'This is beautiful,' I tell Marc, as he places my rucksack on the leather luggage rack.

I notice a huge white cellophane bag on my bed and run my fingers over the thick plastic.

My wedding dress has been delivered.

'Don't go peaking in this bag, will you?' I tease, picking up the hanger and heading for the wardrobe. 'I'm superstitious, if you hadn't worked it out already.'

'I'm fully aware of your superstitions,' says Marc, raising an eyebrow. 'If it was down to me, we'd be sleeping in the same bed tonight.'

He's wearing loose grey cargo trousers and a plain black hoodie. I love that he can transform from James Bond smart to action hero casual, and still look equally mesmerising and handsome.

I'm wearing a light summer dress made of crumpled linen fabric and embroidered with butterflies.

My feet are bare, since I kicked off my sandals the moment we came into the room. I love having bare feet in summer.

My hair is loosely plaited down my back, but as usual, some of it is struggling to escape, and tendrils fall around my face.

'Why tempt bad luck?' I say.

'I don't believe in bad luck. Not with you around.'

Marc opens the French doors and leads me onto the huge ground-floor balcony.

When I see what's waiting on the wooden table outside, I put a hand to my mouth.

'Marc.'

Resting on the varnished wood, beside a bottle of red wine and two gleaming glasses, is an astonishingly beautiful bouquet of flowers.

'Your wedding bouquet,' says Marc with a smile. 'You don't believe it's bad luck for the groom to see the bouquet before the wedding, do you?'

The bouquet is a soft and glimmering orb of ivy, woven with the reddest roses I've ever seen. The ivy and roses are so fresh and natural looking it's as if the bouquet could be growing wild in the woods.

'No.' I shake my head. 'That's one superstition I've never heard of.'

81

We drink wine and watch the sun set over Ivy College.

It's a beautiful warm evening, and the red sky tells me what I already knew – that tomorrow will be perfect sunshine for our wedding.

Marc and I talk and tease and laugh about how we first met. Thinking back to those early days feels so unreal now. It's almost like we're two different people.

'Tell me again what you thought of me at my audition,' I ask Marc, with a teasing smile.

'You know what I thought of you,' says Marc, pouring more wine into my glass. 'I thought you were astonishing.'

I grin. 'Funny. Because you couldn't have been colder towards me. I thought you were angry with me. That my audition hadn't pleased you.'

'I was a master at hiding my feelings back then,' says Marc. 'But now, I'm not so good.' He takes my hands and begins running his thumbs back and forth over my palms, pressing in hard, firm strokes. 'Do you want to know what I'm feeling right now?' His eyes have that primal, hunter look in them.

I laugh. 'It's pretty obvious.'

'I'll be gentle. I promise.'

'You don't have to be.'

Ever since Marc rescued me from PAIN and moved me into the farmhouse, we've had the most amazing, loving, caring sex, and it's been very beautiful. But ... I like the other side of Marc too.

'I've missed your dark side,' I say.

Marc throws me that delicious, devilish smile of his. 'My dark side?'

'Yes. You know what I mean.'

'I thought. After PAIN ...'

'What PAIN did is a world away from what we do together in the bedroom. You dominating me is part of who you are. Who *we* are. It's why we fit so well.'

Marc frowns. The square shape of his pale jaw and the sharp lines of his angular face are so beautiful in the setting sunlight. I find myself, as usual, slightly dazed by his handsomeness.

'Come inside,' says Marc, his voice dropping several notes. 'Now.'

He takes my hand.

I stand, following Marc inside. He closes the French doors and draws the curtains.

'Hmmm ...' Marc scoops me up and lays me onto the bed. The linen is crisp and smells like apples. 'Stay there for a moment. I'll be back.'

82

After ten minutes or so, I hear the bedroom door opening again.

Marc strides into the room.

My thighs tighten when I see what he's holding.

'Where did you get that?' I ask.

'The prop store behind Queen's Theatre.' He's holding a cane – a swishy bamboo rod with bumps all along it. 'I'm only sorry I didn't bring the silk rope with me that I ordered all those months ago.'

Sensing me watching, Marc holds out the cane and flexes it between his fingers.

'Is this an early wedding present?' I breathe, feeling my lips stretch into a smile.

Marc comes to the bed, his beautiful spiky lips twitching into a smile. 'No. This isn't the present. What comes next is the present. Lie back on the bed.'

I rest onto the pillow, my eyes not leaving Marc's. He's got that wicked, deadly look on his face again. The one that leaves me weak at the knees. The one that has me begging for more.

Marc lifts the cane and swishes it through the air. Then he smacks it against his palm.

CRACK!

Oh. How can that little sound make me wet already? But it does.

'Are you sure you still want this side of me?' Marc asks. 'After everything that's happened?'

'Positive,' I breathe, watching the cane as Marc rolls it between his fingers.

Marc lifts my dress with the yellow tip.

'Off,' he instructs.

I struggle out of my dress and lie back on the bed in my underwear – the fairytale set that Marc bought me when we took a trip to his island.

Marc smacks the cane down hard on the bedside table, and a resounding crack echoes through the air.

God, I'm wet now and getting wetter by the minute.

Marc prowls around the bed, swishing the cane back and forth. I squirm a little when I see the outline in his cargo trousers. Huge and hard and fighting to escape.

I feel the tip of the cane at the waistband of my panties. Marc flicks the rod under the elastic, pulling it taut and letting the waistband snap back against my skin.

'*Oh*,' I moan.

'Those too.'

I reach down to pull my panties off, but Marc smacks my fingers lightly with the cane.

I yelp and pull my fingers back.

'Yes sir,' he prompts.

'Yes sir,' I say, putting my smarting hand to my mouth.

'Take them off.'

I wiggle out of my panties and watch Marc as he continues to prowl around the bed.

'Roll over.'

I roll onto my belly, hearing his footsteps still moving around the bed. I hear his deep breathing and try to work out where he is as he moves. Then I feel the tip of the cane under my bra strap.

'This too.'

I undo my bra and pull it over my arms, then fall onto the duvet again, my head still pushed face down into the pillow. I can hear my own breathing and feel the heat of my breath against my face.

Marc stops moving and there's silence.

'Marc?' I whisper into the pillow. 'Are you still there?'

CRACK! Marc whacks the cane against the bedside

table again.

'I didn't say you could speak.'

Oh god, that sounds good.

CRACK!

There it goes again, and now I'm desperate for him.

'Keep still,' Marc barks, and I hear him pacing.

I wait, growing wetter by the minute.

'Spread your legs,' Marc instructs, slipping the cane between my thighs. 'Now.'

I moan and move my legs apart.

CRACK!

This time, Marc smacks the cane hard against my left buttock and I leap an inch from the bed, giving another little yelp.

I hear the swish of the cane and then, CRACK! It comes down hard on my other buttock.

CRACK!

The cane comes down once more on both buttocks, and I flinch in pain – but good pain. I want this so badly. I've been waiting for this side of Marc to come out again, and it feels so good.

'Roll over,' Marc instructs.

I do, rubbing my stinging buttocks. My bra stays on the bed as I roll over, so I when I face Marc I'm completely naked.

I look up at him, and see he's naked too.

'How did you take your clothes off so fast?' I ask breathlessly, taking in his muscular, naked body – the taut lines of his arms, the cut of his abs, his flawless pale skin and the light covering of brown hair on his chest.

I notice that between his legs he is hard and firm, and so, so huge. Looking at him I wonder, as I often do, how on earth he'll fit inside me.

Marc's lips curve into a dangerous smile. 'Don't you know not to speak until you're spoken to?'

'I guess not.'

Marc comes closer and holds the cane up over my thighs.

He brings the cane down fast, but stops inches from my skin.

I flinch, waiting for the blow that doesn't come. I moan as I watch the cane hover over my legs.

Marc raises an eyebrow. 'Did you want something?'

'Hit me. Please.'

Marc gives me that devilish smile and raises the cane. Then he brings it down hard, CRACK, on my thighs, and I moan with pleasure.

As the stinging sensation spreads up my legs, Marc picks up my ankles and rests them over his firm shoulders. Then he runs the cane up my inner thigh, and slowly strokes up, up, up until it reaches between my legs.

I'm so wet that when he begins to slide the cane back and forth between my legs and buttocks, it slips easily up and down, and I moan as I feel the hard joins of the bamboo roll over me, bump, bump, bump.

Just as I'm going insane with the pleasure of it all, Marc slides the cane out from between my legs and rests the tip on my stomach. Slowly, he traces a snaking line back and forth across my belly, and I shudder and shiver as the cane moves up my body.

When the cane reaches my breasts, Marc slides the cane roughly across my nipples, back and forth, back and forth, the joins pushing and pulling at my skin.

Oh god. It's beautiful, delicious teasing agony, but I need more.

'Hit me,' I beg him. 'Please.'

'I don't think you can take it,' Marc says, stroking the cane back and forth.

I nod quickly. 'I can. I can.'

'I would never take you beyond your limits. You know that, don't you?' Marc lifts the cane high above my breasts.

'Yes,' I agree. 'But my boundaries are well and truly stretched.'

'You're sure?'

'I'm sure.'

Marc brings the cane down, once, twice, three times on my breasts, CRACK, CRACK, CRACK.

'Oh god, oh god,' I moan, as my nipples burn white hot and a stinging sensation creeps over my breasts and chest. 'More. Give me more.' I roll over.

CRACK, CRACK, CRACK.

Marc hits me hard on my backside.

CRACK, CRACK, CRACK.

When he stops I almost can't see straight. God, it feels so good. So, so good.

I'm about to beg him for more, but before I can, I feel Marc pushing my legs apart and climbing on top of me, his hardness pressing between my thighs.

'I can only tease you for so long,' Marc says, sliding himself into place, ready to push inside of me. 'You're irresistible to me, do you know that Miss Rose? Absolutely fucking irresistible.'

I hear the tear of a condom packet, and feel myself shaking my head into the duvet.

'Let's do it without.'

'Without?'

'I want to feel you. All of you. We're about to get married. I think it's okay now.'

'Sophia. I don't want anything happening to you that you don't choose. There could be consequences. A baby. Are you ready for that possibility?'

'I'm ready for whatever happens. Are you?'

'Very ready.'

With that, he plunges inside me, all the way in – so hard and fast that it takes my breath away.

'*Ooooh*,' I moan, as I tighten around him, feeling him get as deep as he can. My buttocks sting from the pressure of his hips, and my breasts feel hot as they're pushed into the bed.

It all feels so, so good.

He pushes my legs wider so he can get even deeper, and for a moment I'm not sure I can take it – how deep he's going. But as he starts to move, I realise I can. That we're made for each other, and his body is meant to fit with mine, even if it means pushing me to my limits.

Marc moves hard and fast for a few strokes, pushing me back and forth into the bed like a rag doll. Then he flips me over, still keeping himself inside me, but lifting my ankles onto his shoulders again.

I think I might come just from looking up into those intense, burning eyes of his, but I hold myself just on the brink, just on the verge of losing it.

I see Marc is barely holding on too. His eyelids are fluttering and his jaw is held tight.

'Oh god Sophia,' he groans, his spiky lips curving even higher. He plunges forwards, letting out a long, low moan.

That does it. I can't hold on anymore. An orgasm rises up and up, until it's pushing and pulling, sending waves of warmth and pleasure from between my legs, up over my whole body.

My thighs clench around Marc, pulling him deeper, and I reach out to grab his buttocks, forcing him further inside me.

Marc moans again, and I moan too.

He rubs his hands up and down my legs, creating a gorgeous warm friction that makes my orgasm last even longer. His eyes are closed and he's lost in me, just like I'm lost in him.

After a long, delicious moment, he slides my legs from his shoulders and pulls my body against his.

'You still want to be Mrs Blackwell tomorrow?' he whispers into my hair.

'I've never been surer of anything in my life.'

'It's nearly midnight.'

'Maybe it won't be bad luck for you to stay, after all,' I say, desperate to hold on to this moment.

Marc smiles. 'We've had this discussion. You didn't want to risk it. Remember? I don't want you doing anything you might regret in the morning.'

'Then I guess you'd better go,' I say. 'Before the clock strikes and you turn into a pumpkin.'

'I'll be back for you Cinderella,' says Marc. 'See you in the morning.'

The next day, I wake to the most beautiful sunrise. It's pink and orange and grey and just a whole rainbow of soft pastel colours.

The dark green woodlands of Ivy College look more magnificent today than I've ever seen them.

I've barely got out of bed and brushed my teeth before there's a knock on the door.

'Is there a bride to be in there?' Jen calls.

Smiling, I head across the room to let her in.

'Wow,' says Jen, as I open the door. 'Amazing room.'

'I know. Nice, isn't it?'

For once, Jen isn't all made up and picture perfect. Her long blonde hair is piled up in a messy bun on her head. She's wearing a pink tracksuit and sunglasses, and when she whisks off the sunglasses, her eyes are clear of makeup.

I stand back to let her in. 'Thanks for getting here so early. I know you hate early mornings. And it must have been pretty hard leaving Leo Falkirk in bed …'

'Anything for my best friend.' Jen is carrying her huge metal makeup case. 'Well. Are you ready for me to work my magic?'

I take in a deep breath and let it out. 'Yes. Ready. Let's get started.'

84

After Jen has fixed my hair and makeup, Rodney arrives with croissants and coffee, 'courtesy of Marc Blackwell'. And he brings something else with him. Something even better than breakfast.

Tanya.

'Morning all,' she says, breezing into the Ambassador room. 'I'm not late am I?'

'No,' I tell her. 'Right on time.'

It doesn't take long before Jen starts fixing Tanya's hair and makeup too, and soon we're all prettied up and ready for the big day.

I have to fight Jen off a few times when she hovers with the red lipstick, wanting to 'make the most of those amazing lips', but in the end we keep my makeup soft and natural, just like I want.

The three of us stand side by side in the full-length mirror, grinning like idiots. We make a lovely picture – not because we're all beautified, but because our arms are wrapped around each other and we're all laughing, as Tanya jokes about Tom's outfit for the wedding.

It took him weeks to decide what to wear, apparently. He's been scanning the internet every evening, looking for something suitable.

'He's like a girl when it comes to clothes,' says Tanya. 'But I love him anyway. I think he's a bit jealous of my bridesmaid's dress.'

Tanya's fern green dress is made of loose silk and cut on the bias. She and Jen are wearing exactly the same thing – simple silk gowns, gathered in all the right places. I picked a green that would suit both their colourings.

'I love mine too,' says Jen. 'But not as much as I love your wedding dress, Soph. It's just so *you*. You look like some beautiful woodland princess.'

My wedding dress really is amazing.

Marc took me to the most exclusive boutiques and introduced me to some really famous designers. But in the end, I just wanted something simple that felt like me. So I asked Jen's mum to make my dress. She's a really good seamstress, and knows me inside and out.

When I told her what I wanted, it was like she could read my mind. And the finished dress is perfect, just perfect.

It's made of long, flowing white silk, and has a simple v-shaped bust and tiny silver ivy leaves embroidered on the shoulders. It's so light and loose that it flows around my body when I move, and it makes me feel like a fairy princess.

It's pretty and natural, but best of all I feel really comfortable in it. I didn't want anything that wouldn't let me move freely.

I considered marrying in bare feet, but then Jen found some ivory-satin ballet pumps with silver leaf details over them and gave them to me as my 'something new'. I knew they were perfect as soon as I saw them. Jen knows me so well.

The dress aside, I'm pretty much done. Jen has left my hair kind of natural.

She's put stuff in it so it doesn't puff up, and she's strung pearls on silver thread around my curls, but other than that it's just shiny and loose, like always.

Oh, and Dad gave me my mum's blue jasper stone bracelet as my something old and something blue. And Denise has leant me a tiara from her huge costume collection as my something borrowed.

It's a beautiful silver one, with metal work so delicate that it looks like lace.

So I'm ready. I'm ready to get married.

85

The sun glows overhead as Jen and Tanya lead me across the grass.

I'm holding their hands tightly as we near the woods and I don't let go, even when we near the woodland path.

Jen is holding up the silk skirt of my dress so it doesn't trail along the dew sodden ground. It's still early – 10am – and the sun hasn't chased away the night-time damp just yet.

Tanya is carrying my bouquet.

A gorgeous yellow sun shines down from a clear blue sky, and I can't help smiling as we enter the dark woods, even though my stomach is churning with nervous excitement.

'Deep breaths, deep breaths,' says Jen, squeezing my hand. 'Nearly there now.'

We head along the woodland path, where sunlight speckles the soil and a thick canopy of green leaves cools the air.

We walk carefully over the bumpy, baked ground one step at a time. One, two, one, two. Breathe, breathe, breathe.

As we near the clearing, my smile grows even wider as I see Dad up ahead. He's waiting for me at the entrance of the fairy circle, wearing a brand new tuxedo and beaming with delight as he sees me approach.

'You look beautiful, love. Absolutely beautiful.' He dabs at his eyes.

Jen lifts my hand and gently links it through my father's arm.

Tanya gives my other hand a reassuring squeeze and

hands me my bouquet.

'Ready to give me away?' I ask Dad.

'Ready,' says Dad.

Jen and Tanya come to stand behind me, lifting the silk at the back of my dress.

We begin to walk forward, heading into the clearing.

86

From the woven arches of branches overhead, to the dapples of sunlight shining onto our guests, everything is absolutely perfect.

I decided I didn't want music at the ceremony, just the sounds of the trees and the birds. The stillness that comes from the woods.

At the far side of the clearing is a wooden altar, made by Marc's friend, Peter.

The altar is carved with ivy leaves and roses, and behind it sits Tom, wearing one of the fanciest suits I've ever seen him in – brown with green piping, and paisley swirls on the lapels.

Around the clearing stand our guests, all watching me with huge smiles.

The guest smiling the most has to be Annabel. She's right near the entrance to the clearing, and she looks like a different person these days.

Dressed in a simple light-green summer dress, white daisies woven into her hair, she holds a beautiful little boy in her arms – Daniel, her son.

Daniel rests his head against her shoulder, sucking his thumb and looking totally and utterly content.

Danny Blackwell. Back with his mother at last. I've loved getting to know him over the last few weeks. He's shy and often seems deep in thought, but he's always ready to smile too. I've taken him to the cottage a few times to play with Sammy and the two of them are becoming great friends.

Before I walk into the clearing, I stop to ruffle Daniel's hair.

'Are you liking all the trees, Danny?' I whisper.

He nods shyly and smiles.

Denise is beside Annabel, holding hands with Sammy.

I smile at Denise and kneel down to Sammy.

'What about you, short stuff? Do you like trees?'

Sammy nods and leans against Denise's arm. It hasn't taken long for Sammy to fall in love with Denise, just like Dad has.

When Genoveva found out that Dad was with some-one else, she started calling him. Apparently, her doctor boyfriend went back to his wife and now she has no one.

Dad told her that he didn't want to get back together, but arranged fortnightly visits so she can see Sammy. Sometimes she remembers to visit, sometimes she doesn't.

'Shall you and I climb some trees later?' I ask Sammy.

'YES!' he bellows, a little too loudly.

The crowd laughs.

It's all so perfect, but of course the most perfect thing is Marc, standing by the wooden altar.

He's wearing a fitted, jet-black suit – so black it seems to drink in colour – and his hair is thick around his ears. His long, lean body is perfectly still, waiting for me. Although he has his back to me, I sense there's a smile on his face.

I stand up straight, take a deep breath and link arms with Dad again.

'Ready?' Dad whispers.

I nod, and Dad walks me across the clearing towards Marc.

As we crunch over twigs and old leaves, Marc turns and our eyes meet.

It's the most amazing moment. His eyes are so dark. So intense and stormy. He hasn't lost his dark side. Not completely. But I definitely see light in him.

Lots and lots of light.

His eyes still undo me. For a moment, I lose my footing and Dad has to grip my arm tighter to get me walking straight.

Marc raises an eyebrow, and gives me an 'are you alright?' smile.

I return it with a nod and smile of my own, then take the last few steps towards him.

Dad carefully places my hand in Marc's, and Marc and I stand for a moment, our eyes holding each other.

I have never felt more loved than I do right now, standing beside Marc, among all our friends and family, about to bind my life to his.

Tom clears his throat. 'Okay you two. It's clear to everyone that you *want* to get married. So are you ready to go ahead and do it?'

Gentle laughter fills the clearing.

I nod. 'Yes.'

'I've never been more ready,' says Marc.

Our vows are simple.

We pledge to love each other for the rest of our lives.

Then Tom gives us the rings – two silver bands engraved with weaving roses and ivy.

I slip the band onto Marc's finger, my hand shaking a little. Finally, the ring slides into place and I hold out my own hand for Marc.

When Marc places the wedding band onto my finger, I look up into his deep blue eyes.

'I love you,' I murmur.

'I love you too, Sophia Blackwell,' says Marc. 'Forever and always.'

87

After the ceremony in the woods, Marc and I are driven by limousine to the registry office to sign our marriage papers. I'm shaking for the whole journey, a crazy, sobbing, smiling quivering mess in Marc's arms.

I can't believe it. Marc Blackwell has just made me his wife. To have and to hold. Always.

'I'm praying those are tears of joy, Mrs Blackwell,' Marc whispers. 'Because there's no backing out now. You're mine. Forever.'

'I know,' I manage to sob, trying to get my voice steady. 'I'm so happy.'

Marc lifts my chin, tilting my face so I look up into those strong, burning blue eyes.

'I'm never letting you go again,' he says. 'Ever. I will love you and take care of you for the rest of my life.'

*****

When Marc and I return to Ivy College, we find our guests sitting in a circle around a huge picnic blanket on the lawn. They're drinking champagne and fresh orange juice served by hovering waiters.

A round of applause breaks out as we approach, and I feel strangely shy to be the centre of attention among all these people that I love.

I know I'm an actress, but in real life I'm used to looking after people. It feels strange to be the one everyone is focusing on.

'It's so amazing to see you all,' I manage to say, as Dad and Jen move apart to let Marc and I sit down. 'Thank you so much for being here.'

Marc and I are handed champagne, and we drink and talk and laugh under the sunshine until lunch is served from wicker picnic baskets.

Jen made sure we got the very best food for the picnic, of course – a hand-picked delicatessen lunch from Harrods, delivered with real silver cutlery and china plates.

The hampers are full of delicious pies, sandwiches, scotch eggs, salads, smoked salmon, fresh strawberries and clotted cream.

As the day moves on, I notice that Jen and Leo are talking and laughing away. They're sitting so close that their heads are practically touching.

I smile. Leo is perfect for Jen. And it looks like Leo knows just how perfect Jen is for him, too.

It really is the most amazing, glorious, loving, happy day. To be surrounded by love from my friends and family, but most of all from Marc, well ... I've never felt anything like it.

I didn't organise speeches or anything like that, but as the sun begins to set, Jen raises her glass and says, 'A toast to Mr and Mrs Blackwell.'

Everyone cheers, raising their glasses.

'Oh, wait,' I say, getting to my feet. 'There's something I forgot to do.' I pick up the bouquet of ivy and roses. 'I need to throw this,' I announce, turning my back on the crowd.

I hear murmurs and laughter as female guests get to their feet.

'Ready?' I call. 'One, two, three!' I throw the bouquet high into the air, and turn to see it land between Jen and Tanya, who both catch the ivy and roses with one hand. They turn to each other, laughing with disbelief.

'We both caught it,' laughs Jen.

'Looks like we'll have to have a double wedding,' says Tanya.

'I'm up for it if you are.'

88

When I sit back on the grass, a waiter comes to top up my champagne glass.

'Oh, no thank you,' I say, holding my fingers over it. 'I think I'd better stick to orange juice from now on.'

I feel Marc's arm tighten around my waist. 'Are you okay? Do you need me to take you for a walk? To clear your head?'

'No. I've only had one glass of champagne so far. It's just ... I have a feeling about something.'

'A feeling?'

'Yes. After last night. It was the first time we ever ... I mean without protection.'

Suddenly, I feel like we're the only two people in the whole world.

'Sophia, it's far too soon to know anything like that.'

'But where my body is concerned, my feelings aren't usually wrong. And I feel this pretty strongly.'

'Do you feel ill? Do you need a doctor?'

I shake my head. 'No, it's nothing like that. Nothing physical. It's just ... a feeling.'

Marc slides his hand around to my stomach, his eyes fixed on mine. He pulls me tight into his body.

'Let's hope your feeling is correct.'

'And if it is?'

'Then you, Mrs Blackwell, will be a wonderful mother. And I will be the happiest man in the world.'

Ready for the next Devoted Trilogy? ...

My next book will be out soon! If you want me to tell you the special early release date (so you'll get the book at the lowest price, and be able to read it before everyone else) come and friend me on Facebook or Twitter, and I will share early release news.

I LOVE MY READERS!

Dear Readers,

You truly are the most amazing people. I love meeting you on Facebook and Twitter and finding out about your lives. I truly love and care about every single one of you, and am honoured that you read my books.

If you haven't already, come make friends with me on Facebook and Twitter:

https://www.facebook.com/IvyLessons

https://twitter.com/SK_Quinn

I accept all friendships, and follow everyone who follows me, so don't be shy.

I would also absolutely love you to share your thoughts on Amazon. I read every review, and pay special attention to my favourite reviewers.

It's also good for me to hear critiques and negative feedback, so if there was something you hated about the book please email me at: press@bookgroupbooks.com, and help me become a better writer!

TWEET AND SHARE!

If you enjoyed it, please help your friends discover a good read by tweeting and sharing. I pay attention to tweeters and sharers and will often seek you out and give you free, exclusive reads. Xx